HOW TO MAKE TIME FOR ME

HOW TO MAKE TIME FOR ME

Fiona Perrin

First published in the United Kingdom in 2019 by Aria, an imprint of Head of Zeus Ltd

Copyright © Fiona Perrin, 2019

The moral right of Fiona Perrin to be identified as the author of this work has been asserted in accordance with the Copyright, Designs and Patents Act of 1988.

A CIP catalogue record for this book is available from the British Library.

ISBN 9781788547345

Cover Design © Charlotte Abrams-Simpson

Aria
c/o Head of Zeus
First Floor East
5–8 Hardwick Street
London EC1R 4RG

www.ariafiction.com

To my wonderful Mum

I

I was on my way to wine. That was my first thought when I got knocked off my feet by the Deliveroo rider.

It was a Friday night in April, darkening at six, and I was out of the station, striding with a Sainsbury's bag of food and my handbag, heavy with all the crap you needed with a full-on-job and even-more-full-on-family.

I was cold and knackered but smiling because I was listening to loud rock music (classic Stone Roses, if you're interested) on my headphones, and I could almost smell and feel the warm home waiting for me.

There'd be *life* in it – even if that was just three teenagers who'd look up for about a second from their phones/laptops/other devices to acknowledge that I was there. I'd cook pasta while they lay around doing absolutely nothing. Eventually, we'd all sit around the kitchen table and I'd tell them I was sending them to a Bootcamp for the Perennially

Lazy and they'd say, 'Oh, *FFS*,'* – the acronym, because swearing was not allowed – and I'd say: 'What is the eleventh commandment?' and they'd chorus back: 'Thou shalt not take the piss out of thy mother.' And all that time there'd be wine, and it would be allowed because it was Friday.

The green-blue and black of the cyclist's uniform came from nowhere as I stepped onto the zebra crossing. As he hit me, I felt myself fly upwards in the air, along with my bag for life, earphones and handbag: a firework comprised of a forty-three-year-old woman, dinner for four and wires, tissues, purse and make-up.

I instinctively put my arms out as I hit the striped tarmac. And then, just for a moment, everything went dark.

When I came to – and it was probably just a few seconds later – there was an overwhelming smell of Thai green curry. The food-delivery cyclist was looking down at me, still holding his bike. I could see headlights from cars stopped behind him and hear him shouting, 'Stop, there's been an accident,' in a deep, panicked voice. Then down at me, 'Oh, my God, are you all right?'

I heard car doors slam and the sound of people running towards us. Everything was very woozy, but I was awake and trying to sit up.

He said, 'I just didn't see you, I'm so sorry, I just didn't see you…'

---

* As this story features teenagers who frequently speak a different language from the rest of mankind, I have taken the liberty of adding footnotes throughout to help. FFS means 'For F**k's Sake' and is in wide use on social media by teenagers (and many adults, actually, who should probably know better).

That was when I started to laugh and cry at the same time as I looked up at him from the ground. 'Ha, ha,' I said, 'no one sees me any more.'

I think I passed out again. When I opened my eyes, the cyclist was crouched down beside me. He was about my age, blondish hair poking from his helmet, from what I could see through my blur.

'Curry,' I said. 'Lemongrass.'

'Oh, hurrah, you've opened your eyes,' he said. Relief lit up his face – it was a pleasant face, from where I was lying on the tarmac: blue eyes, skin pink from the exertion of cycling, even if he did seem a bit older than your usual food-delivery rider. Behind him was a giant billboard that greeted people coming out of the station: 'Welcome to Seymour Hill', the name of our market town thirty miles north of London. In front of that was a small circle of people peering down at me; someone was saying an ambulance was on its way.

'Yes, I was delivering it to some people on…' He looked around and I could see cartons of green food along with my pasta and, in my peripheral vision, a smashed bottle of carbonara sauce. 'Seriously, I'm so sorry, but we're going to get you help now. It's all my fault, I just didn't see you.' His eyes were still desperate, a couple of feet from my face.

Ha, ha, I'm the Invisible Woman. This made me laugh again – a mad sort of cackle that didn't sound as if it was coming from me at all. *You've had a bang on the head. You're deranged.*

The cyclist shook his head and smiled back uncertainly. 'I'm so glad you're OK. Are you, do you think? I can't move you until I know nothing's broken.' His voice was low and the sort that people described as English, when they meant no discernible regional accent.

I couldn't feel any searing pain from my body and there was no tunnel full of angels waiting to greet me, even if I had turned into a nutty old fruit loop. 'I think I'm fine,' I managed, but everything was a bit dreamy, as if it were happening to someone else. 'What about the people waiting for their curry?'

He laughed and put his black-gloved hand on my shoulder. 'The ambulance is on its way,' he said. 'Do you want to sit up?'

'Poor love, are you OK?' A woman with a large Russian-style fake fur hat on crouched down beside him.

'He just didn't see me,' I told her, and she looked at me quizzically. 'He just didn't *see* me. I'm the Invisible Woman.' For some reason, I thought I was hilarious and was laughing again.

'I came round the corner but I didn't see anyone on the crossing...' the cyclist started.

I was wearing a coat with a large deep pink band at the bottom of its flared black skirt. I have a full head of brown hair. I'm no short-arse either at 5'6". And while I'm not overweight, I'm no stick insect. That was what I was thinking rationally.

Unfortunately, it's not what I was saying.

As they helped me sit up on the cold floor, I could hear myself repeating over and over again: 'the Invisible Woman, the Invisible Woman' and I was laughing like a drain.

4

Then there was the pah-pah of an ambulance arriving.

It was clear that I wasn't injured, just dazed and confused. I was in the back of an ambulance and a friendly paramedic was telling me I needed to come to A & E to get checked out. The contents of my bag had been gathered up and given back to me by the lady in the hat and everything was there, including my phone, miraculously uncracked. I held my bag on my lap as my vision started to become more normal.

From outside the white shiny doors I could hear people saying things about the lighting near the station not being good enough 'since they fixed the road', and the voice of the hat-lady telling someone that, 'She keeps going on about being invisible.'

'No one sees me any more, that's the joke,' I said to the paramedic who was strapping me into one of the ambulance chairs. I could see this other version of me – the one who'd been sideswiped by Thai green curry – but I couldn't seem to control her. 'I've lost my actual mind,' I said. 'Not just my mind, but my *actual*† one.'

She nodded and smiled. 'We're going to make sure you're OK,' she said in a voice designed to reassure.

'Do I smell of curry?' I asked her, but she was busy plugging in something else.

----

† Using the word 'actual' to reinforce a statement was a habit picked up from my teenage children. Typical use might be 'What the Actual F**k'. You get the gist.

The cyclist appeared in the doorway of the ambulance. 'I'm really, really sorry,' he said again. 'What can I do? Shall I come to the hospital with you?'

I smiled at him, 'the man who thought I was invisible,' and bent over laughing again.

He grinned – a kind grin – but mostly, as you'd expect, he looked confused. I was clearly mad. I'd look confused myself if I came across me.

'You've got to let me do something to help,' he carried on. The paramedic was preparing to leave.

'Wait,' I said. 'Have you got my dinner?' I was still sane, then, because I was thinking about the kids' dinner.

The man handed me the Sainsbury's bag. 'One of the pasta packets split and the jar burst,' he said and then started apologising again. 'Listen, shall I bring some food later? I mean, it's the least I can do and… Look, please, can I have your number? I want to check you're OK.'

'First you knock me down and then you want my number?' Now I was a stand-up comic. But he looked confused again, so I rattled it off twice while he punched it into his phone and then said, 'I live at number 42 Patchett Road.'

The cyclist looked even more confused. 'What a coincidence,' he said. 'I've just moved into number 36.'

'Really?' I hadn't seen him outside in our street even though this was three doors down; I would've remembered a middle-aged man in Lycra.

'So, we're neighbours,' the man went on.

'You could've just come round to borrow a cup of sugar,' I pointed out. 'You didn't need to run me over.'

The cyclist's face crinkled again in a smile, but the paramedic was getting impatient. 'What's your name, love?'

'Callie,' I said. 'Callie Brown.'

She signalled to the cyclist to get out of the way as she wanted to close the doors. He disappeared from view, saying, 'I'll get in touch later and make sure you're OK.'

'Now is there someone we should phone?' the paramedic said. 'Husband, partner – other responsible adult?'

'None of the above,' I said.

She raised an eyebrow and cocked her head to one side. 'What about your parents?'

I thought about my generally batty mum and dad – they meant well but weren't exactly responsible adults. 'They won't be much help. Look, I'll call one of my friends.' She pressed a button to her side, which must have been a signal to the driver as the engine kicked in. 'No blue light?' I asked. 'The traffic's going to be shit.'

She laughed. 'I'm not sure you're an emergency,' she said. 'You haven't broken anything, and you seem all there to me.' Then she muttered to herself, 'Apart from all this stuff about being invisible and curry.'

I was staring at a white ceiling with a halogen strip light in a curtained cubicle. A nurse with beautiful skin like polished teak, and a name badge that read 'Maura', was taking my blood pressure. She'd asked me to remove the jacket I was wearing to go to work and wrapped one of those rubber things round my arm over my white shirt.

I'd messaged the kids on the family groupchat[‡] just telling them that I was going to be late; there was no point worrying them.

Daisy texted back.

Hope you're on the sauce. Have fun Ma!

She spent a lot of time telling me to get a 'like,[§] social life' and was obviously hoping I'd gone out after work.

Lily sent me a single kiss:

x

I imagined her sitting at her desk with her head in a textbook, furiously studying for her GCSEs, which started in a couple of weeks. Alternatively, she'd be thinking, *Hurray, Mum's out,* and getting it on with her boyfriend, Aiden. Call me a modern and progressive parent, but I'd rather she was doing the latter – she was working too hard and was really stressed lately.

There was nothing from Wilf. But then he'd probably got his headphones plugged into his Mac, occasionally looking up at another screen as he mixed beats. Wilf was not my biological son, but I considered him my child. I'd split up with my long-term partner and his father, Ralph, a couple of years back, but he'd been going through a bit of a

---

‡ A forum typically used by my children for useful purposes such as sending me pictures of an empty fridge, to indicate how starving they were.

§ 'Like' is a completely unnecessary addition to most teenage sentences but probably one of Daisy's most frequently used words.

meltdown at the time (to put it mildly), and Wilf had stayed on with me while his dad recovered and got sober. And then afterwards, they'd needed to rebuild a very fractured father-son relationship; some of the scenes when Ralph was at his worst hadn't been pretty. So, Wilf stayed on at our house.

Eventually, Ralph did recover, got into healthy living, and at the gym he'd quickly met a very competitive South African named Petra (I'm not saying a word; honestly, I've tried *really* hard to like her) and, after a few months, moved to her executive home on the other side of Seymour Hill. Then, in a move that had surprised most people who knew Ralph (he wasn't famous for making decisions or taking action) he and Petra had got married. At the time, I'd just been relieved that he was better, and someone instead of me was taking care of him.

Wilf spent quite a bit of time at their house now but didn't show any signs of wanting to take Ralph and Petra up on their invitations to live with them, despite her constantly buying him presents. After everything that had happened between Wilf and his dad, I thought he should make up his own mind where to live and in his own time; secretly, of course, I hoped that he would never pack up his messy bedroom and move to the other side of town. I considered him my special gift in life alongside my own girls.

I felt a tug towards them all as I lay having my blood pressure taken. Well, them and wine. I should be at home by now with a bucket of Sauvignon Blanc. Instead, *this* was my Friday night.

'Now, it's Callie?' Maura said. 'Short for what? Caroline?'

'Calypso,' I said, embarrassed to explain as always. 'Odd parents.'

Maura spent a few seconds looking at the blood-pressure gauge. 'If I was called Calypso, there's no way I'd be shortening it. It's a brilliant name.'

'Now it's the brand name of lemonade or something,' I said. 'But once it was a character in a book that my mother liked called *The Camomile Lawn*. Calypso was always having sex with people she wasn't married to.'

The bang on the head had made me overshare. Maura smiled though – this was probably pretty tame tosh for a night in A & E.

'Free love?' she drawled, arching an eyebrow. 'Now, your blood pressure is fine, Callie. You don't feel any pain?'

'I think I'm going to have a few bruises but that's all.'

'And your vision?'

I look around me at the yellowing walls and the nylon curtain. 'All fine.'

Maura wrote on a chart on a clipboard. Around me I could hear the sounds of a bustling ward: a mix of voices, whirring machines, the pad of soft shoes on the tiles.

'Well, the doctor will be coming along soon to check you out.' Maura looked at the chart again. 'And you don't feel confused?'

'Confused?' I said. Annoyed about being there, numb and a bit emotional, but not *confused* so to speak...

'Well, it says here that post the accident, you seemed confused.'

'Well, I was joking a bit about...'

'Says here that you kept calling yourself the "Invisible Woman",' said Maura, and she raised another majestic eyebrow at me. She was probably about fifty, not much older than me, but I already wished she were my mum.

'It was a joke,' I said weakly. 'The driver kept saying he didn't see me and… he was delivering curry.' I looked down at my trousers. I could still smell lemongrass, but there were no signs of splatters.

'The paramedics said it went all over the kerb.' Maura cocked her head to one side and laughed. She probably laughed a lot; she had that kind of look. 'So, what's all this about being invisible?'

'It was a joke,' I muttered again, colouring. 'Bang on the head.' I was embarrassed now about causing a fuss and making a fool of myself.

'Comes from somewhere, though?' Maura looked knowingly at me. 'You got someone to talk to?'

'It was a *joke*,' I managed, before a waterfall of tears rolled down my face. What was it about someone being nice to you when you felt sorry for yourself that made you blub like a baby?

Maura was quickly beside me, rubbing my shoulder and saying, 'Hey, come on. Maybe you've got a lot on. And that's without some cyclist mowing you down.'

'I was on my way home from work,' I told her in between sobs. How long had it been since I'd cried? It felt strangely good. Cleansing and overdue. 'Going to give the kids dinner.'

'How many have you got?'

'Three: a boy, fourteen, and twin girls. They're sixteen,' I said, as she handed me tissues. 'Although the boy's not mine really. His mum died ages ago, before I met his dad.'

'Families are not that straightforward now, are they?' Maura clicked a few switches. 'Are you with him now? He's not the twins' dad?'

'No to both questions. The girls' dad was a bloke called Dougie – a short thing in my late twenties. I got pregnant and I wanted to keep them; he didn't and, to be fair, had always said he was going to live back in Australia. I was a voluntary single mum.'

'To *twins*? You're a brave woman, Callie.' She mimicked very believably holding two babies up to her impressive bosom. 'Was it like two at a time? Rather you than me.' She winked, and I had to laugh despite the tears.

'But then I got together with Ralph and he already had Wilf and we were together until a couple of years back,' I carried on eventually. 'Ralph had a breakdown and became an alcoholic. He's all right now though.'

'You've been through *a lot*,' Maura mused. 'And you took on his boy?' Her questions were gentle and distracting. She stood still now at the end of the bed and looked as if she really gave a fuck about my complicated family set-up.

'I love him,' I told her, and she just nodded.

'Bet you've got olds to look out for too.'

I thought of Mum and Dad, who lived down the road, and stopped crying. 'Just two extra children in their seventies. My mum is practically deaf now, poor her, and they're both a bit strange.' At least no in-laws that I was responsible for. That was a bonus. And Ralph no longer turned up on my doorstep broke/pissed/useless since he'd got better and married Petra. Somehow, she'd managed to keep him sober – a fact that she was very fond of passively aggressively pointing out to me, as if I still had feelings for her husband. I didn't, I promise. And frankly, although I didn't want him to return to his worst periods, she'd made him quite odd and boring now, like a robot in their beige home. I shook my head and concentrated on Maura. 'What about you?'

'I've got three kids, two grandchildren and three old ones,' she said. I nodded – shit, thank God, no grandkids yet. But then she added, 'In my *house*.' She paused dramatically. 'Sometimes some of them go back to their own places.'

She joined in with my laughing, which dried up the tears. 'It's all the bloody washing,' Maura carried on. She shushed with her finger and looked around her at the curtain, mock-worried about if anyone could hear her. 'I'm not supposed to swear in front of patients, but you try putting up with this shit. The only good thing about it is getting out of that house.' That old female joke – I come to work to have a rest. Maura carried on. 'All that, "do you know where my rugby socks are", and, "can I have a twenty to go out and get wankered?" And that's from my *husband*.'

She winked once more but she'd set me off again – this time more tears with my laughing.

Maura did nothing to silence me, but she stepped forward to rub my shoulders again. 'You let it out,' was all she said. 'Mrs Invisible? They didn't have her in the superheroes movies.'

'I'm no superhero,' I said.

'Sometimes it feels like you have to be, though, doesn't it?' Maura said. She sat down on the end of the bed. 'Where do you work, hun?'

I told her about my unbelievably pointless job running the HR team of a small car-leasing company. Well, pointless apart from it being necessary as I was economically responsible for three teenagers, a dog and, quite often, my parents.

'Here's to having it all,' whispered Maura. 'What do you think of that, Mrs Invisible? Now, haven't you got a new man?' She then clearly remembered that she'd been on a course on how to be more liberal because she hastily added, 'Or a woman? Or...'

'No man,' I said. 'There just doesn't seem to be any time.' I knew this was an excuse. But now, faced with a choice of lying on the sofa guiltily reading *Grazia* or doing all the plucking, waxing and trying to remember how to flirt that went with going on a date, I'd choose the couch and celebrity gossip every time.

'You must go out? Gorgeous woman like you.' I smiled politely at the compliment. Not gorgeous. Not any more, although I was dimly aware of a time when I'd been attractive enough to have a steady stream of lovers and lover applicants. God, it felt so long ago. Now I was a pale shadow of that confident, fun person.

'Have you done that Match.com thing?' Maura gestured to her head and then her pelvis. 'Full head of hair? Bald. Six foot two? Bonsai in real life. Big cock? Can't even see it, mister.' I loved Maura, just loved her. She winked, getting up. 'Well, the doc will probably say you need ibuprofen and a lie-down, but I recommend a shag.'

We laughed a bit more and then she looked reluctantly at her watch. 'Now, I reckon the crash has made you a bit shaken, but the doc will give you the once-over, Mrs Invisible.' She looked at me kindly; I bet her grandkids loved her.

'I'll be fine.' *I've only got the same shit going on as everyone else.* A bang on the head had turned me into a temporary batshit-crazy nutjob, who cried and made unnecessary jokes and felt sorry for herself, that was all. I shook my head.

Maura nodded. 'Look after yourself.'

Please don't go. I need you to look after me as well as your extensive family. 'Thank you for cheering me up.'

She blew me a kiss and disappeared round the curtain.

My best friend Marvin came to pick me up. He appeared in the bay from nowhere, like Mr Tumnus in Narnia, his goatee beard in a really good point. He was wearing mascara, striped black and red leggings and a floaty, theatrical coat. 'You get knocked down, but you get up again...' he sang tunelessly but dramatically.

'I'm sorry, were you going out?' I said.

'You know damn well this is what I always look like to watch TV on a Friday night,' Marvin replied, then, as I went to get down from the trolley bed, he rushed towards me. 'You stay there. Now what did the doctor say?'

'I'm fine,' I said. 'Take co-codamol, watch out in case I puke as that means concussion. Have a kip.'

'The lady takes to her bed.' Marvin did his best Oscar Wilde impression. 'You will receive visitors in the shape of me, Ajay and Abby.' He meant our two other best friends, who we called the 'AAs' because they should've been at a meeting years ago.

He put one of his weedy arms underneath me and I pretended this would help. We hobbled along the corridor, passing all the people who were coughing or wheeling oxygen cylinders, but on their way to have a fag. I told him about the crash. 'I went a bit nuts for a minute though,' I said in the end.

'What kind of nuts?'

'I kept calling myself the Invisible Woman. It was because of how the cyclist – who turns out to be my new neighbour, by the way – kept saying that he didn't see me. But I was deranged.'

'You're all right now?'

'I just feel stupid. But then there was this nurse who was great. Told me about her family. I mean, *she's* got grandkids.'

'Oh, my God, not grandkids,' Marvin groaned. 'You're already like one of those lactating animals with someone dependent hanging off every teat.'

It was the kind of joke we made from knowing each other so long but I started to cry again in the corridor. Marvin swung round and hugged me quickly. 'Oh, God, my stupid big mouth, I'm so sorry, you know I didn't mean it like that, Callie…'

I shuddered into his bony shoulder. 'I know, I'm sorry,' I said. 'It's just, you know, I feel so old and knackered and…'

'You're just tired,' Marv said diplomatically.

'I suppose it's just what happens to you around my age.'

'Sandwich generation,' said Marvin. 'You get the kids, the parents, the whole lot.'

'All those people and yet we still make the sandwiches,' I said, and we started towards the car park. 'Seriously, Marv, sod getting old.'

Marvin squeezed my shoulder. 'You're in a rage against age. Oooh. That's good: a rage against age. Go me.'

'Go you,' I said. 'You're a sage in my rage against age.'

'Just a stage in your rage against age,' Marvin went on.

'Turn the page on your rage…'

'I think we're done, don't you?' He smiled, and we carried on down the corridor.

As we tried to work the car-park machine, Marvin asked, 'Was he hot?'

'Who?' I handed him my purse.

'The Deliveroo guy?'

'I have no idea. He was about our age: older than your usual delivery dude and quite middle class. Maybe he's hit hard times.'

Marvin managed to get the machine to spit out a yellow token. 'Look what happens when Seymour Hill becomes hip.'

His point was that Deliveroo had only just set up in our town, alongside loads of other hipster stuff. Google had built a new office at the London end of our trainline and lots of millennial families had moved to leafy Seymour Hill overnight – our parks had become full of thirty-something men carrying skateboards with babies strapped to their chests in slings; we'd got a sushi bar, a craft beer shop and a vinyl record store too. I secretly approved.

Marvin had a date. He told me he'd texted her – Marvin was extremely camp but resolutely heterosexual – to tell her that he'd had an emergency and would be late.

We got almost to my house in his Fiat 500 before he said, 'You look absolutely fine to me, Cal. Bit shaken, you know, but fine. Do you think, what with chatting her up on Tinder for ages... that you'd mind if I went to the date? And the kids are at home, aren't they? Or some of them?'

'I'll be fine,' I said. We swung into our Victorian terrace. All I wanted to do was sleep. I'd tell the kids what'd happened, and they'd sort themselves out. And then I'd postpone having that bucket of wine and see if I could sleep all this off and start again tomorrow. 'You go and get laid.'

Marvin didn't bother to deny that this was his sole intention. 'I love you,' he said as he drew up. 'I'll come round tomorrow.'

I picked up the Sainsbury's bag. 'Thank you so much for coming to get me.' We hugged. I felt the first twinges of the bruises I'd have in the morning.

It was only as I got out of the car that I realised there was someone leaning on the post by my front gate.

He carried a paper food bag and was still wearing greeny-blue and black Lycra.

'Oh, thank God for that,' he said in greeting. 'You're all right.'

'Not gone totally fruit bat yet,' I said as I came into the light from the lamp post. 'Sorry about all that.'

'It's me who should be sorry.' He moved forward as if he wanted to help me. 'Look, I really hope you like sushi.'

2

I f-ing love sushi. Well, actually, cold, slimy, raw sashimi. Preferably salmon or tuna. And I love edamame beans. And the inside-out rolls with crab and mango.

The maki sticky rice with bits of cucumber in it, not so much. I wondered what he'd bought – expensive, raw fish or basic rolls? I looked at the food bag and it had the logo of the new sushi restaurant, No Fusion, that had opened in the high street but that I hadn't been to yet, what with it being completely booked out by hipsters in lumberjack shirts.

I looked at him and tried to work out the likely success rate of him handing over the sushi but then buggering off to let me sleep.

'That's really kind of you,' I said. His face was smiling and contrite in the darkness. It was a calm face, now that he'd stopped looking so panicked, no unnecessary facial hair and no wanky hairdo that looked as if he was trying too hard, just a mop of white stuff that had probably been crushed by his cycle helmet. He was just above average height and, in his Lycra, a bit on the skinny side for a man who was, I guessed, in his forties – but that probably came from cycling up and down the hills of our town delivering Thai curry and sushi to the people of Seymour Hill. I wondered vaguely how he'd tipped up in my street and how he could afford the home counties rental price, if he was riding a bike for a living. Then, instead, I thought about getting my hands on the sushi and getting into my house.

He could very well be a serial killer. Frankly, he'd already mowed me down on a Friday night – his creds as a potential slayer of women had been sealed when I'd faceplanted the tarmac outside the station.

Still, *sushi*. And probably pretty good sushi. And the kids were in. If he tried anything I could just get them to shout 'no win, no fee' really loudly.

But he held up the sushi bag. 'You can just take it,' he said, and I blushed because it was as if he'd just read my brain or I'd been saying my thoughts out loud. 'I just wanted to say sorry again and make sure you were OK. Look, is there anything else I can do to make it up to you?'

'I'm just exhausted,' I said, 'that's all. It was an accident and it happened and...' I took the bag of sushi and it felt satisfyingly heavy. 'You didn't need to do this.'

'It was the least I could do,' he said but looked relieved. 'Look, I know I live just there—' he indicated a blue door on our side of the street '—but can I give you my number? In case you have any lasting injuries or something?'

'Don't worry, I won't sue your arse.' I smiled.

'That wasn't what...' he said. 'I just wanted you to have my number in case...'

I couldn't think of what other 'in case' there would be, but I got my phone out and he smiled.

'My name's Patrick,' he said.

'I'll file it under Bloke in Lycra,' I said and put that into my contacts.

'Not the best outfit,' he said, looking down at his uniform, which made me glance at his legs (muscly and long, if I were noticing, but I wasn't) and then hastily look away. I wasn't in the habit of sexually assessing any man at that point, let alone my new neighbourhood food-delivery person.

He told me his number and I punched that in too.

'Thanks for the sushi.' I turned to go.

'Sorry again.' He started to wheel his bike up the street. 'Really glad you're OK.'

You could hear the din of an epic teenage row before I'd even got halfway up the path that led round the side of our house to the back door into the kitchen. I sighed. That would be the twins, then. Daisy and Lily passionately loved each other – it came from hanging out in the same over-stretched uterus together for nine months, I guessed, one egg fertilised by the same swimming sperm – but they also argued with just as much feeling.

About pretty much anything.

'Fuck that,'¶ Daisy was shouting. 'I didn't know there was a speed restriction on the fucking** broadband. What

---

¶ Yes, I understand that it's not the done thing for a sixteen-year-old girl to swear like a drunken sailor, but this was a particular phase Daisy was going through, more of which later.
** Yep, as above.

is this? A developing nation? Who doesn't have super-fast broadband?'

'But I can't do my revision,' Lily shouted back, only marginally more quietly.

Lugging both food bags and my handbag, I felt like turning round and going back out again but I took a deep breath and got to the back door. I could see their silhouettes behind the glass of the window, one either side of the kitchen table, two tall skinny figures, leaning forward in aggression.

As I pushed open the door, they both turned to me. Even in fury their similarities were as obvious as their differences – their faces were curled into identical snarls, even though Daisy's face was rounder, her nose more pronounced and her eyes bigger than Lily's more delicate, pensive features. Their hair was the same though – both refused to cut it and it fell down their backs, so dark it was almost black, almost to their bottoms.

Wilf was in the kitchen too, although he was sitting at the table with his noise-cancelling headphones on – wise, I thought – and was prodding at his iPhone. He didn't even seem to notice that I'd come in, although this wasn't unusual.

The dog, Bodger – a small and, most people might say, scruffy springer spaniel of dubious hygiene – was sitting under the table with his face curled in agony. Bodger was generally a good reflection of the emotive state of my household, his face being particularly expressive for a dog.

'What's going on?' I said.

The twins both started talking at once.

'Right, so I'm trying to do online past papers and it's against the clock and the wireless was really slow and that's because Daisy was streaming *Riverdale*.'†† Lily, accusing and red in the face.

'Apparently, we don't have enough fucking broadband.' Daisy, definitely in the wrong, was already fighting back.

'Please stop swearing,' I begged, dropping the shopping and holding onto the kitchen cabinet with one hand. The drugs from the hospital were wearing off – I could feel my headache coming back with a vengeance, sharp and throbbing at my temples.

I held up my hand. They both took no notice.

'So, her watching some crap TV show is more important than my education.'

'It's *Riverdale*! Everyone's watching it. Literally everyone. It's, like, social death‡‡ not to have watched it.'

'Social death? You're such a drama queen.'

Bodger let out a small moan; Wilf was oblivious.

'Please shut up,' I said less quietly, holding my hand to my head.

Wilf looked up then and, seeing me, he smiled his lovely lopsided grin. 'Hi, Cal,' he said extra loudly as he was wearing headphones. It hurt my head, but I smiled back, and his dark hair flopped into his eyes. He was still wearing his school shirt and blazer, tie knot so loose it was halfway down his chest. He removed the headphones and said more quietly, 'I know you're not a feeding machine, but is there any dinner?'

The feeding machine was one of our jokes. When Wilf was younger he used to wait at the kitchen table for me to

---

†† A TV series from the US; apart from that, it doesn't really matter.
‡‡ Generally, not getting invited to all the right parties.

come in the door, Bodger also looking up hopefully, and I'd say, with a hint of humour, 'What do you think I am, a feeding machine?' Now it had become a standard source of him teasing me.

I pointed to the two food bags on the floor and he nodded contentedly and put his headphones back on.

'That's selfish, Daisy,' I said.

'You'll have to get a, like, job and pay for better broadband yourself.' Lily was gleeful. 'You could get a job at Maccy D's.'

'There is no way I'm wearing a nylon tunic,' Daisy spat. 'And I'd stink of animal fat...' She was a vegetarian, I think at that point, but it was quite confusing as she also sometimes claimed to be a pescatarian, lactose intolerant, a flexitarian§§ and various other things, depending on her mood or political/ideological persuasion that week. Sometimes, she forgot all of these things and ate a standard bacon sandwich, generally when she'd spent a few weeks demanding I buy gluten-free bread and that the whole house stop eating meat.

'Can we deal with this later?' I clutched my head again. 'I've had quite a difficult evening as it is and...'

They were still at it though when the door opened again. I knew it was my parents – who I love dearly, of course – and let out a big sigh.

Mum came in first, all bent from the cold, her practical grey snood pulled over her white hair. 'Calypso? We thought you'd be home by now. Hello, kids.' She said it very loudly

§§ Vegetarian as and when she felt like it – helpful for food shopping and menu planning, I agree.

as she was quite deaf and refused to switch on her hearing aid, due to her belief that the toxicity of radio waves from hearing aids damaged the brain. I secretly thought it was because she liked having an excuse to withdraw from the world.

'All right, Lois?' the twins mumbled, but at least it made them stop arguing. Wilf indicated that he'd seen them arrive by doing a pretend fist bump in the air. Mum did one back. My parents refused to be called anything 'age-defining' like Gran and Grandad.

Dad – Lorca to the kids – came in after her, as tall as she was short, bending his head in the doorway. He had a hat on too and pulled his overcoat tight round his thin frame. His face was lit up in his usual smile but there was five days' worth of grey stubble covering his chin. I wondered what I needed to do to get my folks to look after themselves: did they actually shower? His face itched mine as he kissed me, but he didn't seem to smell.

Mum threw off her coat and sat down at the table beside Daisy. 'Lily's been such a twat,' she immediately started telling her gran.

'Daisy, please, I've had *enough* of this language,' I said, my head throbbing even more now from the collection of humanity around me. They were my family, sure, and I loved them to death, but that didn't mean they didn't make me feel demented, *all the time.*

'Twat's not even a swear word,' Daisy said. 'Although it is in America. There it's pronounced twot and it's just like saying c—'

I shouted, 'Daisy!' just in time and she grinned as if she'd outsmarted me. Of course, she had.

Lily told Mum about the broadband issue.

'It's corporations wanting to take advantage of the vulnerability of the young,' shouted my mother when she'd finished.

Dad had managed to get Wilf's headphones off him. 'We had ones like that at the silent rave,' he told Wilf, who managed to not look too shocked about his adoptive grandparents knowing what a silent rave was, let alone attending one.

'That's so cool,' he said kindly. 'You and Lois throwing some shapes.'

'It's at this new centre we've found out about.' Dad addressed us all now. 'It's a multigenerational meeting place. You can live there too.'

The kids and I looked blank. Dad was always finding new 'experiences' and believed very strongly that there should be no limit on personal development at any age. 'Going to be dead soon,' he'd say cheerfully, 'so no reason not to have a go at everything on offer'. Recently he'd started talking about going to the Burning Man festival in the desert near Vegas, which was wild and hippy and full of psychedelic drugs. We tried not to mention the fact that he was seventy-nine and sometimes couldn't seem to get from his house, a few streets away, to ours without getting lost, let alone mainline acid in forty degrees in Nevada. He tried very hard to keep up with the kids, particularly the EDM DJs that Wilf adored.¶¶

¶¶ Electronic dance music. In essence, repetitive beeps and other noises, with no discernible melody.

But none of us knew what a multigenerational centre was. I didn't know if I cared at that point – I was standing by the kitchen cabinets with my coat on and *still* no one knew that I'd come there straight from A & E.

'It's called Yoof and a Roof,' Dad went on. 'It's a concept from Holland. Young people get somewhere to live and us oldies live alongside them – everyone benefits as our brains are being stretched and we get to do stuff that keeps us active. We're thinking of moving there.'

'We had a brilliant time,' shouted Mum.

This was too much to take in, so I tried not to. My folks lived in the home I'd grown up in. From the outside, it looked like one of those terraced houses on the TV on programmes about hoarders. Inside, the sofas were over-stuffed, sagging but comfortable. The kitchen was full of whatever fad they'd got hooked on last – there'd been a film screen for a while in front of the sink while they binge-watched *Game of Thrones*, which made washing up quite hard. It was messy and mad, but it was where they lived.

I turned and took my coat off. 'Where's it at, Lorca?' Wilf asked politely.

'Down by the park. They've taken over Seymour House,' Dad went on enthusiastically. 'The old boys' school.' He was talking about a particularly Hogwarty building with gothic spires.

'It's painted in colours to help people with dementia,' shouted Mum.

'Cool,' said Wilf.

'What will you do with your house?' Lily said, ever practical.

'Oh, sell it or rent it or something,' Mum said vaguely.

The thought of getting rid of the stuff in my folks' house and preparing it for someone else to live in it made my head hurt even harder. That was days/weeks/years of effort. Whole Saturdays and Sundays for decades, probably. And all down to me. I mused how selfish it was of them to have had only one child – me – when I could really do with some super-helpful siblings to share the strain – and pleasure, of course – of their lovely company.

They'd crossed a line in about the last six months and were less endearing-crazy than stop-the-world-I-want-to-get-off-nuts. The idea of someone else making sure they were feeding themselves and washing in an old people's home was quite appealing.

Lily went out of the room, probably to do more revision. And still no one had noticed that I was a shell of the woman who'd left the house this morning. I'd just got out of A & E, for God's sake, and none of them had shut up long enough for me to tell them. I desperately wanted – needed – to lie down.

'We'll have to think about all that,' I said as calmly as I could. 'And not now... I've had quite a day and...' I started to unpack the bags.

No one got up to help or asked me why my day had been such a bastard. I tried to work out if my parents had eaten already or had popped round hoping to be fed.

My precious sushi. I'd still not peeked in any of the bags to work out the sashimi quotient; if I drew attention to the bag itself, its contents, raw fish or otherwise, would be devoured.

'Poor Cal,' Wilf did say, but then put his headphones back on while Daisy got her laptop out, so they could show her the old people's home on the web. They were all poking at the screen and saying things like, 'Can you make the text any bigger?' when Lily came storming back in.

'Daisy,' she shrieked. 'WTF!*** It's still going really slowly because of you...' and the whole argument about how crap our broadband was and how selfish Daisy was started again.

My parents ignored them. 'Is there any spare food going?' Dad said. I felt the bruises in my ribs hurt as I reached into the fridge. 'You were going to make dinner, weren't you?'

I started to cry but this time in outrage. I also started shouting – I'm not proud of any of it. 'Does any of you know or *care* what's happened to me tonight?'

Wilf couldn't hear, of course, but the twins and Mum and Dad all immediately stopped talking and looked up from the table.

'Mum, are you all right?' Daisy said as I clutched my head with one hand and the kitchen bench with the other.

'NO! I am not all right,' I went on. 'I'm seriously not all right. I've been knocked down...'

Daisy leapt to her feet and rushed to me. Mum and Dad both looked at me with slack jaws. Lily was wide-eyed with anxiety. It made my heart ping. She was desperately worried about the exams, but also lately she had an air – like a bird on a wire waiting for the next reason to fly away. My tears were coming wet and fast although I was trying to stop them for her sake.

*** What the F**k – I apologise now, wholeheartedly and repeatedly, for the state of my offspring and the inadequate parenting that should have stopped this kind of behaviour.

Daisy threw her arms around me. They were skinny and inadequate, but I clung to her ribcage and she let me cry into her shoulder. She smelt like she did as a baby despite the overall waft of Hollister body spray. 'Awwww, Ma,' she said. 'What do you mean, knocked down?'

In between humphs of woe, I let go of her, tried to explain about Patrick, the ambulance, going to A & E and Marvin bringing me home. I had to stop in the middle as we'd forgotten Wilf, who was told to take off his headphones by Mum.

'Is there something going down?' he asked and was given a quick summary by Daisy.

'Bad shit, Callie,' he said after this. 'Are you OK?'

His eyes looked baleful – like Bambi. He picked up the stripy blue and white scarf he always wore and wrapped it round his neck as if to protect himself.

'I'm fine,' I said. 'Just need to go to bed.'

'Man,' said Wilf, 'no shit.'

I held up the bag of sushi from No Fusion and for a tenth of a second Lily's face lit up, like it used to. 'Let's see what's in it. Maybe get the chopsticks out?' Mum and Dad were salivating. 'Someone needs to cook something else though. The bloke bought it for one – or two – not six.'

'We'll get Domino's or something?' Wilf said with carbohydrate hope in his voice.

I am pleased to report there was a six-slice box of mixed sashimi as well as lots of sushi, complete with wasabi, soy sauce and ginger. I got two slices of sashimi through epic negotiation, which included drawing on the fact that I was the only person who'd been to A & E that evening. Lily ate her maki rolls with her shoulders bent. Daisy took a photo. 'It's gram-able,'[†††] she said.

Wilf got his quasi-grandies to pay for a massive pizza and similarly sized garlic bread by showing them how cool the Domino's app was.

It was all lovely, but the idea of a pillow was lovelier. 'I'm going to bed.'

Lily came up the stairs with me and fussed around. 'I can't believe this happened to you,' she said.

I tried to reassure her while I cleaned my teeth and then had a quick look at my bruises while she was fetching me some arnica. I was going to have a pattern of purple cascading down one side of my body; it would turn yellow from there: attractive. Still, it wasn't as if I were going to be showing my body to anyone else. That sort of thing didn't happen to me any more.

I pulled on my pyjamas and sat on the edge of the bed to swallow the arnica tablets with a glass of water. I also necked a couple more co-codamol to try and control the throb of my head.

Lily encouraged me into bed and then gave me a kiss as if I were the child and she the mum. 'I love you,' she said and tiptoed out of the room as if I were already asleep.

My phone tinged in my bag and I picked it up to see a text from Marvin.

[†††] Food that was aesthetically pleasing and aspirational enough to be posted on her Instagram feed, making all regular meals seem inadequate.

DAAAAAAATTTTTTEEEEEEEE

It read, which meant he'd managed to pull a hot one, then:

Hope you're OK Cal, will check in with you tomorrow, big love Mx

I sent him a simple kiss back and saw that I had unread emails. Mostly junk promotions.

'Night, Cal,' said Wilf through the door. 'Hope you feel a bit better soon.' And he was gone, his teenage body going down the stairs two at a time. I smiled despite everything. It was hard not to, when Wilf was around.

I lay back on the pillows and desultorily deleted another couple of junk promotions. Then I clicked on an email that had been sent earlier that day, from an address I didn't recognise –

Roger.Balmain@Balmainandpartners.com

with the subject,

Attachment for Ms Calypso Brown

It was probably one of those scams requesting my banking details to secure an amazing deal in Nigeria where I'd make millions, I thought woozily.

But instead, the email sprang into life on my screen.

And my world fell apart.

3

Dear Ms Brown,
Read the very official-looking attachment on letterheaded paper from a solicitor's practice with an address in the town centre.

> We are instructed on behalf of Mr Ralph Colesdown and Mrs Petra Colesdown of 46 Sycamore Close, Seymour Hill, to officially inform you that they intend to take the minor Master Wilf Colesdown ('Wilf') with them when they move in July to Cape Town, South Africa.

South Africa? What was this about South Africa? They were going to take Wilf to South Africa? On holiday? To visit Petra's folks?
'when they move in July,'
No, they meant for good.

Oh, no. Oh, no. Oh, God, no. Not Wilf. Being taken away – and not to live on the other side of town but the bottom of another hemisphere.

My worst nightmare had become reality via words on a screen.

Why hadn't Ralph said anything? I'd seen him two days previously when I'd gone to pick up Wilf with his bike. He hadn't met my eyes as he'd come to the door of their house, standing on the faux-Georgian porch steps and hurriedly going to help Wilf load the bike into the back of my estate, but I'd written that off as just being Ralph. 'All right, Cal?' he'd said and that had been it.

The coward. The unbelievable shifty coward. He'd known then that this letter was coming but said nothing because he hated confrontation. Having to be the bearer of bad news was anathema to Ralph. My left fist clenched into a ball as I held the phone with my right. I read on:

Mr and Mrs Colesdown believe that this official communication, whereby they give notice of their intention to emigrate with Mr Colesdown's son, Wilf, recognises the role that you have played latterly acting in loco parentis to Wilf,

Loco parentis? Was that what they called looking after him for eight years? I remembered the six-year-old boy who'd walked through the door, shyly holding onto his dad's hand all that time ago. He'd mumbled, 'Yes, please,' when I gave him a drink, had played happily enough with Lily and Daisy, who had treated him like a pet kitten, but had avoided directly meeting my eyes.

Newly in love with Ralph – and yes, it was love back then – and the idea that we could create a more perfect family from interlacing our two imperfect ones, I'd silently promised to always be there for Wilf. And he was always a very easy child to love – sweet natured and quietly clever; blackly funny in a way that made you gasp for breath before you laughed, a dark mop of hair that had come from his mother, tragically dead of a brain tumour when he was just two. I made a promise to Sylvia to look after her son, while never forgetting her.

My heart was beating fast in my chest. I was supposed to be going to sleep to recover but these surges of anger had made me feel more awake than I'd ever been.

Was this Petra? Certainly, in the last few months, she'd bought Wilf even more presents – new devices for his Mac, but never quite the one he really, really wanted; clothes that he politely accepted and then threw to the back of his cupboard – and cooked him dinner whenever he was visiting his father. Wilf said most of her food tasted like polystyrene, which I pointed out wasn't kind at all, but, of course, I was secretly pleased.

Ralph had also tried to talk to me about Wilf moving in with them for good, but I knew how to brush him off. All I had to do was ask whether Wilf had said anything himself about it and I knew I'd won a reprieve. Ralph was, fundamentally, a lazy bastard and he hated any kind of difficult conversation. And while a combination of anti-depressants and Petra had made him much more subdued than he used to be, he still steered clear of any kind of confrontation. So, all I'd had to do when he'd brought it up again, a bit more forcefully this time, was slightly raise my voice and he'd slunk off.

But had they been plotting other ways to get Wilf under their roof? I thought the way Petra tried to love Wilf was quite bogus. On the few occasions when I'd seen them together, she'd made quite a display of affection for him, but her hugs were wooden and her shrill voice over-solicitous. And she seemed to always be looking out of the corner of her eye at me to see if her behaviour was having any impact: it was as if she was playing at being a better mother than I was. She also spent a lot of time talking about how she'd transformed Ralph, as if she cared more about being seen as an angel of mercy to him and his motherless son than actually being a real mother figure to Wilf.

It had never occurred to me that she would want to move Wilf to a whole different country. Or that Ralph would ever have thought about it either.

I read on:

but provides sufficient time for you to emotionally prepare for the departure.

How could I emotionally prepare? And what about Wilf? How was he supposed to emotionally prepare?

It also recognises that this is the appropriate time in Wilf's education to make the move, giving him two years to prepare for his secondary school examinations under the SA system.

Christ. As if they would even think about his education. I wasn't even sure that Ralph knew what he was choosing in his GCSE options. It was me who went to the school briefings and helped him fill in the forms, trying to find a way he could do music tech as well as drama. The timing would be nothing to do with Wilf's education.

This had to be down to Petra – and I'd clearly underestimated her as being a slightly strange, but ultimately harmless do-gooder, who got a kick out of turning my ex-partner into a reformed character.

When she first got together with Ralph, my reaction, along with Marv, Abby and Ajay, had been 'What the F**k?' She had a sleek head of blonde hair and wore very efficient block-colour trouser suits – as if she were going to one day become Hilary Clinton – and she worked as a corporate lawyer somewhere in London. What did she see in feckless, scruffy, bohemian Ralph? But the truth was that, after a couple of years when we'd all played a part in collecting him from whatever bar he was passed out in, or trying to protect the kids from seeing the worst of his drunken excesses, we were just glad that someone else was helping him. And Petra had managed to get him to stay sober and out of trouble. He'd even started up his graphic design business again. Then eventually he'd asked Wilf to be his best man at his wedding – a simple thing with very few guests at the town hall. Petra, I'd thought, despite really not liking her at all, was generally, in her determination to fix broken people like Ralph, a force for good. Well, I'd got that wrong. Very wrong indeed.

Mr and Mrs Colesdown trust that suitable ongoing visiting rights should be established between you and Wilf on an annual basis and regularly via Skype or a similar platform.

What? I'd see him once a year? Pick him up from the plane they'd put him on, hardly recognising him because he'd have grown? And we'd use Skype. As if that made up for seeing him sitting at the kitchen table with his headphones on, eating a bowl of cereal.

I bit my hand while I read on.

Mr and Mrs Colesdown believe that the use of a solicitor in the case provides for appropriate third-party arbitration but trust that this will not be necessary, given their right to assert Mr Colesdown's parental responsibility and rights in the case of Wilf.

Ralph certainly had rights. I'd never adopted Wilf when we were together – to do that we'd have had to get married. That was out of the question in the beginning as we never had any money. And after the early years together, I wasn't sure I wanted to marry Ralph and I think he was relieved. I became more of a carer than a partner when he was really drinking, very sad that I couldn't seem to help him, but also focused hard on looking after the kids. When we eventually split up, I was very glad I hadn't married him. But that meant that Ralph was Wilf's father and Petra was his stepmother and I was... well, acting in loco parentis or whatever it was the lawyer had called it.

I must have some legal leg to stand on, then, I thought in desperation. And what about Wilf? Didn't he have a right to say what he wanted to do? I knew he would hate to leave me.

My headache was succumbing to the drugs I'd swallowed but there was no escaping the new tension that was stiffening every bone in my bruised body.

I thought about the girls, who considered him their quite annoying and smelly sibling, but who could barely remember a time when he hadn't been their wingman. They called him 'Bro' and he called them 'One' (Daisy) and 'Two' (Lily). They'd grown up together and would all protect each other from anything, despite it being very, very uncool to express affection for each other out loud. What about the effect on Lily, already so raw from whatever was going on in her head? With Wilf gone there'd be an empty seat at that kitchen table, so maddeningly full of life.

I had to be able to fight this. I was a strong and capable woman.

I turned off my phone and rolled over into my pillow. There were noises from the kids and my folks still occasionally coming up the stairs. Laughter. I could hear the noise of Mum and Dad eventually slowly shuffling out of the back door, which banged with a click I knew so well.

I was shaking with cold despite the heat of my duvet and the dark of the room. Why couldn't Ralph go to South Africa if he wanted to be with Petra but leave Wilf behind? Petra didn't really want Wilf; I was sure of that, deep down. And Ralph loved his son deeply, of course, but had been happy to let me have the lion's share of parenting. Wilf could fly out and see him and he could visit, and I'd look after him, and he would be stable and…

My best bet was to make Ralph and Petra see this, I thought as the drugs and drama of the day took over. I'd make them understand.

Knocked out by life as well as a cyclist, I fell into sleep. Tomorrow I'd sort it all out.

4

I woke up the next morning because something was rustling round in my bedroom. I opened one super-heavy eye, still deep in delirium, and there, in the shafts of bright morning light coming around the curtains, creeping across to *my* chest of drawers with an exaggerated tiptoe, was the unmistakable shape of Daisy.

'Ummpppfffhhh, I can see you, madam,' I managed.

'Oh,' she tried to laugh, 'but I've got no knickers and—'

'You've loads of clean ones. Get your own bloody pants,' I hissed. Daisy frequently stole my underwear rather than look through the pile of clean washing I would have put on her bed a couple of days back, which would now be mixed up with the fetid heap of books, clothes and general teenage debris that was knee-deep on her bedroom floor. It was not unusual for me to get out of the shower wet, rushing for work, and open my drawer to find myself completely out of knickers, due to my dear, dear daughters.

'But I'm late for the meeting,' she said, her hand still going for the drawer. She meant the Saturday morning meeting of the local youth charity, which was called GenZ.[‡‡‡] She loved it, talking politics with other young people who were 'woke'[§§§] and occasionally they went on a march, normally to raise awareness of something really peripheral like saving Madagascan otters or the inalienable right to communicate at school through only dolphin song.

'Well, go commando,' I said, rolling over onto my pillow and becoming freshly aware of my bruised body. 'No one will know if you wear a real skirt.' She was wearing something that looked like a long jumper, which came just past her arse. 'Or trousers. Actual trousers that cover your legs.'

'It's because of my dress that I need your knickers,' she said. 'Big black ones.' This was one of my rules – the non-negotiable wearing of boy short pants with any miniskirts – and I knew she'd won one over on me.

I couldn't be bothered to fight on, sighed and shut my eye again: 'All I want are my own knickers, just for me.' This was a frequent refrain.

'How do you feel now?' asked Daisy, rustling away in my drawer. As I tried to answer her it came back – not the pain in my body or the dull throb of my head, but, with a slightly delayed wham, the knowledge that Ralph and Petra wanted to take Wilf away from me. I gulped back the lump in my throat.

[‡‡‡] The group was named for the generation of people born between 1995 and 2015. What happens to the next lot?

[§§§] 'I was sleeping but now I'm woke' = being alive to new ideas and philosophies. Daisy loved people who were 'woke'.

'I'll be OK,' I said brightly. 'What's the meeting about today?' Maybe if I put her off knowing what was going on with her brother, I could put off having to face it myself.

'Youth mental health,' said Daisy. Oh, something *useful* for once. 'We've got someone coming from Resilient, who's going to run a programme in the town to make teenagers better able to cope with being part of the most pressured generation *ever.*'

I wasn't exactly sure what these pressures were for Daisy – she was popular, social and attractive and didn't seem fazed by anything, but her sister was a different ball game altogether. I was also impressed: Resilient was a national charity that had hit the headlines by getting famous people from all walks of life – musicians, politicians, actors – to make a film talking about their own struggles with mental health as teenagers. 'That sounds really interesting. Can't you take Lily?'

'She said she's got too much revising to do.' Daisy slammed the drawer – noise, ouch. 'I'm going for coffee afterwards and a party tonight, remember?'

'Revision, madam,' I said, hopelessly. 'Your exams start soon.' But she was gone, my knickers in her hand, pretending she didn't hear me.

'Why does everything have to f-ing beep?' I groaned as I went into the kitchen a few minutes later. Someone, astonishingly, had put the dishwasher on and it was reminding me very loudly, about every ten seconds, that it was finished with a shrill, repetitive beep. I kicked it pathetically with my slippered foot and then pushed the 'off' button with my fist.

Wilf was sitting at the kitchen table prodding away at his Mac, headphones on. As it was Saturday, he was wearing a T-shirt with an obscure DJ's name on it with his blue and white scarf wrapped round his neck; I made a mental note to wash it one day when he stopped wearing it for a minute. Bodger had his head on Wilf's knee: even the dog was going to miss him. I wanted to rush over and hug all the blood out of him as his head bobbed ever so slightly along with the music, but instead, I just stood and stared at him as if by doing so I could make him stay in our kitchen, safe from the world forever. *I'll fight this,* I told him silently as I flicked the kettle switch.

It was the smell of coffee, and me sitting down at the table opposite him, that finally made him sit up and pull off one headphone, smile his wonky grin – so like his dad – and say, 'Hey, Cal.'

'Hey,' I said.

'You don't look injured or anything.'

'I'm fine,' I said. 'There's a purple one here...' I lifted a corner of my long fringe, where there was a quite impressive bruise the size of a small tangerine, tender to my touch, but which was going to be easily covered by make-up and hair. I showed him my left shin too, rolling up my pyjama trousers. 'They're like that all up this side.'

'Man,' said Wilf. 'You need to stay in bed all day, Cal.'

'What are you up to?' I said. *Don't say you're going to your Dad and Petra's.*

'Going to the vinyl shop then jamming in Jowan's garage,' Wilf said, looking as if this was his nirvana. 'Then pizza tonight at his sleepover. You remembered that I'm staying round at his?'

'Yes, of course. Have you recorded anything yet that I can listen to, you and Jowan?' I said this while hoping that he wouldn't offer to play me a track – it was one up from the dishwasher beeping in terms of harmony.

'We've nearly got a new one.' Wilf's face lit up. He gently pushed Bodger's head off his leg, picked up the cereal bowl beside him and then, seeing me look at him, made for the dishwasher. On opening it he looked relieved to find out it was full and lobbed his bowl into the sink as usual.

'How's your dad?' I pushed gently. Although Wilf refused to talk about it, Ralph's breakdown had hurt him very much.

'He's OK,' said Wilf.

'What's he up to? Got much work?'

'Something about finishing some jobs off.' Wilf shrugged. 'He's got a new coat, though, that Petra got him for his birthday. Quite flashy.'

I nodded. We both silently acknowledged that his dad, who'd been borderline hobo in his darkest days of drunkenness, and always a bit 'I'm with the band' in his dress and looks, had sharpened up his act since Petra had come along. Now he sometimes looked nearly conventional, but the shiny end of conventional, as if she'd polished him with Pledge and a good duster.

He grimaced though. 'She said she'd get me something, but it was a bit roadman,¶¶¶ so I said I'd rather have a new microphone.'

¶¶¶ A reference to a particularly flash teen tribe that wears famous brands of sportswear and walks with a hunched slouch; related to 'chavs'.

'It's not your birthday for ages,' I said lightly.

'Petra got a bonus or something.' Wilf shrugged. 'See you tomorrow, Cal, hope you feel better,' and he was gone.

I waited until I'd heard his bike go down the side passage before I banged the table with my fist. They were trying to win Wilf over with more presents. Very expensive presents when it wasn't Christmas or his birthday.

I went to have a shower, thinking about when I'd met Ralph. He'd sat down by me at a school concert, coming in the back door of the hall, late like me, and being forced to sit on the added-on row of chairs reserved for tardy parents, right at the back. He was panting but I felt only sympathy – the mad dash to the school concert was something I knew only too well. I moved over slightly but I didn't look up – I was too busy wondering how I was going to get through listening to the Year 3 Grade 1 violins and recorders, play another number. This time it seemed to be vaguely recognisable as Madonna's 'Holiday', which Daisy and Lily had been practising for a week or two, but with additional full-on screeches and plenty of bum notes.

I must have clenched my teeth and clutched my chair extra hard because he looked at me through the gloom of the hall and grinned, rolling his eyes.

It was interpretative dance next from Year 4 and I had to bite the insides of my face as they came on in leotards tacked with long pieces of green chiffon and wafted (the better dancers) or clunked (those who were never really going to have moves) around the stage pretending to be the sea. He seemed to be shaking beside me, but I couldn't look at him or I was going to lose it. Year 5 did a mash-up of

Rolling Stones songs next with plenty of wannabe Jaggers, probably coached by their dads.

During the cheering that followed I glanced at him. He was clapping as enthusiastically as the rest. He had overlong brown hair and a sheepskin jacket that had probably never seen a dry-cleaner's. In profile his nose was straight and long; his forehead crinkled with his mouth as he smiled.

At the end, the head congratulated the kids on their hard work and told us to wait in the foyer for them. The man beside me stood up, turned to me and said, 'Those violins,' and bent over laughing until I was snorting away with him. His voice had a hint of the artist.

'Mine were in the recorders,' I told him. 'The rehearsals have been hell.' I picked up my bag and went with him into the queue.

His face fell as we shuffled forward together. 'I missed my son – he's in Year 1. I ran all the way, but I missed it.'

Oh, poor him. Fancy having tried that hard and still missing his young son sing. 'It was good. They sang—'

'Abba, I know. We've been practising. His favourite was *Waterloo*. I don't know what to tell him.' He looked stricken. 'I got held up at work and then…'

'It happens to all of us,' I said. 'You have two choices – tell him the truth or tell him you were at the back and he was brilliant. They really were.'

'I can't lie to him,' he said. 'I can't.'

'Well, then, I'll tell him how good he was,' I said, and he looked at me and smiled.

So that was how I met Wilf, a tiny version of his dad, as he came in a line with all his classmates excited to see the pleasure on their parents' faces. He looked up to see the man beside me and gave a grin that sloped to one side with something between shyness and irrepressibility and, as soon as he was able to, ran the few feet to his dad and grabbed his legs.

The man bent down and, putting his arms round him, said something in his ear. And for a tiny moment the smile on his face receded but then, as if he was used to having to deal with bad things, it came back, and he glanced shyly up at me.

'I thought you were absolutely brilliant,' I said and tried to give him a high five. He missed but came back to try again and eventually his tiny palm met mine. '*Waterloo* was the best bit for me. Were you in the front row or second?'

'Front,' said Wilf with a hint of pride.

'What's your name? I need to look out for you when you're famous.'

'Wilf,' he said. 'Not short for Wilfred. Just Wilf.'

'I'm Callie,' I said, not bothering to tell him that that was short for something.

'And I'm Ralph,' said the man beside me.

As I got out of the shower, still deep in this memory, my phone rang from where I'd tossed it on the bed. *Bloke in Lycra.* I sighed but wrapped a towel round me and answered.

'Hello? Callie?'

'Yes, BiL,' I said.

'My name's Patrick, not Bill, but never mind.'

'It's because of the Bloke in Lycra, that I stored your number in on my phone.'

'You can call me whatever you like, but it may take me a while to answer to Bill. What with actually being called Patrick.'

I hmmed for a while but said nothing. I did have stuff to do and while I needed to be polite to my new neighbour it didn't warrant that much effort. Still, he was very solicitous.

'Anyway, I just wanted to make sure you were still feeling all right after last night.'

'Few bruises, that's all.'

'And what about…?'

'You mean am I still crazy?'

'Your words, not mine. But are you still feeling invisible?'

'Only to my immediate family of children and old people,' I said. 'I haven't ventured out into the world yet today.'

'How can you be invisible to your own children? How many of them, anyway?'

'Three,' I sighed. 'They loved the sushi, by the way.'

'If I'd known, I'd have bought more,' he said in a voice that sounded as if he meant it. 'I can't get over what happened. I haven't been doing this gig very long.'

I didn't want to ask why a forty-something man was fetching other people's dinner for a living, so I hmmmed again.

'And I just didn't see you… not that that makes you invisible. In fact, I wanted to say I didn't know how you could ever be invisible…'

'Hmmm.' I needed to get this man off the phone. We'd met because of an unfortunate accident, and it turned out he lived a few doors down, but I didn't need his guilt or clumsy compliments. 'It's sweet of you to call but I have to get on now. There's something I have to deal with. But cheers, BiL,' I said, my thumb hovering over the red 'finish call' button.

'I'm going to go with the Bill thing. Everyone I meet today, I'm going to tell them to call me Bill. Anyway, I'm just glad you're OK.'

If you only knew, I thought as I said goodbye. *If you only knew.*

Lily's door was firmly shut against the new day. Even thinking about her for that brief second of passing made me feel the shiver I associated with her now: worry. It was always there in the background and I spent long hours trying, firstly, to work out what it was that was troubling her so much and, secondly, how to fix it.

I gently pushed the door open and put my head round it. There was a lump in the bed clothes, the covers pulled right over her head as if she was not just sleeping but hiding.

'Lily, are you getting up?' I asked in a whisper. 'It's a new day.'

'Same shit,' came the unmistakable whisper from under the covers.

I sighed. 'Come on, I got knocked over last night and I'm still...'

She sat up then, blinking long lashes heavy with effort and concern as she looked at me. 'But you're all right now, though?'

'Bit bruised but fine.' I sat down on the edge of her bed and held her hand, which lay limply on top of the duvet. 'What about you?'

What I meant was, *What's really going on with you, my darling? You're breaking my heart with all this not quite knowing.*

49

'Just tired with all the revising,' she said in a voice designed to ward me off.

'Well, maybe have a bit of time off today? Daisy's gone to her group; she's not revising today.'

'She holds all of it in her head better than me,' Lily said.

'Not true.' Daisy *could* sink facts into her head for the short amount of time it took to remember them for the test, but the real difference was in her confidence about doing it. 'You need a rest from all the late nights.' I thought about passing her door and finding a light still on into the early hours. I wondered how I was going to hold off her finding out about this terrible issue with Wilf.

'What's Aiden up to today?' I asked, crossing my fingers that her boyfriend was in a mood where he wanted to spend time with her.

'He's coming round to revise with me.' She got up and stretched.

'Well, maybe go out for a walk or go to the cinema instead?' I rustled in my bag. 'Here's a twenty.'

'The exams start so soon, Mum,' she said as if I understood nothing.

It was one of those things that no one told you when you had really young children: that they would need you as much when they were teenagers and in such a different way than they did when they were small and snot-nosed.

'I still think it would be better for you to have a break,' was all I said.

My heart hurt for her, but I focused hard on what I had to do next – making sure that the boy she considered her brother wasn't going to be taken away from us forever.

5

I pulled up outside Petra and Ralph's house. It was a rental on an estate on the edge of the town – a cul-de-sac with spacious detached houses along it, the sort I secretly thought were soulless and vulgar. The lawns were immaculate, but the flower beds were too new to be full; there were shiny cars in front of several of them but no real signs of what I would call *life*. This was the environment Ralph hung out in now – maybe all this newness had painted over his sense of morality too.

I tried to compose myself in the car but instead felt my outrage rise. I strode up the path and, as I rang the front bell, I tried to breathe but tapped my toes impatiently. My strategy had to be to get to Ralph and implore him to go wherever he wanted with Petra, but to leave Wilf very much with me.

There was the sound of steps echoing inside. It didn't sound like Ralph; it was the brisk tap-tap of someone with somewhere to go and places to be, moving down a hallway. Petra, then.

I pulled my body to its full height. Petra was small, but her perfect proportions and upright stance shouted 'brisk and efficient'. I could see her working out it was me through the glass of the door; there was a brief pause before she pulled it open. She was wearing very clean dark jeans and Converse that looked as if they'd just come out of the box, with a pale pink cashmere jumper; her face was set in what I imagined was her version of a sympathetic smile.

How dare you feel sorry for me? I determinedly did not smile back.

'Hello, Calypso,' she said, and tried to make the smile even wider. Her voice was louder and shriller than it should have been, disguising the lilt of her South African accent. I was also sure she knew how much I hated being called the long version of my name, but she carried on using it anyway, even though I'd heard Ralph correct her a couple of times.

'Petra,' I said. 'You won't be surprised to see me. Is Ralph in?'

'I'm so sorry but, no, he is not,' she said, extending the sentence for far too long. 'Would you like me to tell him that you reached out to him?'

I wanted to scream, 'Reach out? Are you a member of the Four Tops?' But I bit my lip instead. 'When will he be back, Petra?'

I thought about the very few occasions when I'd previously been in the same space as her: there'd been a couple of school football matches where we'd stood uncomfortably on the sidelines, me trying to be super-civilised like the post-marital celebrity couples you always saw in magazines, who managed to have brunch with each other's new partners while smiling for the cameras. We'd made polite chit-chat, mostly about the importance of Ralph taking vitamins and mindfulness classes as he got better, and how 'dear Wilf' was progressing at football. There were the times I'd picked up Wilf from her house and, again, she'd only take the opportunity to big up her role in Ralph and Wilf's lives.

'It's like she wants to get one over on me in a way that I couldn't care less about,' I'd grumbled to Marvin.

She hesitated for a brief moment, and I knew she was lying. She was smaller than me and I stood a good chance of getting past her. Ralph was hiding inside. 'He's here, isn't he?' I said, trying to shuffle past and see into the hallway. 'I want to see him, Petra.'

'I'm sorry, that's not possible, Calypso.' She did a little dance in the doorway and I ducked and dived, trying to look over her shoulder.

'Ralph,' I shouted. 'You cowardly bastard. Come down here.'

'There is no need to use such aggressive and inappropriate language,' Petra said sniffily.

'I don't want to talk to you. I want to talk to Wilf's father.' Then I pushed her aside. She was even lighter than I'd imagined, like a feather in a breeze, but she resisted me. In the end, though, I was bigger than her and much, much angrier.

'A court will note physical violence,' she spat as I strode into the hallway.

She was already talking about the law – well, she was a lawyer. I focused on the bigger task – getting hold of my spineless ex-boyfriend, who was hiding somewhere in this house.

The hallway was wide, painted an expensive magnolia colour with fake floorboards. There were few pictures on the wall – it gave the air of somewhere Petra had no intention of putting down roots. There was a door I'd been through before on the right, which led to the sitting room – sparsely furnished in taupe-coloured soft furnishings – and, I knew, another door to a dining room on the right. It had made me laugh when I'd seen it – trying to imagine Ralph, albeit sober and having been dragged upmarket by Petra, sitting at the head of the big veneered table Petra had put in it, complete with candelabra.

I started pushing at the doors and scuttling behind the sofas while she stood back with folded arms. 'Ralph, I know you're here,' I shouted, throwing open the door at the back of the hallway where an expanse of kitchen spread across the back of the house. Everything shone in a way that was impossible in a house with three messy teenagers. I spun quickly on my heel, my face in a snarl, my pace picking up.

Petra made a feeble attempt to stop me going up the stairs, but I moved with determination. 'You want to come out and talk to me about it?'

As I raced to the top Petra cried, 'Ralph, babe, she's gone mad...' and then suddenly, there he was, emerging from one of the bedroom doors and holding up both hands in a gesture of surrender.

'Callie, come on, there's no need...' He was wearing jeans and one of the polo shirts that Petra had bought him – today's one in an incongruous pink with more than a hint of smoked salmon. But his face was white with fear – and that made me even angrier. He was terrified of a confrontation with me – but he wasn't sorry.

I stopped at the top stair and looked at him with disgust. 'How could you do this to me? How could you do this to Wilf?'

Petra was halfway up the stairs behind me and said, 'He has every right to live with his real parents.'

Ralph held up his hands again at this and mumbled, 'Petra, babe, it might be better if—'

'I'm not going anywhere,' she said. 'We need to protect our legal position.'

I turned on her. 'You might be a lawyer, but this isn't about a legal position,' I said as quietly as I could. 'This is about the future of a child; it's about his happiness.'

'Callie, babe—'

'Don't babe me,' I snapped at him. Since when had he called me – or anyone else – babe?

'What I mean is, we need to sit down and talk about it...'

'And that's what you wanted when you sent me a solicitor's letter?' He must have heard the betrayal in my voice because his face took on a new shade of grey.

'That was to protect us against precisely this sort of scene,' Petra said, as if she was quoting some sort of law book again. She probably was. 'You hadn't been very forthcoming in our strategy to move forward as a family. We thought you might understand legal communication.'

'Did you think I wasn't going to fight for him?' I asked her. What had she thought? I would meekly read their letter and then nip into Wilf's room and start packing his suitcases?

'But now we should sit down and talk about it like adults,' said Ralph with some of her sanctimonious air. Christ, he'd changed. 'Come on, Cal, we need to explain.'

'Yes, you do,' I said and burst into tears.

Petra looked at me and folded her arms, as if to say, 'I knew we could expect this kind of emotion from *her*.' But I ignored her as the tears rolled.

'I can't believe you would take Wilf away from me, after all this time.'

'We're not taking him away from you.' Ralph came closer to me but stopped short of touching me on the shoulder.

'You're taking him to the other end of the world. You know I think of him as my son.'

'Come and sit down,' said Ralph. Helplessly, I started to move downstairs, Petra leading the way into the beige-zone of the sitting room. She tried to offer me a box of tissues, but I pushed them away angrily.

'Could we talk alone?' I asked Ralph, glaring at Petra.

'I'm his stepmother,' Petra said, 'and that counts for a lot in the eyes of the law.'

'Will you please stop talking about the law?' I howled through tears that were now flowing like Niagara on the day of a rainstorm.

I grabbed one of the tissues from the box and collapsed onto one of their sofas, which looked soft but was hard. Ralph sat down on the one opposite. He looked ridiculously healthy, as if he was mainlining vitamins and sleeping properly too. I wondered if Petra had also booked him in for Botox as part of her Rehabilitation-of-Ralph programme.

She sat down beside him and held his hand in a gesture of coupledom. 'We thought,' she began, speaking slowly as if I were a child of six rather than a grown woman, 'that it would be easier for you to receive a letter from an independent person...'

'Than his own father? Ralph? What's going on?'

He had the grace to blush, which made his face clash with his salmon shirt; he let go of Petra's hand. 'You see, Pet's got offered the most brilliant job in Cape Town and...'

So, it *was* about Petra and her career. Or at least that was why they were moving.

'Congratulations,' I said, 'but why do you have to take Wilf? I mean, he's happy, his GCSEs are in a couple of years...'

'That's just it,' said 'Pet' in the same patronising voice. 'It's important that we take the chance to maximise Wilf's educational chances by moving him at the right time in his development. And we don't want to affect his opportunities in the vital late stage of adolescence.'

OK, she'd not only been swotting up on the laws on parenthood, she'd been reading books of bollocks on how to bring up kids. I took a deep breath. 'Do you reckon you could let Ralph speak?'

'Yeah, so I can't leave Wilf here,' Ralph said. 'I know he's been living with you for the past couple of years without me, due to what went on. But he's my blood, Cal, even though I've let him down, and I want to carry on making it up to him.'

I knew Ralph's guilt too well. After every episode of bad parenting, drunkenness or drugginess, he would crawl back to me and plead how awful he was – and for a long while I'd believed him: he would change, stop, grow up, get better. More importantly, at the point of his abject remorse, he'd believed it himself too. And despite everything that had gone on, Wilf was his only child and I'd never doubted that he loved him very much. 'So, I can't go without him, especially now I'm better and in recovery.'

I acknowledged this with a nod. 'But he's happy with us,' I said, 'and it works, and I love him. And what about the girls?'

'Well, I thought they'd come and visit us too,' said Ralph. 'I'll have loads of time, what with not being able to work for a while with the visa thing, so I could hang with them and Wilf. Daisy and Lily would love a trip to South Africa.'

They probably would, but I'm not sure that would make up for losing the kid they thought of as their *brother*. 'You know Lily is so...'

'Yeah, Wilf said she's got a bit jumpy,' Ralph said. 'Exams?'

'I think it's more than that.' I put the tissue to my eyes again and spoke quietly.

Petra looked at me with more pity. 'So, you've got quite a lot on your plate?'

Ralph turned and raised eyebrows at her. 'Worrying time,' he said, direct to me.

'And you're going to make it so much worse for her,' I said. 'She'll react badly to think she's losing Wilf.'

'With respect,' said Petra, 'she's not losing him, he's just relocating.' She obviously wasn't kissed by the empathy fairy as she fell to earth.

'Why can't you go without him if you have to go? He could come and visit you instead.'

'I just can't leave him,' Ralph said. 'Even when he's stayed at yours, I've seen him a few times a week and we're really getting back on track. I miss him all the time. But you know how grateful I am to you for keeping him when everything was going wrong for me.'

Keeping him? He made it sound as if I'd been doing him a favour rather than revelling in raising his son. I remembered the quick conversation when Ralph had finally left. Wilf had looked up at me in the kitchen and said, 'I can stay here, Cal, can't I?'

And I'd just hugged him and said, 'Forever.'

'We're both really grateful,' said Petra. I shook my head and grimaced; all this anger dried my tears though. 'But Ralph has also consistently expressed a desire that Wilf now move in with us as his proper parents.'

'How long have you known about this?' I asked Ralph, but she jumped in to answer.

'I got approached a couple of months ago for a key new position offering me an excellent career opportunity with outstanding development potential,' she began. 'And, of course, the recruitment process was especially rigorous, so it's only been solidified in the last few weeks. Then my husband and I...' I raised my eyebrows again at her – seriously? '... had a lot of productive discussion and we made a decision, and then we aimed to provide as much notice as we could to you and dear Wilf.'

Dear Wilf? Ralph sat silently while she spoke all this bullshit. 'And why the solicitor? Why couldn't you have just come and talked to me?'

'Pet thought it would take the emotion out of the situation,' he mumbled.

'Cowardly.' He blushed.

'The law is quite clear,' Petra said, back in her lawyer tones. 'You have no rights over Wilf, as a minor.'

'But you must know he won't want to go.'

'He'll want to be with me, though?' Ralph said. 'Seriously, Cal, I've been working really hard on rebuilding my relationship with him. And he's getting on all right with Petra now…'

'It really is a significant opportunity and provides me with the platform to return to my own motherland,' Petra said. 'I have family back home too, you know.'

'So, you always meant to go back?' I asked her. 'And take Wilf with you?'

'Well, when Ralph and I were lucky enough to seal our special union,' she started. Did she speak like this all the time? How did Ralph not throttle her in her sleep? 'We were focused on ensuring that that element was successful. Ralph was very vulnerable.' She actually patted his hand as she said this, and he looked at her with calf eyes. He was like an unfinished project to her, I thought – that was what she got out of it. She'd always deserve his gratitude for fixing him. 'But as we progressed, we recognised that a new start would be of further benefit to him…' what, going to another country? '… and, of course, that will always include our son.'

'*Our* son?' I blinked at them both and tears came back into my eyes.

'We know how much you will miss him,' continued Petra.

'No, you don't,' I whispered. 'How could you ever know that? And when in this *plan* were you thinking of asking Wilf what he wants?'

'We'll talk to Wilf once dates are settled, but we hope to move at the end of the term,' Petra said. 'That will give him a couple of months to orientate himself and spend quality time with his father and stepmother…' now she was talking about herself in the third person '... before he commences the next stage of his education.'

I stood up. 'Make no mistake, I am going to fight you every single step of the way.' I put my hands on my hips and glared. 'I will find the money to get legal support. I won't let you take the child I have raised since he was six away from me.' Petra nodded as if she'd expected no less and her eyes narrowed. Ralph flinched. 'And you will not talk to Wilf about it.'

'We have every right,' Petra said.

'Just give her a few days, babe,' Ralph said and shrugged at me.

'Maybe we need to schedule another meeting? At the solicitor's office? To keep momentum on the timeline?' Petra said, standing up and acting as if this were a standard work meeting, where we would now swap pleasantries on the way to the lift. 'I'd hope that we'd be able to meet a mediated solution in a few days' time.'

'I'll be in touch.' I ran out of the room and the front door.

In the background I could hear Petra turn to Ralph and say, '*Well*, can you believe that?' as if she was surprised at any expression of a woman faced with losing her son.

6

I wanted to go home and rage. But there is no such thing as privacy in my house – Lily was there and probably Aiden by now. So, I wiped the tears from my face furiously with the back of my hand, drove round the corner and screeched to a halt by another kerb. Then I let myself thump the steering wheel and shout obscenities for a good minute, ignoring anyone who walked past on the pavement.

Then I FaceTimed Marvin.

'Doll,' he said. 'I was going to give you a bell. How's the bruises?' But then he saw my face. 'Oh, my God, are you OK? What is it?'

'Ralph wants to take Wilf away,' was all I could manage in between breaths.

'Are you serious?'

'Petra and him – they want to take him to Cape Town to *live*.'

Marvin was sitting on his sofa, which showed clear signs of recent sex. The sofa cushions were all shoved up one end and it looked as if it had moved on its castors through some vigorous thrusting. Through the door to his bedroom, I could see his colourful duvets, quilts and pillows strewn across the floor. I was used to this – and much worse, frankly – on a standard Saturday morning, so I said nothing, just thought, *Ewww, bodily fluids.*

'Wow,' Marv said. 'Who'd have thought that Ralph would move to the bottom of the earth?'

'With Petra! Oh, my God, you should've seen her. All legal this and legal that and she's got him by—'

'Sounds like she missed out the short and curlies and went straight for his balls,' Marv interrupted. It was crude, but also accurate.

'He's completely dependent on her,' I said. 'Like a broken man with Stockholm Syndrome. Now he has no money, no nothing – except life in this horrible, bland box of a house, with a robot wife. So, she says: "*Babe*, we're off to South Africa," and he says, "Great idea, *babe*," but then remembers he has a son.'

'And so, she says, "Babe, the son can come too," and that's that. *Bitch,*' added Marvin, acting out a petulant Petra on the screen.

'He calls her "Pet".'

Marv looked quizzical. 'In a northern way?'

'No, because it's short for Petra.' For some reason this made me start to laugh, great shudders of irrepressible giggles from my stomach to my mouth, and Marvin joined in, until I remembered that this was the kind of behaviour that had been happening in the hospital the previous night and stopped. I was clearly now a sandwich short of a picnic.

'All this after the crash last night too,' Marv said. 'How are your bruises? Are you in pain?'

'I'll be fine,' I said. 'The cyclist bought me sushi. Anyway, what am I going to *do*? I've got about three grand in the bank and I don't know how much lawyer that gets you... and Petra will be getting mates' rates through work and—'

'We need to make a plan,' Marv said. 'Involving the AAs. We'll do it tonight.'

'All the kids *are* going out,' I said. Daisy was going to a party; Lily would be with Aiden and Wilf was at Jowan's sleepover.

'It's *vital* that we make a plan.' Marv was a man with a mission and one that meant noisily guzzling Sauvignon Blanc. 'Eight o'clock here. I'll make cheese straws.'

'Yum, but make loads as Ajay always eats them all,' I said, starting up the engine and feeling as if at least I would have some support from my friends in my battle for my family.

Next, I drove to my parents' house. Every time I pulled up outside their house I vowed to get around to doing something about the front 'garden'. In their growing disarray over the last year or two it had got worse.

The kids always asked me whether it was like this when I was growing up and I'd honestly been able to say, 'No, of course not or I'd have had no friends'. In my childhood, Mum and Dad had been great parents in most ways: Dad especially was willing to play endless games of dressing up and make believe. When I got older, my mates thought it was great to have a dad who always wanted to give us a lift and knew the names of all our fave bands, as long as he wasn't *their* dad. My mother had banged on a lot about the destructive nature of capitalism, but it was about the time that we were all getting into *Das Kapital*, so my friends didn't mind her either.

Now, though, as I clambered out of the car, it did occur to me that moving them into a permanent place where someone had some sort of eye on them wasn't a mad idea.

They mostly lived in the kitchen, and had chosen a year ago to move their double bed into the front room ('Just like Charlie and the Chocolate Factory,' Wilf had said) for reasons my mother said were related to minimising global warming, but were probably more about the effort of Dad climbing the stairs. I'd hired and watch them fire a series of cleaners over the years: 'She was all right, but she talked to us like we were old people,' Dad had said when he'd got rid of the last one. Then there was the one who had left herself in horror at my mother's insistence on nudity when she was in a phase of trying to get in touch with her inner ying. It might have been yang. It doesn't matter – no cleaner could handle it.

Lately, I'd been coming at least once a week to push a Hoover round their bed/sitting room and the kitchen, wash the floor and clean the kitchen and bathroom. They generally sat at the table while I did it, with my mother occasionally mentioning something about how over-cleaning was fuelling diseases like Ebola. Their very worst characteristic was an absolute refusal to admit that they needed me. 'Your ma is such a stresshead,' my mum would bellow to the kids as I ran around trying to cook after work. I had to bite my lip hard when I heard that one.

Still, it was also worth remembering that they were people of considerable achievement. My dad had been a relatively successful scientist and, as leader of the UK's Academy of Science Communicators (slogan 'Just ASC'), spent his time appearing on local radio stations, where listeners would call in with questions like, 'Why does my water go down the plughole that way?' Mum had been one of the original radical feminists, joining the picket lines at Greenham Common, reading *Spare Rib*, and denouncing Margaret Thatcher, Milk Snatcher.

I opened their kitchen door to find them both sitting at the table. I couldn't spot any more chaos than usual.

'Just me,' I said loudly enough to attract Mum's attention.

'Hello, love,' Dad said. He was reading a copy of Wilf's music mag, glasses perched on the end of his long nose and still wearing his pyjamas, with a cardigan over them, even though it was past lunchtime. Mum, at least, was dressed – in very practical dungarees – and seemed to be looking down at her iPad, prodding it with one finger now gnarled with arthritis. She clicked her hearing aid on as she saw me; she'd obviously been pretending to hear my dad for the morning.

'Are you all right after yesterday?' she asked in a normal tone of voice, peering at me.

'I'll be fine,' I said. They didn't need to know yet that a much greater shock had swung into my life.

'It was nice of him to give us the fish, though,' Mum went on. 'I hope he's told that nasty conglomerate he works for of the unsafe conditions in which they place their staff.'

I sighed. 'Tell me more about this place you've been going to – with the young people.'

'Brilliant concept, isn't it?' Dad beamed, putting down the magazine.

'Lovely, light apartments,' Mum joined in. 'They're all around a giant courtyard to provide a sense of community.'

I put three teabags into some cleanish mugs. 'And where do the young people live?'

'Well, they share flats too but on the top floor, as not many of the older people want the bother of the stairs or a lift; then everyone meets up for activities and mealtimes in a big hall. It's all very colourful.'

'And it's actually called "Yoof and a Roof"?' I asked dubiously.

'No, it's actually called Seymour House, but the kids gave it the nickname.'

Seymour House. That sounded much more respectable. I sat down at the table.

'It's got lovely period features,' Mum went on. 'And the standard of renovation is superb.' For someone who lived in a house that was one up from a hovel, she had very high expectations.

'We were shown round by such a nice young man,' Dad said.

'A real commitment to ending world poverty,' Mum added.

'Pete,' Dad said. 'His name is Pete and he's just moved in there.'

'Does he have a job as well as living in the...'

'Community,' Dad said. 'They use the word "community".'

I could see why this would appeal wholeheartedly to my parents. 'And Pete is studying to be a sound engineer,' Mum went on. 'He's just starting out and finding his feet, so the set-up makes sense to him. The younger members spend two hours or so a few days a week either helping to run the home or managing an activity or an outing, and their rent is paid for them.'

'So bright and colourful,' said Dad. 'None of that smell you get in old people's homes. It's a highly proven model in Holland.'

'It does sound great,' I said. 'How does it work financially?'

'Well,' said Dad, 'this is the clever bit. To ensure that community members are making the right decisions about permanently relocating, the house encourages a trial period. There's a membership fee — a thousand pounds...' I gasped but Dad ignored me '... but we've got that saved up and then you effectively move in, with some of your belongings, but not all, for a month to see how you like it.'

'And if you decide you do, then you pay monthly rent, like anyone else,' Mum said.

'And if you don't, you've wasted a grand?' I asked.

'No!' Mum was triumphant. 'Because then you can use it for day facilities – like going to the raves and the yoga. The fee would cover us for a year after that.'

'The facts are,' Dad said, picking up his mug of tea, 'that it's a failsafe scheme.'

'And if we did want to move in, we'd sell this place,' Mum went on, as if she were closing the deal.

Even if this was their latest fad, it seemed to be one with quite a lot going for it. I looked round at the mess and then got up, much more enthusiastically than usual, in order to start the cleaning. It might be one of the last times I'd have to do this. 'I'd better book in with you to go and have a look round.'

7

The AAs were happy to be invited to top up their alcohol intake at Marv's. Ajay claimed not to have been up long – he'd been at a party the night before, which apparently hadn't ended until 6 a.m., so a big glass of Sauv Blanc was his breakfast. Abby had been out too, but as usual there was no sign of it in her capable, line-free face.

Ajay – all polished metrosexual, carefully curated clothes and slicked hair, despite the hangover – was seated at Marvin's kitchen table when I arrived. He was clutching a big glass of breakfast wine and saying, 'No... the absolute tosser, *seriously*, what a wanker...' as I let myself in and went into the kitchen. The kitchen smelt of baking and melted cheese.

Abby was wearing a white shirt and tucked under the table would be blue jeans and her feet in a pair of ballet pumps, her standard weekend uniform. Her face was a muted expression of horror. Abby didn't really do visible emotion – this expression of rage was about as good as it got. 'Bastard,' she hissed.

'Come on in, come on in,' fussed Marv, pulling out a chair and hugging me. I blew kisses to the AAs across the table.

Ajay got up and hugged me to his chest with his tight, fitted shirt, overwhelming me with the smell of Bleu de Chanel. 'Poor baby,' he said.

'And you haven't heard yet about her getting knocked over by a Deliveroo rider,' Marv went on, and proceeded to tell them all how he'd found me 'deranged and a bit hysterical' in A & E.

'I mean, how deranged exactly?' Abby asked Marv.

'Not quite full-on batshit, but out there.'

'And then she had to find this out about Wilf.'

'I am here, you know,' I said.

'After all that stuff about being invisible last night, are you sure?' Marv raised his eyebrows and cocked his head to the side.

'Ha, ha, very funny,' I said. I was halfway through my first glass of cold wine and it was finally lifting my spirits.

'Right.' Ajay picked up a cheese straw and I eyed him suspiciously; I'd calculated that there were four each and he'd already had two. 'What are we going to do about Ralph-the-child-stealer, then?'

I loved the 'we' in that. They might be my slightly mad, mostly drunk friends, but they were on my side.

We'd met at uni, sharing a corridor and fighting about whose turn it was to clean the kitchen. We came together in a shared hatred of a boy called Adrian who lived next door to Marv and, instead of washing up his dishes, simply opened his cutlery drawer and put all the filthy plates in there, refusing to do anything about it. The dishes stayed in the drawer for about a month before flies started buzzing near it and Marv dramatically cleared it out wearing a pair of Marigolds.

Ajay was from Berkshire, clever, twisty, a natural software geek who, at eighteen, tried very visibly to be cooler than the average tech guy. Abby was studying biology and, even then, she was the same wiry, practical, almost emotionless blonde. I was what I was – a home counties girl from a creative household, trying as hard as I possibly could to be cool now that I was away at Sussex Uni in Brighton.

Marv was the magnet who pulled us into his gravity. He was flamboyant, like a late-teens Oscar Wilde who'd grown up in an age of grunge and rave. He wore robes then, quite consistently, long flowing kimonos in spectacular colours that he'd found in charity shops. He was colourful, bearded and full of drama.

'Like a bogus Jesus,' muttered Abby under her breath as we all met that first day in the kitchen.

'But quite a cool one,' I said as Marv got us all out to a bar and we all got very drunk. Twenty years passed and, while we'd all lived in different places, when I'd ended up back in my home town – now handily classified as 'one of the most desirable places to live' with its country feel, but just outside London – Marv had come to rent a flat and Ajay and Abby, all of them still childless and single off and on, had come a year or two later.

'You can't choose your family,' Marv would say, 'but you can choose your friends and I choose you. My *logical* family.'

Now Marv – always the ringleader – drew our kitchen-table meeting together. He put down his glass and looked each of us in the eye, one by one. Abby picked up a cheese straw and I took my second. Ajay reached out for his third. I resisted saying anything.

'First we need to check out the legals,' Abby started.

'Have you looked up your rights, Cal?' Marv asked.

I'd spent the rest of the day reading various family law websites. Certainly, it looked as if, without some sort of specific injunction and child care order, I had very few rights. I wasn't Wilf's stepmother legally; his views would be considered, but not as much as they would if he were sixteen rather than fourteen. And would Wilf really say he wanted to stay with me, in front of his own father, in court? I thought about asking him to do that and how traumatic it would be for him.

The fact that Ralph had left our house only eighteen months previously and had been sober all that time, didn't help. Neither would the fact that he'd had constant contact with Wilf over that time and they were undeniably close.

I explained this to my friends. Marv, who was poised with a pad and pen for the plan, wrote down: 'Find qualified expert lawyer' and then wrote '1' beside it and circled it emphatically.

'I'll ask around at work,' said Abby. She worked in London at one of those flash management consultancies with a big glass building on the South Bank. 'Someone must know a family lawyer. And I'll lend you money, Cal, if you run out.'

This was very sweet of her, but she was easily the richest of the four of us, having bounded up her career ladder and with no partner or children to spend it on. 'Thank you, Abs,' I said and reached over to squeeze her hand. She looked embarrassed, as she normally did at any expression of emotion, and gently pushed my hand away.

'I've got savings too,' Ajay said and then bitterly added, 'Raul didn't take it all.' Ajay had split up with his long-term love, Raul, a few months previously, in one of the most acrimonious splits you could imagine – all broken windows at six in the morning, clothes piled in dustbin liners on the small front garden of the flat they'd bought together. Now they were arguing over who owned it.

'You need all that for the flat,' I said. 'But thank you.'

Marv didn't offer me any money simply because he rarely had any. Marv was what he dismissively called 'a retweeter' – in actual fact, a social media manager for minor celebrities. His working day was principally moving from his bed to his kitchen table – the one we were all sitting at now – and putting out propaganda for has-beens who 'are so Z-list they've been kicked out of the alphabet'.

'But as well as a legal attack, how do we get Ralph to understand how awful he's being? Petra's brainwashed him.'

'I know, right?' said Ajay. 'I saw them in Waitrose and he looked so *clean* and her trolley was full of superfoods.'

'Ralph is now made of blueberries and kale,' Marv said with disgust. 'And *quinoa*.' He pronounced it kwinoah.

'Is that how you say it? I never say it out loud in case it makes me sound like a twat.'

'Yeah, kwinoah,' Abby confirmed. 'And they haven't said anything to Wilf yet?'

'I made them promise they'd give me a few days,' I said. Marv poured me another large glass of wine and went to the fridge to get another bottle. Ajay reached out for his fourth cheese straw. I grabbed one too, just to make sure he knew that I was on his case, but he didn't seem to notice, just carried on munching away.

'I can go and talk to Ralph,' Marv went on. 'I'll do it on Monday. I'll text him and invite myself for a coffee. He can't really say no to that.'

'Well, he can ignore the text,' I said. 'It's not like he's that great at communication. You'd better just go round there and lurk until you see him.'

'I'm good at lurking,' Marv pointed out and we saw no reason to disagree with him.

Over the next two hours, we got rambunctiously drunk. We ripped Petra apart first, sending up her shrill voice and her precise ways.

'She'll reach out to you,' I groaned.

'And socialise the results of her thinking,' Abby said. 'That's a new one at work – sharing information becomes "socialising" it.' She downed the rest of her glass and ate another cheese straw.

It was at that point that Ajay also tried to reach out for another. 'No way, Jose.' Marv pulled the plate away. 'You've had your four, you greedy bastard.'

'Have I?' He feigned innocence.

We moved on to hearing about Marv's date the night before, as we opened bottle number four. I thought about the horror of the hangover that was coming my way in the morning but then figured that I was probably too drunk to escape it now.

'She was absolutely gorgeous – lives a few miles away, really athletic,' Marvin started.

'Then why are you already talking about her in the past tense?' I despaired of Marvin ever finding someone who lasted more than a few dates.

'There was a bit of an embarrassment when her false eyelashes caught in my beard and just came off.'

'Yuck, like having spiders on your face?' Abby asked.

'It was a bit of a passion killer,' Marv agreed. 'But she was all upset about it – said that no one ever saw her without her lashes on. After that she wouldn't let me look at her face, so we tried to... improvise... but we'd kind of lost it.'

God, it felt good to have time out from what was going on in my life.

Daisy and then Lily texted that they were home and going to bed. This was the rule – you had to text when you got in. I messaged Wilf to find out if he was having fun at the sleepover and he texted back:

Yeah, good.

'So, I think we should play a game now,' Marv said. He was always the instigator of games – particularly 'Snog, Marry, Avoid'. One of us would choose someone to 'snog' and Marv would go on for the next two hours about it. 'But I always think of Ed Miliband as talking as if he has an over-sized tongue?' or, 'I can't believe you'd go there with Mary Berry.' That kind of thing.

So now we all groaned but Marvin ignored us. 'It's a new one. It's called "Who'd be on your team in the face of a zombie apocalypse?"'

'Who are you allowed to have?' Abby wanted to know the rules of engagement.

'Well, anyone that you want, but your team has to be two famous people and then one person you know in the room.'

'But that means some of us won't get picked each time,' I said.

'It's called life, Cal, and it's not fair,' Marv said. 'We're all big enough and strong enough…'

'*All right,*' I said. They were always accusing me of being too soft.

'So, you have to pick them and tell us who is in on your team and why,' Marv continued. 'Ultimately, we have to decide on whose team would beat off the zombies and survive.'

'Very dystopian.' Ajay looked keen.

'I'll start,' Marv went on, 'because I've been able to think about it for longer. So, mine would be Kim Kardashian, as she would distract the zombies and then she could turn around and the zombies would bounce off her arse.'

We nodded, and he went on. 'And then I'd also have Boadicea. I mean, she's got form.'

'And one of those chariots with knives coming out of the wheels.' Abby approved.

'And you, of course,' Marv said, turning to her. 'Abby's just the kind of kick-arse woman you want on your team in the face of a zombie apocalypse.'

Ajay nodded. 'So, yours is an all-female action squad. *Nice.*'

Abby looked mildly pleased about being part of it. 'Goals,' she said. 'Right, mine would be Ajay as he is a secretly greedy bastard and would fight like a beast to make sure we were eating.'

This made sense. 'And I'd be a mean fighter.' We all waved our wine glasses at her in agreement. 'Then my celebrities would be people who are unafraid in the face of danger. Like Vin Diesel. Or Arnold Schwarzenegger.'

'Pretty standard boring choices there, Abs,' said Ajay.

'All right, let's hear you be so original,' she said huffily.

'Easy. My celebs would be people who were clever enough to find a way to defeat the zombies without direct confrontation. Amal Clooney, natch.'

We all sighed because *we* hadn't come up with Amal. We adored her and in recent years had turned our standard question in the face of any decision-making from, 'So what would Beyoncé do?' to, 'What would Amal do?'

'Then, I'd have Steven Hawking,' Ajay continued.

Marv considered for a minute. 'I think you're allowed dead people,' he said.

'Marv had Boadicea. So, I think I'm good with Steven.'

'Which one of us though?'

'You,' Ajay said without hesitation. 'You're a devious little shit who'd come up with a way to charm the shit out of the zombies.'

'Hmmm.' I tried not to feel too outraged. 'What about me? Why wouldn't any of you pick me to face into the zombies?'

They seemed, through my drunken blur, to be sharing a moment. Marv picked up my hand and said in a gentle voice, 'I mean, it's not really your thing, is it?'

'I kind of think you'd be there,' Ajay continued, 'but, you know, with more of a back-seat role. Making the tea or something.' Abby looked horrified for a second, but then she couldn't stop herself and burst out laughing, getting louder as the full impact of what Ajay had just said obviously registered on my face.

'Sorry,' I spluttered. 'Did you just say that in the face of a zombie apocalypse, I'd be making the *tea*?'

'Don't take it the wrong way or anything.'

How was it possible not to take this the wrong way? 'Making the tea?' I asked again in outrage. 'Seriously, that's all you'd think I'd be up to?'

'He's winding you up.' But Abby was laughing and laughing, and Marvin was joining in. I felt every bone in my feminist body, probably fuelled by drink, respond with rage.

'It'd be great tea,' Ajay went on with a completely straight face. 'Nice and strong, with just the right amount of milk.'

'That's so mean of you,' I said and, although I found myself laughing with them at this point, it did hurt. Was that what they really thought of me? That I'd be in the background and in a support role in the face of imminent danger? *Invisible*, my drunken head said. *Invisible*.

Marv caught my eye as he stopped laughing. He was remembering the state of me in A & E. 'Back off, Ajay, she's not in the right mood.'

'Only teasing.' Ajay held my hand.

'I can't believe I'm getting upset about my hypothetical role in an event that's never going to happen.'

'You can have my last cheese straw if you forgive me,' Ajay said, which meant that we all forgot about a game where the mythical walking dead were coming to take over the world and started going on about how he was a greedy bastard again.

It was midnight when I got to my house and I'm not proud to say I wobbled up the path to the back door, over-enthusiastically shushing myself to make sure that I was quiet. Teenagers can be remarkably judgemental about their parents, considering that they spend a lot of time desperately trying to do the things we get up to – like get drunk at a good night out with their mates. This was the kind of deep thought running through my brain when I nearly tripped over a small pastel-coloured carrier bag on the doorstep.

Bending down, I picked it up to see what was in it. It certainly looked like a gift – it was pink, and the bag was made of expensive logo-less paper. Inside was a cardboard box – the sort you got in posh patisseries. Ah, probably a gift from a boy to Daisy.

But there was a small card on top of the box and it clearly read: 'Callie' and underneath it said:

Hope you're feeling better, from a Bloke-newly-called-Bill.

Ah, another guilt offering from the Deliveroo rider. Still, at least he knew that the way to my heart was through my stomach – even if the old adage was only supposed to apply to men. And he'd gone to the new funky late-night bakery near the church to get this box for me – I recognised the posh hipster pinkness. I worried briefly about him being able to afford it but then I picked up the bag and it smelt of warm pastries. Lifting the lid, I could see four beautiful pastry shapes covered in sugar.

I put them on the top shelf of the medicine cupboard so that anyone getting up unnaturally early wouldn't eat them all. Then I wobbled my way up the stairs with a clear aim of sleeping for a very long time.

⋆

But it was 4 a.m. when I woke, my head throbbing from the wine. I gulped down the glass of water by my bed in three slugs and then got up to go and get more from the bathroom tap.

The Fear came fast and furious as I climbed back into bed. Even while I knew that the extreme paranoia surging round my capillaries was caused by drinking too much while I was miserable, it wasn't going anywhere. I gripped my head as I listened to my own brain doing me in.

What if Wilf – I thought about him on the floor in his sleeping bag at his friend's sleepover with a rush of love – *wanted* to go to Cape Town and have a new start with his dad?

Next came the familiar worries about Lily. Should I take her to a doctor to discuss her obvious anxiety? How did I find ways to make her more resilient? I should ask Daisy about the talk she'd been to.

I longed for the days when my kids were so young that you always understood all their emotions – simply because when they were sad or angry they cried and could be cuddled better; when they were happy, they laughed and ran around with joy.

I rolled over in my bed, trying to make the feelings go away, but my headache and self-loathing came with me. And look, a whole half a bed that was empty and had been ever since I'd split up with Ralph.

For a moment, I thought about the twins' dad and how young and brave I'd been when I'd met him. I'd been in my late twenties; he'd been in London on a working visa from

Australia. We hadn't fallen madly in love but we'd definitely had fun and when I'd found out I was pregnant – one of those 1 per cent who still got pregnant while following the contraceptive instructions exactly – I'd wanted them very much indeed and it hadn't occurred to me to be scared. I'd chosen to keep the babies; Dougie had made it clear he was going back down under and, while he would help pay for them, kids weren't part of his plans. I'd moved back to Seymour Hill to be near my folks, full of energy and courage now: willing single mother, career woman, and still young and eager for life. Then eventually I'd met Ralph and Wilf.

Now I was ugly and old, and it was only going to get worse. I pulled at my neck – it was impossible to ignore that it had grown a turkey-like saggy bit at the front. My face was descending too, with extra bits of skin slightly flapping under my jaw, and the crow's feet round my eyes were turning into big bird footprints.

My fearful head went on obsessively: if you had a man you'd have someone to help you now. But the last thing I'd wanted for the last few years was a man, the more reasonable part of my early morning brain countered – I hadn't had the time or the energy.

But in the meantime, they'd stopped thinking about me. I wondered how long it was since I'd been chatted up or flirted with. There was the guy outside the Tube at work who always shouted, 'Cheer up, gorgeous,' when he was sober enough as I passed at the end of the day – but I wasn't sure that homeless suitors counted.

Even Ajay thought I was so *background* that I was only good for making the tea in the face of a zombie apocalypse.

The whole world seemed to think I no longer counted or mattered.

Oh, The Fear! I shook my sore head from side to side and remembered how stupid and paranoid I could be at 4 a.m. with a liver trying to process too much wine. And it was inevitable that I would wake with the worry of Wilf and lie here, trying to work out what to do. But what if I'd become so ineffectual that I was incapable of helping him? I rubbed my eyes furiously as tears of self-pity started to flood onto my pillow. Feeling sorry for myself wasn't going to help.

Getting my shit together – that was what mattered.

8

Abby was as good as her word and by Sunday evening had arranged for me to speak on the phone to a solicitor friend. He was called Dominic and it was easy to tell that, while he felt sorry for my situation, he didn't think I had a leg to stand on. I was hiding in my bedroom and speaking very quietly as the kids were downstairs.

'The problem is, Callie,' he said after I'd given him a precis of the situation, 'that you didn't marry your ex-partner or adopt his son. And you tell me that the living arrangement with Wilf has always been informal?'

'Well, yes, his father and I lived with each other for six years, but we never got round to being married. And then when his father was ill, Wilf stayed on with me, and he asked to stay even when his dad recently married. He thinks of me and my children as his family.'

'And he's fourteen, you say? A judge will take his wishes into consideration, but the problem is that it seems to be that the only person in this situation with parental responsibility is your ex-partner.'

'So, his new wife has no responsibility either?'

'No, not unless she adopts Wilf,' Dominic went on. He was more or less just reinforcing what I'd learned about our situation online, but the idea of Petra trying to become more officially Wilf's mother than me sent a sharp new jab of pain through me. 'But that would be a provocative gesture and not one that she would probably go near unless the child really wanted it.'

'But what if Wilf simply says he's not going to Cape Town?' Even as I said it, I knew that unless this was what Wilf came up with himself, I could never beg him to stand up to his father.

'Well, it would count for quite a lot, but there would have to be a special court order and that would be highly unusual,' said Dominic. 'Sorry, when Abby told me what was happening, I did tell her that on the face of it I wouldn't be able to give you good news.'

'But could you act as my lawyer, you know, if I paid the proper fees?'

'I couldn't take your money,' said Dominic gently. 'Firstly, I can only advise you that any lawyer taking on your case should recognise that it has little hope of success. So, I can clarify your position and so on, but there's no need to give me any money. Not as a friend of Abby's.'

I thanked him profusely and he went on about how I had to be realistic about my chances before he said anxiously, 'Is Abby a close friend of yours? Will you tell her I was as helpful as I could be?'

Ah, one of Abby's long list of admirers. One who didn't know where he stood at all with her because she showed so little of her feelings. I told him I would absolutely tell Abby how helpful he'd been and thanked him again before I put the phone down in abject despair.

Downstairs, our sitting room, which used to seem spacious when the kids were smaller, now seemed to be overcrowded with teenagers. Aiden and Lily were in one corner of the sofa, their arms round each other; they'd probably been snogging but had stopped at the sound of my footsteps on the stairs. Aiden's tattoo of a bird – probably an eagle – that rose from the back of his T-shirt was just visible over the back of the sofa. I knew it was one of many, having met him a few times on our landing in his pants on the way to the bathroom, when he'd stayed over on the floor in Wilf's room. He'd got some quite feminine roses across the bottom of his back and some Eastern symbols on his arms.

At the other end of the sofa was Wilf, who'd returned that morning from his sleepover and gone straight back to bed for a few hours. Now, he seemed to have recovered from what he'd said was an 'all-night jam' and was holding fast onto the remote. Holding it meant absolute power – and at the moment that meant *Doctor Who* on catch up. Daisy was in the armchair watching it too.

Earlier, we'd enjoyed the pastries from Patrick; the kids had been impressed about this flash breakfast. I texted him.

Thanks for the delicious breakfast, New Bill. You've said
sorry now, so are we done?

He texted back:

Why would we be done? I like making you feel visible.

My only admirer in years appeared to be a guy who
delivered food on a bike. In any other circumstances he
might be attractive, and he was certainly generous, but I'd
spent enough years with Ralph, who earned very little, and
didn't need another penniless partner – or a partner at all.

In my hungover state, I couldn't really think about it.
Life had to go on. That had meant dropping my folks home
after a late afternoon Sunday lunch, which I'd tried to
pretend was just like any other. There had been the standard
moaning about my home-made gravy: 'Why do we have to
have posh gravy when all we really want is Bisto?'

We'd talked about Seymour House – 'Sounds cool as,
Lorca' (Wilf); and we'd talked about how Aiden and Lily
had gone bowling the night before. I was pleased that she
seemed to be following my advice and taking some time out
this weekend.

'Then we came here to Netflix and chill,'**** said Aiden. All
the kids tried not to giggle as I pretended not to know what this
meant. I still found it very difficult to think of my daughter as
a potentially sexually active human being, although I'd taken
the decision six months ago, when she'd come home and told

**** Stay in pretending to watch TV but actually get it on. Come on,
you've heard this one.

me that she was on the pill and that Aiden's mum had said she was cool with her staying round there, to also welcome him, as her long-term boyfriend, to our house.

'I don't know if it's the right thing to do or not,' I'd moaned to Marvin at the time. 'I put them in separate rooms but there's no mistaking it's probably going on.'

'Well, where did you go at her age?' he'd asked, and I'd thought of losing my virginity in the summer house (read, shed with mattress) of my then-boyfriend's house because I hadn't wanted to talk to Mum and Dad about sex. I was afraid that Mum would act as if I was being oppressed sexually by the patriarchy and that Dad would try to tell me stuff about his early sex life to relate to me.

'I was at least a year older than she is, though,' I'd worried on. 'She says they're in love.'

'You just have to be cool.'

This was easier said than done when your daughter was being ravished two rooms away as you went to sleep.

'Want to tell me more about the visit yesterday?' I sat on the arm of Daisy's chair and stroked her long hair. Perhaps she'd found out something that would help her sister.

'All right, I've seen this one anyway,' she said. 'And I want to go to some other meetings this week – our group's got really good and passionate.'

'Shhhhhh,' howled Lily and Wilf.

'Come in the kitchen,' I said. 'I'll put the kettle on.'

Over a couple of cups of camomile, my oldest – by half an hour – daughter became really animated. 'There was this really cool guy who came to talk to us and who's going to be heading up the Resilient campaign here,' she said. 'He's called Sunil.'

'Where is he from?'

'This is the cool part,' she said. 'He's been part of the Corbyn campaign in London, but he got disillusioned so now he's decided to dedicate his politics to helping those who can most make a difference in the future – the young.'

'That sounds noble,' I said.

'No, he really *cares*, Mum. And he really listens to us all – after the talk yesterday, we all sat and brainstormed how we could really take action to address the lack of funding in youth mental health.'

'But what about tips to make your generation more resilient?' I asked. 'Or what parents should be doing to spot the signs?'

'He said that parents just need to be available for their kids and let them know they are there,' she said. 'Like you're always there for us.'

I smiled and clasped her hand. If only always being there for them were enough; it didn't stop the pressures that seemed to be an inherent part of being sixteen today. Having to get brilliant exams and still manage to have decent 'extra-curricular' on your CV; getting amazing internships and part-time jobs; being politically correct and coping with a sexual world where boys were raised on porn; having 'on fleek'†††† eyebrows, a Kim K arse and skinny waist.

'All that time you spend on social media doesn't help, though.' One of the things I hated most about watching my

---

†††† Eyebrows are the single most important element of teenage girldom. On fleek eyebrows are the ultimate bushy yet groomed arched shape.

children grow up was how 'out there' they were via Twitter, Instagram and Snapchat (Facebook clearly being for old people like my age group); how they longed for 'likes' and counted them; how they all spent so long trying to take selfies with the right filter.

'You're right about that, Mum, according to Sunil.' *OK, so Sunil says it and suddenly it counts.* 'He's really big on IRL‡‡‡‡ social interaction.'

'OK...'

'Social media subscribes to a world view that puts beauty above intelligence.' He might be right, but Sunil did sound a very serious person. Still, if it made my kids spend less time staring at their iPhones, bring it on.

'He sounds fantastic,' I said. 'How old is he?'

'Oh, *old*. Like a few years younger than you. But still cool,' Daisy said, and then added when she saw my grimace, 'Not that you're not cool. And he's going to come round and meet you, so that you know who I'm hanging out with,' Daisy said. 'As he's going to be giving me a lift sometimes to demos and stuff. It's part of safeguarding.' Daisy shrugged. 'Right, do you mind if I go? There's an online hangout with the kids from the group, talking about reducing screentime.'

She didn't seem to see the irony in this, so I let it slide.

The BBC put costume dramas on Sunday evenings as a service to all us licence-fee payers: if we could be transported to a rose-tinted time in history we would forget about

---

‡‡‡‡ In Real Life.

the grim reality of a modern Monday. I settled down to be anaesthetised from my worry by whatever this week's version was. The kids had all disappeared upstairs.

Then, though, the doorbell rang. Weary and still weak from my hangover, I went to answer it in my old pyjama trousers and a long-sleeved top that had a fading picture of a kitten on it. I pulled open the door on its chain and peered through the gap.

There, not wearing a cyclist uniform, but instead what seemed to be a perfectly normal jumper and jeans, was Patrick aka BiL I felt instantly embarrassed about my make-up-less face and then irritation: he might be trying to make me feel more visible, but just *calling round without an invitation* wasn't the way it was supposed to work.

'Callie?'

'Umm, yes?'

'I found this dog outside your gate and wondered whether it was yours.'

I looked down and there, in the gap, was Bodger's face. His eyes were wide as if he knew he was in the wrong.

'Oh, what was he doing outside?' I slid open the chain and he came bounding in and jumped up at me as if he had been lost forever, rather than having gone for a lone, late evening stroll. 'Bodger? What have you been up to? Oh, thank you.'

Patrick hopped from one jeaned leg to another on the doorstep. He looked bigger somehow without his Lycra on. 'Least I could do,' he said. 'Are you OK? I mean, you seem to still be in one piece.' He didn't do anything suggestive or stalkery by looking me up and down, but, given the state of me, I glowered anyway and looked down at my pyjamas.

'Yep, one piece. Thanks for bringing Bodger back.' I tried to close the door into the silence that followed.

'Why's he called Bodger?' Patrick asked as if he didn't know I felt ridiculous, standing in the doorway in my gruesome home-alone outfit.

'He was a mongrel runt,' I explained. 'I called him a "bodge job of a dog" and it stuck with the kids.'

'He's cute.' Patrick bent down and gave Bodger a stroke. He responded enthusiastically. He knew he wasn't cute really – mangy, stunted with stinking breath was a better description – so the unexpected affection was a bonus for the dog; he had to get his compliments wherever he could. 'Bet the kids love him.'

It seemed that BiL was willing to stand on my doorstep telling blatant untruths about my dog and making polite chit-chat. Didn't he know that the busy people of Seymour Hill didn't do doorstep small talk *and* that there was a BBC bodice-ripper on the box?

I edged the door closer and said cheerfully, 'They loved the pastries, cheers again.'

'I'm thinking of giving up the food-delivery business.' He smiled on. I raised my eyebrow politely. 'Not sure I excel at it. Two days into it, I knocked you over, so it's not my best career move. Probably better to stick to the day job.'

Without being rude, I couldn't now not ask him what that was, although the practical part of me, which worried about how people paid the rent, was pleased he had another source of income. 'What's that?' I mumbled.

'I'm a teacher,' he said bouncily. 'I start at Whitebury in September.' He was talking about the sink comprehensive in the next town. It wasn't just in special measures, it had been a frequent backdrop to a segment on *Crimewatch*. Surely, this had to be the equivalent of teacher hell and damnation.

Despite myself I was interested. 'You're going to need a flak jacket to survive a morning in that place.'

'I take a personal thrill in daily survival,' he said. 'And a flak jacket is one up on Lycra. Anyway, this job is a bit of a step up and all that stuff from my last one. I'm going to be Head of PE.'

I looked duly impressed and simultaneously made a note that, in terms of status, having a respectable teacher pay me unsolicited attention was one up from having a food-delivery worker in hot pursuit. 'Head of PE sounds like a lot of room for personal injury,' I noted, 'but I'm sure you've done a risk assessment.'

It was clear that this new job was a source of pride. 'They've had a couple of really good athletes in the past. I'm hoping to channel some of the energy from running county lines into running on a track.' This was a gang/drug reference, and not a bad joke. I smirked and jiggled from foot to foot, worried about whether my nipples were standing up in the cold through my T-shirt. This was turning into the kind of conversation that should warrant a friendly, 'Fancy a cup of tea?' but it was Sunday night, I was hungover and exhausted, and I looked like shit. He didn't seem to notice and carried on chatting away. 'So that's why I've moved to Seymour Hill. And I just thought, while I waited for the job to start, I might as well earn some money and keep fit but, like I said, it's not for me.'

I wondered if he was really lonely: he wanted to string out neighbourly conversations on a doorstep; he hadn't mentioned a partner or kids.

'Bit of a change from South London,' he went on blithely. 'Newly trendy Seymour Hill.'

'Where in South London?' And, more interestingly, why had he moved for a job five months before the start of a new term?

'Balham,' he said. 'But Seymour Hill is properly bougie.'

'It didn't used to be,' I said. 'It's the impact of Google.'

'Yeah, it's geek central here.' BiL smiled. He was quite funny, I'd admit that much. 'I particularly like the range of facial hair.' He rubbed his own clean-shaven chin. 'I mean, to be really cool now you have to have a full-on fake jihadi.'

'Do you live on your own?' I asked, realising that I'd been standing on my doorstep for a good five minutes, probably with my nipples on parade in the light of the streetlight.

'Yes, now I do,' he said, and a small cloud passed over his face. 'I broke up with my long-term girlfriend and changed jobs all at the same time, so it's a new start for me in newly trendy Seymour Hill. As a hobby, I'm going to start up a craft brewery, I reckon, with fermentation based on obscure Mongolian methods with foraged herbs. It'll go down a storm here.'

'The rule is that you're allowed to take the piss out of the place if you come from here. If not, it's a no-no,' I told him sternly, crossing my arms across my chest.

'You see? I was made to run into you so that you could make sure I know this stuff.'

This was moving into distinctly flirty waters in which I was not prepared to paddle, so I nodded: 'Thank you for the food and for bringing my dog back.'

'Swiftly delivered food, I think you'll agree.'

'Five-star delivery,' I agreed.

He turned, giving Bodger a big stroke. 'I think he knows I'm the guy who's delivered food. So, he sat outside in the hope for more.'

I swear Bodger gave an almost imperceptible nod. This seemed like collusion to me and I pushed the dog back into the hallway. 'Thanks again for bringing him back. See you round, BiL.'

9

There were people in life who were lucky enough to love their jobs, who relished every challenging, satisfying hour they spent completing their daily tasks *and* got paid for it.

Unfortunately, I was not one of them.

My job – Head of HR at a car leasing company– was completely unsatisfying in every sense of the word. I worked in a dingy office at the Angel in Islington. My basic daily tasks typically involved trying to get employees to stay with the firm; refereeing arguments between alpha male managers; and responding to the public who filed daily complaints about our delivery drivers speeding while on their mobile phones and harassing customers and so on. I had a particularly great one to deal with at the moment: one of our workers had been caught snorting cocaine in a customer's toilet after delivering a new Mercedes C class in Kent. It was the stupidity of it that got me – I could just about get my head round doing Class As at work, but why choose the polished porcelain ledge of a customer's loo and then leave a white powder residue?

Of course, not everyone who worked at Carter's Cars was a complete moron, but I'd be lying if I didn't say that most of them were. It was because of the culture that started with my boss, Eli Carter, who was one up from Neanderthal in terms of evolution. Because he hired people who didn't challenge him and, indeed, supported his warped, prehistoric world view, the place was full of people who would have been more at home as cave-based hunter-gatherers.

How had I ended up with such a fantastically crap career and why didn't I leave? Both good questions. The answer was money. Because it was such a terrible role for any self-respecting HR person, it was quite well paid. Back in the days when Ralph and I were bringing up three kids while managing what seemed a mammoth mortgage, and his contribution was, at best, minimal, I'd left my exciting job doing HR in a media company in Soho and, attracted by an extra £10k a year, gone to work at Carter's Cars of north London. And the money had made a huge difference to our family, despite me hating pretty much every hour of every day, so I'd stuck it out. Then when I tried to leave (which happened every two years or so, when I realised anew quite how awful my job was) Eli Carter would phone me up from whatever golf course he was on and up my salary again. Then I would think about how broke we always were despite everything and decide to stay. And when Ralph had left, any money that he *had* been contributing had vanished with him, so I'd just got on with it.

I was thinking about having to fire the coke-snorting driver when I arrived at the office on Monday morning.

My little team was already there, all three of them, looking forward to another five days in this daily grind.

I knew it was my job as the boss to rally the team and made a pathetic effort. 'Good weekend, everyone? And here's to a great week ahead.'

'Oh, don't be so fucking bogus, Cal,' said Greg, the recruitment manager, who was a dour, potty-mouthed Welshman. He had an online gambling habit and was continually in debt, so through the same mechanism of colleague retention – bungs in his pay cheque – I'd managed to get him to stay for three years now.

'Another Monday in this hellhole,' muttered Ayesha, who sat next to Greg. I figured Ayesha would last about another six weeks in the role before she left to go somewhere where she didn't have to deal with daily racism and hourly sexism.

'Oh, come on, I'm only trying to get a bit of *joie de vivre* into the place,' I said. 'What about you, Charles? Did you have a good weekend?' We currently had a young nephew of Eli's working with us on what had been loosely called 'an internship'. He was extremely posh, turning up every day in a Prince of Wales check suit, tie, shirt and cufflinks and was very friendly. He was also completely, utterly useless at any task we set him, so we just avoided giving him any jobs. This meant that he spent most of his day on Instagram.

'I had a fantastic time at the motor racing,' Charles said. It was the sort of posh thing he spent his weekends doing, so I didn't look surprised. 'And now I'm ready for the challenges of the week.'

'Finding new followers on Insta,' grunted Greg. 'Really challenging.'

'Ha, ha! I would love to help you this week, Greg, and gain some of your valuable experience,' said Charles, who was immune to sarcasm.

Greg looked absolutely horrified and when his desk phone rang picked it up with alacrity and much more enthusiasm than usual. 'Hello? Greg speaking.'

If I didn't have enough on my plate, this was my daily bread and butter.

Lucky me. Monday morning was also the operational management meeting. It was the standard dirge. I successfully managed to outsource firing the coked-up driver to one of the regional managers. I was feeling that this was a result when my colleagues – all men, white and in their forties and fifties – started to debate the most important issue of the day: lunch.

'Did anyone organise any?' asked the ops director.

Six heads turned to look my way before they realised what they'd done. As my eyebrows went up in rage, they all looked hurriedly down at their notebooks or picked up their phones.

'Seriously?' I said.

I might be invisible, I thought, but I was also deeply *angry*. Not necessarily a healthy combo.

'Of course, we didn't mean to look at you for the lunch,' soothed Eli, leaning back in his chair, but giving the little eye-roll he always made when faced with issues of political correctness.

'It's that thing you made us go on the course about – unconscious bias – in action,' said the finance director.

'Because we're pre-programmed by our upbringing to think of women in that role, we all looked at you at the mention of food.'

The other members of the meeting tried to work out whether he was talking crap or had got them out of a hole. The ops director said, 'Sorry, love,' but the others all started going on about their mothers.

'My mum always handed me a packed lunch when I was leaving the house,' Eli said. 'The wife won't do it – she only believes in eating out. Or not eating.' He was currently married to a glamorous younger blonde called Mariella, who despised everything about him, except for his money and his massive house in Gants Hill.

'My mum would never go to bed before she'd made my sandwiches,' said one of the regional managers. 'And once there were microwaves, she'd make me a pie or a casserole for a treat.'

'Is this meeting finished?' I asked, getting up and gathering my stuff. 'It's just I need to go and ensure that my non-existent husband has a home-cooked casserole for his lunch tomorrow.'

I slammed the door but knew it would make very little difference. They were probably all discussing why feminism had got in the way of making the world a very nice place to live in if you were a man.

While I typed a report that afternoon, I waited to hear whether Marvin had managed to speak to Ralph. Instead at about 2 p.m. there was a text from BiL.

People keep calling me Patrick and it's getting difficult to explain that I changed my name over the weekend.

This was quite funny, but really there was so much else to think about. I ignored it and texted Marv instead.

Any luck with the bastard ex?

The screen showed that he was immediately typing back.

Call me.

I hurried outside the dirty swing doors to the office stairwell and pressed Marv's name on my phone.

'Can you talk?' He sounded as if he was walking fast down a road – out of breath, car noises in the background.

'Yes, what happened?' This didn't sound hopeful.

'Well, I waited until lunchtime and, well, I lurked and then he came down the path, on his way to buy some milk or fags—'

'Petra's even managed to get him to give up smoking.'

'So, I sprang out at him from behind a lamp post and he wasn't best pleased. Says, "Oh, right, knew you'd show up," which I think was quite rude considering how I managed to get him home quite a few times when he was legless…'

'Please tell me what happened.'

'So, he says that Petra says that he can't talk to me or any of your friends as it will compromise the legal position, so I said he didn't have to talk, he just had to listen.' Marv paused while a siren went past at a pace. 'So then I told him how he was completely breaking your heart, how you'd always been a perfect parent to Wilf and how he was going to destroy both of your lives.'

I'd known that Marv's love of drama would ensure that he didn't mince his words. 'Wow,' I said, 'thanks.'

'And he listened but he just kept shrugging and then he said he knew you'd been amazing, but life moved on and his life was moving on – and that meant Cape Town with Petra and "my son". And he was sorry for you, but you'd still have a relationship with Wilf and that blood was thicker than water.'

'When did he become so heartless?'

'Maybe it's the drugs he's on,' Marv said. 'I couldn't believe it was the same guy as used to be *your* Ralph. It was like he'd been brainwashed.'

'I know, it's horrifying,' I said, collapsing onto the top step of the staircase. 'Oh, God, what am I going to do?'

'Poor Cal. Poor Wilf. Anyway, I tried but, I'm sorry, I didn't get anywhere.'

'Oh, I'm so grateful, Marv, you know I am. I couldn't ask for a better friend. But how can things get any worse?'

There was a pause and then Marv told me precisely how they were going to get worse: 'I'm so sorry, Cal, but Ralph says he's going to tell Wilf today.'

Oh, no, oh, no. I looked at the time on my phone. 'Marv, I've got to go, if I am going to get back in time.'

All I knew was I needed to be there for Wilf.

10

I tried both Ralph's and Wilf's phones frenetically as the train edged up the line. Wilf's rang and rang, but he'd never been that keen on answering a call. I texted him.

Call me before you go to your dad's

But the chances were he wouldn't have looked at that either, just have jumped on his bike and started cycling round there. Ralph's phone continued to be switched off.

I willed the train to go faster. At the station, I remembered to look both ways as I came to the zebra crossing, ran across it and straight to the taxi rank, jumping into the first minicab and giving Petra's address. As the car sped off on its five-minute journey, I tried to stop the sick feeling of doom that was coming from my stomach and, instead, rang Wilf's phone again and again with no luck.

As the cab pulled round the corner into the cul-de-sac, the sickness became unbearable. Thrown casually against a lamp post and lazily locked, was Wilf's bike. I was too late. Too late. Too late for what, though? To sugar coat a message that he was going to hear at some point anyway?

Worse, though. As the cab drew to the kerb, it pulled up behind a shiny Mini, with the unmistakable number plate: PE T5A. They must have planned that she would come home from work and help break the news to Wilf. I raged anew, thrust five pounds at the driver and told him to keep the change, got out of the car and stopped myself from running up the path because I knew that I had to be calm for Wilf.

Calm for Wilf. Calm for Wilf. But I felt anything but calm.

As I rang the doorbell I tried to peer through the window into the beige sitting room. It was ranged as if it were a posh doctor's surgery and Wilf were a new patient and, sure enough, I could see the outlines of Petra and Ralph, sitting side by side as they had with me, with the floppy-haired shadow of Wilf on the sofa opposite. From the movement of her head, it looked as if Petra was talking.

She jumped at the sound of the bell and Ralph and Wilf did too. It was Ralph who got to his feet, though, and moved towards the door. I saw him through the glass, clearly shaking his head as he saw that the unexpected visitor was me.

'Oh, no, *Cal*,' I could hear him groan, then, also clearly staying civilised for Wilf, he pulled the door open.

I glared at him, giving him the sort of look of laser-focused derision I used to use when he finally came round on the sofa after one of his binges. Then I mouthed the words 'lying bastard' before saying out loud, 'I thought I'd drop in and see how it was going with Wilf,' in as cheery a tone as I could manage.

'Callie!' Wilf was obviously surprised but delighted it was me at the door. I came into the sitting room ahead of Ralph and he stood up and moved towards me, then, remembering that Petra was also in the room, instinctively stopped short of giving me a hug. His school tie hung loosely round his neck, his trousers were down round his skinny hips and his shirt showed splodges of lunch. He was filthy, he was probably hungry as it was after school and he was always hungry, and I wanted to gather him into my arms and refuse to let anyone take him anywhere.

Petra said, 'Calypso, how nice to see you, again,' in a bogus voice that was particularly high-pitched. 'Please, sit down. We were just saying to Wilf how amazing Cape Town is and how much he'll enjoy all the sports that are available in the area.'

I bit my lips. Yeah, Wilf played a bit of football, but his big passion was music. Didn't his bloody stepmother know *anything*?

Wilf looked at me, his gentle face a mix of disbelief and dismay, but his eyes pleaded with me to provide some reassurance.

Ralph said into the silence, 'And a whole heap of great bands come from Cape Town too.'

'Yeah?' mumbled Wilf, swivelling to look at him. 'I mean like who…?'

'Generation Great, for one,' Ralph said confidently. He'd obviously looked this up in order to impress his son. 'And there's a good EDM scene.'

'But what about my band here? With Jowan and stuff?'

'Hey, there's going to be loads of holidays, back here.' Ralph had a slightly desperate tone. 'It's a really beautiful environment on the coast too.'

'But I can't stay?' He looked round at me, begging.

Petra started to speak. 'It's a great opportunity to broaden your horizons alongside your biological parent...' but she must have realised that she wasn't being listened to as her voice tapered off. It was as if she had learned a bunch of points to win the debate, noted them down in bullet-point format and then recited them at the poor kid.

'You'll always have a home with me,' I said, my eyes filling with tears. I moved towards him and he came towards me and, for a brief moment, he let me hug him. Petra caught my eye and her face flushed with competitive spirit. I stared defiantly back at her as Wilf pushed me away from him.

'You're not sending me away, then? Is it because I'm messy? Or eat too much?'

'Don't be silly.' I tucked a strand of his floppy hair behind his ear. 'I'd never send you away.'

'But I want you to come with us very much,' said Ralph.

'*We* want you to come with us,' reproved Petra. I wondered again how much she really wanted Wilf; how much she was doing this because Ralph had refused to leave without his son; how much of it was her own personal sense of one-upmanship. Parenting is not a competition, I wanted to hiss, but said nothing.

'I think we'll have a great time,' Ralph finished lamely.

Wilf looked bereft but didn't say anything. I could feel his primal urge not to upset his dad after the last few years.

He was trying to find out if he had a choice, but he was also desperate not to hurt anyone's feelings.

'It's going to be fantastic,' Ralph continued with more than a hint of his old optimistic charm. 'We'll be able to be outdoors a lot; I won't be at work for a while until I get a permit, so you and I can hang out and I can really help with your schooling...'

'Where will I go?' Wilf said.

'We've conducted a thorough audit of secondary school options for you, Wilf, but in the end we thought we'd let you make the choice of where to pursue your education. There are some fantastic options...' Petra waffled on. Wilf didn't look at her and he didn't look convinced.

'And there's one school not far away from where we'll live, with the most amazing sound-engineering programme,' Ralph leapt in. 'It's a course that's famous across the continent.'

A flicker of interest crossed Wilf's face, but then he looked pleadingly at me. 'Cal, what do you think?'

I bit the bottom of my lip; I'd vowed to always look after him and that meant telling him the truth. 'I don't want you to go. I'll miss you so much.' Ralph grimaced, and Petra put her hands on her hips.

'So, I could stay with you?' Petra glared at me as if daring me to give him this possibility; Ralph looked at me pleadingly.

I struggled hard for a second but then I said, 'Of course you *could*. But the law says...' Petra looked triumphant. *She thinks she's won. She probably has.* 'The law says that you should live with your dad, Wilf. And... he and Petra want you to go with them.' My voice was bleak – I was trying hard to balance my need for him with the fact that I had to help him.

'But if I said—' Wilf started but Ralph leapt in, leaning forward and banging his son hard on the back of his skinny ribcage.

'It's going to be cool as,' he enthused. 'You and me hanging out, all the time in the world, and, now I'm better, I want to make up for being a bit of a shit dad a couple of years back and—'

'Doesn't matter,' Wilf muttered. When anyone brought up Ralph's breakdown, Wilf always acted as if it were a small thing that happened; he rarely talked about it and batted it off if anyone else did.

'Mate, we'll go surfing…' Ralph was selling it to him. 'And rock climbing. You want to go look up the school I was thinking about?'

Wilf shrugged and looked beaten. 'OK.'

Petra didn't bother not to gloat. 'I'll see you at home later, then, Wilf?' I said mock cheerfully. The word home now sounded temporary and inappropriate.

'Do One and Two know yet?' Wilf asked me.

'Umm, no, they don't,' I said.

'We had to tell you first,' Ralph said.

'They're going to be…' Wilf went on and then stopped.

'Yes,' I said. 'I'll go and talk to them about it now, shall I?'

'You'd better,' Petra said in a tone that really said, 'Get the fuck out of my house.'

Daisy and Lily were both in their bedrooms at home, both with earbuds in, Daisy staring at her phone, Lily at a textbook. I walked up to Lily's bed before she heard me approach; as she looked at me, I saw the unmistakable signs that she'd been crying – her eyes were red and bruised, her cheeks hollow. How much more pain was I about to inflict on her?

'Are you OK?' I sat down on her bed and she pulled the earbuds from her ears.

'Yeah, just doing some chemistry catch-up,' she said. I took a moment to hate the government for its commitment to making GCSEs harder, all over again.

'You need to get a bit of balance with this revision,' I said. 'You mustn't get into such a state. You can only do your best.'

'You always say that, but what if my best isn't good enough?'

'Oh, shush,' I said, putting my arms round her. 'Now, can you come downstairs for a minute? I need to talk to you and your sister.'

Daisy joined us at the table; both their faces were serious and worried.

'Right, so…' I hesitated, then pushed on. I was the grown-up here. I had to reassure them and make a shit situation seem better than it was. 'Ralph and Petra are moving to South Africa—'

'Oh, is that it?' Daisy was clearly relieved. 'I thought you were going to tell us you had cancer.'

This floored me. 'God, no.' I shuddered and reached out to both of them. 'I'm absolutely fine.'

'Thank fuck, Ma,' Daisy said. I ignored the swearing.

'Yeah.' Lily's face cleared. 'I mean, we'll miss Ralph and everything, but, you know, he hasn't lived here for a year and a half, so it's not like we saw him every day.'

The true consequences of Ralph moving didn't occur to them. 'But, you see,' I said very gently, 'they want to take Wilf with them.'

Lily's face went white; Daisy's purple with rage. Their reactions were unique to them but so expected. 'Fuck that,' shouted Daisy.

'Oh, no, oh, no.' Tears came into Lily's big round eyes. They flooded into mine too. 'How can Ralph do this to us?'

'I mean, he knows that Wilf lives with us!' Daisy cried. 'What a bastard. Complete bastard.'

'Wilf will be so lonely without us,' Lily whispered. 'Just think of him alone, in another country.'

I wanted to bend over with the pain as they said out loud the things I'd been thinking for the last couple of days. They'd always mothered him as well as been his older sisters. They did it in their different ways: Daisy saw it as her job to educate her younger 'bro' in the ways of the world: I'm pretty sure he'd had his first sex conversation with her.

Lily just cared and comforted. An image flashed into my head: a day out a few years back, in the still-holding-it-together bit of my relationship with Ralph, when all of them were just about tall enough to meet some of the height requirements for rides at Thorpe Park. The girls had topknots for hair to help them reach that ruler; Wilf had a pointy anorak, but on one particular ride that wasn't enough, and he couldn't go on. The girls pulled Ralph with them; I tried to comfort Wilf, who was really upset about not being able to scare the living daylights out of himself. Eventually, I took him to an ice-cream kiosk to bribe him with sugar into looking as if the world hadn't ended. But as I turned to pay, Wilf stuck his head through the railings next to the kiosk – and there was no way it was coming out.

Eventually, after a lot of chaos and general screaming by Wilf, me and half the other parents in the park, he was sawn out by a very patient maintenance man. And it was Lily who pulled him straight into her arms when he was finally free and who cuddled him in the back of the car all the way round the M25, while I sat in the front, furious with myself for not keeping a better eye on him. That was in the days when they weren't too cool to show obvious emotions to each other, of course; and the days when having a kid's head stuck in railings was my only problem.

'I mean, we won't let him go. We just won't,' Daisy raged on. 'He won't want to go, and we won't let him.'

'It's not as simple as that,' I said. 'I've spent the last few days checking out the law and, unfortunately, they *can* take him. He's fourteen. He'd have to say point blank that he didn't want to go and—'

'But isn't that what he *is* saying?' demanded Daisy.

'It'd be difficult for him, though, to say that to Ralph,' whispered Lily. Her face was stricken. I wanted to hold her tight, force red blood cells round her veins, until the colour flooded back into her cheeks. 'It's his dad.'

There was a brief moment while the lack of their own father hung in the room. Daisy always said that she was going to go and find Dougie when she was eighteen; Lily said that she 'had enough family already, thanks', but still I felt keenly that they'd been born into the world without a father. For a while, of course, there had been Ralph – and he'd done as good a job as he could – but both girls had distanced themselves from him as he'd disintegrated and, now, didn't seem keen to re-establish that relationship. I'd tried to be parent enough for everyone, including Wilf, but in the end perhaps DNA counted more than love and support.

Shaking off these thoughts, I gave them a summary of what the lawyer had told me. Daisy thumped the table in anger as I talked. 'I can't believe Ralph would do this to us all,' she kept saying.

'Ralph can't leave Wilf, because of Sylvia,' Lily said. 'I mean, he must imagine she's looking down at him and telling him to get on with being a proper dad.'

I gasped inwardly at the acuteness of her insight. Was it this ability to feel so much that made her so worried about the world? She'd certainly hit the nail on the head about the reasons for Ralph's ultimate breakdown: years of stored-up guilt about his poor wife dying so young that had crept up on him and eventually destroyed him.

'Yeah. I don't think it's Petra. She's only worried about what she looks like to other people,' said Daisy.

'What makes you say that?' I asked, having been extremely careful to never ever diss Petra in front of the kids (only Marv and the AAs; I'm not that nice).

'Well, there was the time she came to Wilf's DJ thing.' I remembered the sweaty school hall, the showcase of dance music, Wilf's excitement about 'releasing his track'. It was not long after Petra and Ralph got married and she'd started to appear at some school events, fiercely clinging onto his arm while beaming munificently about her.

'So, she was properly bogus, then. Really nice to me and Lily in front of Wilf and Ralph, but giving you daggers.'

I can't remember noticing; I was busy being nervous for Wilf in case something went wrong and feeling relieved that Ralph had turned up – still sober. My overwhelming feeling at the time had been gratitude. She was strange, sure, a bit of a corporate freak, yeah – but she'd also managed to make Ralph well again.

'She can't love him like we do,' said Lily quietly.

'I reckon Ralph's said he's not going without Bro and she's thinking, *Gonna lose my man or gain a kid; OK, let's have the kid*,' Daisy went on. My only defence of her was that she watched a lot of American TV.

'Look, Wilf's going to come home soon—' I said that word again: *home* '—and we have to be strong for him.'

'We're not going to fight at all?' Daisy got up and strode to the back door. 'Well, I'm not taking this lying down. I'm going to go down to the centre and see what Sunil says. He says there's always action you can take against injustice.' She pulled open the door in a heated rage. 'There must be something you could do.' Then she was gone.

Lily looked at me appraisingly as if she too was judging me for my inaction, pulled her hand across her face and ran out of the kitchen door and up the stairs.

Oh, that hurt. I put my face in my hands and cried too, helpless as my little family collapsed, like the house made of straw under attack from the Big Bad Wolf.

11

Wilf looked as if an earthquake had gone off somewhere deep in his soul as he came into the kitchen. I'd roasted a chicken and was pounding potatoes into mash – it was Wilf's favourite dinner, the one he always called 'Winner, winner'. This time, though, he eyed the chicken but said nothing, instead not meeting my eyes. I'd gone upstairs to try to comfort Lily, but she'd refused to open her bedroom door. She was blaming me for what was going on, and, while I understood it, it seemed terribly unfair. There'd been no sign of Daisy – probably off raging about stupid adults to Perfect Sunil.

I said, 'How are you doing?'

'Fine.' He thrust his hands deep into the pockets of his school trousers and looked at the floor.

'You know, it's the last thing I expected.' I gulped back the lump in my throat. 'And I meant it, you've always got a home here and—'

'Yeah, but I've got to go with my dad,' Wilf said. 'Because you're not my real mum.'

Could anything hurt more than those short words 'not my real mum'? Wilf hovered awkwardly: 'I didn't mean that, you know… I didn't mean it like that – just that's what the law says, according to Dad and Petra.'

He wasn't criticising me; he was just repeating what they'd told him.

'Yes, I know, and we'll really, really miss you,' I said and went to hug him. He was nearly taller than me now and it occurred to me that I wouldn't be around to see him through his next adolescent growth spurt. In a year, he'd be six foot and gangly. He let me hold him for a while.

'It'll be all right there, though?' Wilf mumbled.

'Hey, I'm sure Cape Town is really cool,' I said as brightly as I could. 'It's supposed to be one of the best lifestyles on earth. And the course your dad was talking about sounds great.'

'Yeah,' said Wilf. 'We looked it up and the school has got amazing studios. The kids looked OK.'

'And you're getting on really well with your dad now,' I pointed out.

'It's all right when he's not talking shit that Petra says,' Wilf muttered. I was shocked: he rarely had a bad word to say about anyone.

'Hey, come on, she's… she's great in loads of ways. She's been really good for your dad.'

'Yeah, I didn't mean that,' Wilf said. 'It's just that sometimes he seems to talk like her now, even when she's not there.'

He was talking about the new anaesthetised version of Ralph, who seemed to have lost his capacity for irony along with his drinking habit. It had to be medication as well as Petra, of course. 'He'll become more and more like himself over time,' I said. 'He's worked so hard to get better.'

'I know you couldn't stay with him, but I wish you had,' Wilf said then, and I wanted to howl with guilt. 'I'm not blaming you.'

'Thanks, it was...' But he hated talking about the past. He didn't want to remember Ralph already in bed when he came home from school or, alternatively, rolling in after dinner, loud and pie-eyed after facing into the bottom of a glass for a few hours of blessed blankness. 'Anyway, if you go—' I was still thinking of it as 'if' rather than 'when' '—we'll come and see you and you'll come back here,' I finished in a bright, false falsetto.

'What did the girls say?' Wilf asked then. It wasn't as if they ever said out loud how much they loved each other. They expressed affection for each other by making the 'L' sign on their foreheads.

'The truth is they're gutted,' I said. 'Like me.'

He looked pleased for a moment and then there was the sign of tears in his big eyes. 'I'm going to miss you all too,' he said and stumbled from the room, because there was no way he would want any of us to see him crying. I grabbed the potato masher and pounded the mash harder and harder.

It was as I was putting the chicken onto the table and shouting, 'Lily, Wilf, dinner!' that the back door opened, and Daisy appeared with a man behind her.

He was Asian and tall, a thick head of black hair above a strong face, a neck wrapped in a dark scarf. His eyes were large and looking at me with sympathy, as if he knew I would be distressed. This was obviously Sunil, campaigner for local youth justice and general all-round hero to Daisy.

The problem was she'd forgotten to mention that he was utterly gorgeous.

'Mum, this is Sunil,' Daisy confirmed as I registered that my hair was in a rough ponytail on the top of my head, my face was puffy from anger and I was still wearing my really Mumsy work clothes, but now with a butcher's pinny over the top. Not that any of that really mattered but he was… well, at least the most attractive man who'd ever come into my kitchen.

I put down the gravy jug and went forward to shake his hand. It was warm and large. 'Come in, come in,' I said. 'You've been such an inspiration to Daisy.' Bodger sniffed him and looked suspicious.

His lovely face lit up in a big smile. 'Hey, thanks, she's a great kid and they're a great group.' He said kid, but he seemed so young to me; what had Daisy said – mid-thirties?

Daisy made a mock-barfing gesture. 'So, Sunil said there probably wasn't much we could do, but why didn't he come round here and chat it through?'

'I wanted to introduce myself anyway,' Sunil said. 'I thought it was right, what with driving Daisy to a rally in Westminster on Sunday week, if she's allowed.'

'Please, sit down,' I said, gesturing towards the table. It was, however, clear from the plates and cutlery that we'd been about to eat.

'Hey, you're going to have dinner,' Sunil said. 'I won't stop. I was just wondering if there was anything I could do to help with the situation with Daisy's brother, but another time.'

'Will you join us?' I asked politely while I internally wrestled with myself. I looked awful and the kids didn't need a guest for dinner tonight. But, on the other hand, God, he was gorgeous – and maybe he did have some sort of miraculous solution.

'Oh, no, but thanks,' Sunil said with a big smile. 'Look, I know some family lawyers and stuff through my work.'

'There must be someone.' Daisy put her hands on her hips.

'From the advice we've had so far, I don't think there is,' I said as gently as I could. 'And I know that's hard.'

'It's a tough one.' Sunil turned to Daisy. She looked up at him in open admiration. I joined in. He had an empathetic air, and did I mention the overall gorgeousness? My body had a reaction that felt quite alien after all this time: a hot flush and a faster beating heart. I'd completely forgotten that a stranger could walk into your immediate surroundings and your first reaction would be, 'OMG, I want to jump your bones, right now.' I tried hard not to let this show in my face.

But in addition to being gorgeous, he was a man who understood teenage brains. He might not be able to help me with Wilf, but resilience was precisely what he *and* Lily needed right now. 'I'd love to talk to you more about your work.'

Lily came into the kitchen then, her eyes avoiding mine. Sunil said, 'Woah, two of you.'

'My twin, Lily,' Daisy confirmed. 'This is Sunil from Resilient.'

His eyes flicked from her to me. I sometimes thought you could feel and smell Lily's vulnerability when you were in the same space as her; Sunil certainly seemed to get it in a moment.

'Hey, Lily,' he said. 'Any time you want to come and hang out with us, let me know.'

Daisy was clearly annoyed about this potential invasion of her space; Lily nodded non-committally. 'Maybe after the exams,' she said.

'So...' He looked at me as he turned to go.

'Callie,' I heard my voice squeak.

'Callie, shall I give you my number, in case you want to chat, or anything comes up about the rally?' I nodded slightly too keenly and he held out a card. I took it and resisted the urge to look at it too much. He was just being a professional youth worker. That was all.

'Thanks,' I squeaked again as he went out of the door.

'Mum, you were, like, so grafting§§§§ on Sunil,' Daisy grumbled, sitting down at the table.

'What does that mean?' I turned to pick up the gravy.

'Like coming on to him,' Lily said. 'It's from *Love Island*.'¶¶¶¶ They'd both glued themselves to the telly for hours the previous summer to watch a series of girls in very small bikinis flirt with and kiss a bunch of boys with biceps the size of small mountain ranges.

---

§§§§ Sorry, new one on me too.

¶¶¶¶ The biggest cultural phenomenon for teenagers, like, EVER. Where have you been? Obviously not watching ITV2 all summer.

'I was *not* coming on to him or whatever you call it.'

'He'll really mug you off, you melt,'***** said Daisy, quoting more *Love Island* at me. I looked at her but knew better than to encourage it. 'He is quite hot for an older dude, I suppose,' she went on when she didn't get a rise out of me, grabbing the plate of chicken from me before I could even put it on the table. 'A DILF.'†††††

'Daisy!' I was outraged. 'That's very sexist. He can't be older than thirty-five.'

'Yeah, maybe,' she agreed, stuffing a piece of chicken skin in her mouth. She obviously wasn't a vegetarian today.

I went out of the door and yelled up the stairs to Wilf.

'I think he was crying,' Lily said quietly. 'I could kind of hear him.'

'Don't say anything about that,' I hissed as I eventually heard his lope down the stairs. 'We need to be supportive, while letting him know how much we'll miss him.'

'Winner, winner,' Wilf mumbled as he sat at the table and we all smiled in relief. I sat down too and then got up again. It *was* Monday, certainly not a designated wine day, but there was half a bottle of wine in the fridge and I knew I needed a big glass of it.

'South Africa: there's wild animals and everything,' said Daisy.

'Lions and tigers and bears and things,' added Lily. It was a saying from *The Wizard of Oz* – a film they'd all loved as children. Now they all quoted it in hushed tones,

---

***** Generally useless person.

††††† Dad I'd Like to Fxxk. I apologise again for my daughter.

in exactly the same way as they'd done when they were young children, gradually getting louder and louder.

And I was back all those years – the same kids, the same house, the same family sayings we all knew. Except it would never be like this again.

12

Eli called me into his office and looking down, mumbled, 'Any issues about all that woman stuff from yesterday?' and I'd wanted to laugh and tell him that a bit of everyday sexism in the workplace was the least of my problems. Instead I just told him I would up my focus on gender balance, which pissed him off.

Daisy and Lily had study leave, which made Daisy lie around watching videos on YouTube and pick up her books when I came into the room and Lily sit upright at her desk, a look of outright terror growing in her pale face. I did everything I could to support her, but it didn't feel enough.

There was silence from Ralph. Wilf went round there after school as usual, but said very little. I spent a few hours at work, pretending I needed quiet time to write a report and taking myself off into a meeting room, where I obsessively stalked Petra on Facebook (wholesome, gushing and cheesy; obsessed with clean eating; not that many friends) and Twitter (just gushy), and trying to find out more about

Cape Town (very beautiful) and my rights with regard to Wilf. Ralph's solicitor sent me an email halfway through that day inviting me to a mediation session with Mr and Mrs Colesdown. I ignored it – what was the point of a talking shop when the outcome was a foregone conclusion? And I wasn't sure I could sit in a room with sanctimonious Petra without punching her. Ralph? It was as if he'd stamped on all the years we'd spent together trying to be a family.

And all the time, GCSE start day was getting closer.

I'd thought, with the absence of food parcels and texts, that Patrick had assuaged his guilt. That was if I thought about it at all. I didn't have time to worry about men or being invisible to them and if I had, well, I'd certainly have used my brain space on thinking about gorgeous Sunil. I mean, Patrick certainly wasn't bad-looking but Sunil was a whole different ballgame – he knocked every other man out of the park.

I mean, yum.

Just yum.

I wasn't used to it at all – that unexpected churning feeling of being attracted to someone – and overall it made me a bit *hot*. I don't mean I suddenly became really attractive to others, I mean it made my body heat up so that I wanted to take off my coat.

The next night, though, there he was – not in my kitchen but in front of me on the local TV news. There was a special focus on Resilient and the role it was playing in campaigning for more funds and Sunil, much to Daisy's obvious glee, and my much more surreptitious viewing delight, was the central spokesperson. His lovely face shone from the screen as he told the journalist, very earnestly, that he would fight the impact of government austerity on teenagers in an 'unceasing personal war'.

'Ooooooh,' said Daisy.

'The government must understand the impact they've had on a generation; I will always use my public platform to campaign for justice,' Sunil went on.

'Ooooh,' I said and then tried to pretend that my stomach wasn't doing a disco dance at his obvious ardour. Imagine, said the much-underused sex synapses in my head, if that passion were directed at *you*. Then I told myself off for being a stupid, deluded middle-aged wreck of a woman who should know better and told Daisy to get off to bed.

Earlier that evening, I'd gone to see Mum and Dad so that I could tell them about Wilf. Inside their kitchen there was a faint smell of rotting vegetables, but it didn't look too catastrophic. Mum was sitting at the kitchen table wearing a blue boiler suit, which she considered a very practical garment for every day.

'Hello,' I said in the loud voice she needed to hear me.

'No need to shout, Callie.' She sniffed. She'd obviously got her hearing aid turned on for once.

My dad came into the kitchen and smiled at me. 'I can't wait to show you Seymour House,' he said. 'We'll make an appointment.'

They were both more upbeat than I'd seen them in a while – it was usually the way as they got involved in a new passion or project. Now I was going to have to make them miserable again.

'Listen.' I sat down at the table and nodded to Dad to sit down too. 'I've got something terrible to tell you.' And, as I related how they were going to have to get used to living without Wilf down the road, I watched their faces fall in disgust.

'I always thought that Ralph was a feckless bastard,' Mum said ferociously as the news sank in. This wasn't strictly true – when I'd first got together with Ralph, they'd been really keen on him. Mum had thought that it was good that he was domesticated and seemed to want to stick around; Dad had had another pair of ears forced to listen to him. And the fact that Ralph also gave them a proxy grandson had counted in his favour.

I had the now familiar conversation about how there wasn't really much we could do about it legally. Mum reacted just like Daisy – wanting to fight for Wilf and their right to be with him. Dad was more ponderous and kept saying, 'The facts aren't on our side, Lois. It's unfortunate but the law is an ass.'

'You're an ass!' Mum hissed when he'd said this for the eighth time.

When my folks fought, it was ferocious and childish, so I leapt in quickly. 'I've got to go, but I'll come and pick you up for the tour of the centre tomorrow.'

'I'm turning you off now, Lorca.' Mum pressed a switch behind her ear as I went out of the door.

When I got home later that week, there was a carrier bag containing food on my doorstep again. There was a note on top of a pile of silver-foil containers; I pushed that aside for now and took the bag inside to unpack it. I was hungry, and the containers contained a still-warm Chinese – noodles, seaweed toast, prawn crackers, spring rolls, special fried rice and delicate lemon chicken. And there was enough for four people. Salivating, I wondered how long this fantastic service was going to go on for. I knew I should discourage it, but it *was* great, not having to knock up dinners for my household.

I shouted to the kids, put it on the table and picked up the note with one hand as I got plates out of the cupboard with the other.

Wilf came piling into the kitchen and said, 'Yum, Chinese.'

'Ace,' said Daisy, coming in on his heels.

Only Lily looked at the food in an uninterested way, throwing herself into the chair, stress emanating from every pore. 'I will *never* pass chemistry,' she said, reaching for a plate and a fork.

'Is this from the Deliveroo guy?' Daisy asked, digging in. 'Maybe he fancies you after he tried to mow you down.'

'Meals on wheels,' Wilf said.

'Just save me some.' I pushed Wilf's hand from the noodles. You had to try quite hard in my family to make sure you got the required amount of daily nutrition.

I opened the note from Patrick: it was on exercise-book paper and in scrawling round handwriting.

Dear Very Visible Callie, sorry for not bringing you food for a bit – I got some supply work in London. I hope this meets the required rules for living in Seymour Hill. I've decided that the full version of Bill – William – is more suited to my station in life, so have adopted that instead. Yours sincerely, the aforementioned William.

I should message him once and for all and tell him to stop.

'I saw him earlier,' Wilf carried on, chomping his way through a spring roll. 'He's got quite a cool bike, but he says sometimes he delivered the food in his car.'

I shook my head. 'You mean you spoke to Patrick?'

'Yeah,' Wilf said. 'I was walking Bodger back from the park—' the dog looked up expectantly at hearing his name '—and Bodger started wagging his tail and bounded up to him on our way back, so we had a chat. I didn't realise he lived so close.'

'Hmm,' I said and glared at Bodger, who looked confused as to what he'd done wrong. I spooned lemon chicken onto my plate before the kids could eat it all.

'Anyway, I said cheers for the grub and stuff and he said, did I like Chinese and I said, yeah, everyone likes Chinese and he said, there's four of you, right? And I said yeah, but sometimes there's Lois and Lorca, and he said who's Lois and Lorca and I said, Nan and Grandad in normal families.'

'Oh,' I said. This was quite a long monologue by Wilf standards. There were four spring rolls not six, so probably even Patrick thought having to feed a family of six through guilt was a bit much, even for someone who had made me go to A & E. Wilf finished up, 'He was a nice guy. I told him you were fine. We talked about his bike.'

This conversation had obviously gone on for a while, then. 'I hope you told him not to bring any more food round.'

'Nah, I mean it's goals,‡‡‡‡‡ free food.' Wilf shook his head.

'We're not a charity case.'

---

‡‡‡‡‡ An aim in life = goals.

'No, he *wants* to bring us food. To make up for knocking you down,' Wilf said, with all the logic of a permanently starving boy. 'We had a chat about bikes and I told him I'd have to get a new one in South Africa. And I talked to him about why I was going and stuff.'

A really long conversation, then, for Wilf, who could never be described as loquacious. 'He's a PE teacher,' Wilf went on. 'He hasn't moved here long and he's going to teach at Whitebury in September.'

'Full of Fuck Boys,'§§§§§ said Daisy under her breath.

'Daisy!' I was outraged. 'I have had enough of your terrible language. Every time you swear from now on I will add two pounds to the amount you already owe me from your allowance.'

Lily looked up and smiled for a moment and I met her eyes. She liked getting one over on her sister.

'It's just an *expression*,' said Daisy. 'Jeez.'

'Don't cheek me, madam,' I seethed. She looked down, but I could see a small smirk on her face.

'The basic definition, by the way,' she went on, in a sweet voice, 'is a lad who shags around and hurts girls' feelings just to get his tiny dick wet.'¶¶¶¶¶

'DAISY!' I roared. 'Upstairs now. *Grounded* now.'

'You said don't swear, I'm just quoting basic biology,' she said. I shook my head, determined not to let her rile me even more, but I glared back. She knew just how to push my buttons.

---

§§§§§ I will spare you this one.

¶¶¶¶¶ Sorry couldn't spare you. In my defence, I'm only recounting what happened. I apologise AGAIN for my daughter.

She got up, objective of shocking me achieved, and sauntered out of the room. Wilf and Lily immediately tried to grab her plate; she'd made the classic Daisy mistake of behaving appallingly *before* finishing her dinner.

'We will ignore her. If we take no notice of her, she will eventually stop.' I determinedly ate on and tried to count to ten in my head. The problem was that as I got to five, my brain was flooded with rage at Daisy. Our relationship had always been heated; right now, it felt volcanic. I tried to remember that she was behaving badly because exams were coming, and her brother was going.

I decided to focus on the conversation we'd been having. 'But Patrick's a stranger, really,' I said. 'You shouldn't talk to strangers.'

'He isn't really, though, is he?' Wilf said. 'I mean, he knocked you down and stuff. And he's our neighbour.'

I turned to Lily, who was eating really fast, and said gently, 'Hey, slow down.'

'I need to get back to revising,' she said, her mouth half full.

'You've got to chill a bit,' I said.

Wilf and Lily both chorused in the sarcastic voice they used to mimic me: 'You can only do your best.'

Later, I hovered outside Lily's door for a while and then, a bit desperately, pushed it open with: 'Why don't we all go to Nando's at the weekend?'

'But what about physics?' Lily's voice was anguished. 'I need every hour of every day.' She was sitting at her little desk, surrounded by open books and highlighter pens.

'Is there anything you want?' I asked.

'No, no,' she said and looked down again while furiously biting the skin around her thumb. 'I just need to get on.'

I went back out onto the landing and peered through Daisy's door. In contrast, she was sitting at her desk, but with one leg swung over the arm of the chair, and her phone pinging with notifications. 'Phone OFF,' I said as I walked in the room and grabbed it from her hand. 'You can't behave like that, you do know that? It's not fair on your sister, your brother or me.'

Daisy immediately looked contrite. You could never tell with her whether she meant it or not, but at least it was an effort. 'Sorry,' she said. 'It's like something gets inside me.'

'A devil. A potty-mouthed devil gets inside you. Now I've had *enough* of it. Revision or sleep, those are your two choices.'

'But I was swapping notes on *Hamlet* with Clare,' she pleaded, 'so I need my phone. It's group revision, Mum.'

'Seriously? Was I kissed by the gullible fairy when I fell from heaven?' And I pocketed the phone.

Resilience, that was the word Sunil had used. I wondered how to make Lily have even half the resilience of her sister.

Thank you so much for the lovely Chinese. I am fine, thank you. Wilf enjoyed talking to you. All the food parcels are sufficient now as a way of saying sorry though, so please stop! Thanks again Callie.

I took a while to compose this text to Patrick, wanting to balance gratitude with a firm request to stop. I resisted any humour to make it clear I meant it. I was busy looking up community reviews for the Dutch company that ran Seymour House when Patrick pinged a message back.

Hi Callie, thank you for the message. Just a bloke called William.

Not a very grown-up one, I thought. But the food-delivery dude turned teacher was definitely hitting on me. This wasn't good.

Firstly, no one had hit on me in a very long time and I didn't have a clue what you *did* any more. Flirting was something that happened to other people. It was OK to fancy someone as young, gorgeous and unattainable as Sunil from afar: it meant perspiring a bit more than usual, but it was safe. But to actually have to avoid the bloke down the road was a bit much.

It was a long while back, when the kids were at primary school, but I'd used up loads of energy avoiding the school-gate dad I'd gone out with a couple of times. He'd turned out to want to talk about polygamy and other open relationships much more than he'd wanted to compare homework schedules. After I'd said no to another night out, I'd had to skulk around for at least a year.

Patrick was also recently out of a previous relationship – one he'd described as 'long term'. I didn't want to be a shoulder to cry on; that was what I needed myself.

He was quite attractive, particularly when he wasn't wearing Lycra. But he was new to the area and, therefore, just out to make some friends. Once he stopped feeling so guilty about me, he'd probably find much less complicated, younger and more attractive women to pursue with food deliveries. And then I'd have to go through the embarrassment of avoiding him every time I bumped into him in the street. Eventually, I'd see him with another woman walking up the road and have to think of a supercool way of saying 'hello' while looking exactly as if I didn't care at all. And with him being my neighbour meant something as simple as putting the wheelie bin out would become an epic exercise in wearing make-up and something other than pyjamas.

But mostly, aside from my harmless dreaming about Sunil, I needed every element of strength and focus I had to concentrate on my family.

13

Seymour House had been part of the landscape between our town and the countryside since Victorian times. It was all gargoyles and leaded windows. Dad explained, as we drove there, that it was a really common practice now in progressive Holland to mix generations in the quest for an agile brain in later years. 'All the facts support the impact on refreshing life in the third age.'******

As we went through the big front door, we were pounced on by a member of the Yoof. He was tall and hairy, and wearing a Breton T-shirt and bright red trousers. His blond hair stuck up in spikes from his head. The overall impression was that he was a trainee clown. 'Hello! Hello!' he said. 'Lois, Lorca, welcome back to Seymour House. I guess you wanted to "see more", ha, ha, ha.'

****** OK, now I have to explain what my parents are saying too? He means being old. He just doesn't like saying it.

Loads of LOLZ. I mean loads. I looked at him suspiciously, but Mum and Dad were shaking his hand enthusiastically.

'Pete,' Mum said. 'This is our daughter, Calypso.'

He looked at me and smiled a toothy grin. 'Come to check out the pad for the parents?' Then he grabbed my hand in his clammy one and started pumping my arm. 'Well, let's get going, then!'

I didn't know whether I could handle an hour in the company of someone this *keen*. And as he came closer, there was the distinct smell of fish – the exact same waft you'd get if you were passing the wet fish counter in Tesco. I drew back instinctively, but my folks didn't seem to notice the unfortunate odour of dead marine life.

Mum and Dad both seemed to have a spring in their step as they followed Fishy Pete into a hallway painted in bright colours. From an open doorway came the sound of badly played rock: 'Just band practice!' said Pete, and on the other side, in another room, about ten old people and a couple of women in their twenties were all doing the downward dog. 'And yoga!' It was as if everything he said came with unnecessary exclamation marks, but Mum and Dad looked excited. Even I could see that band practice and yoga were one up on your standard old people's home.

'It's all about keeping us active, Lois.' Pete put his arm through Mum's. Then he pointed to another doorway where a few more old people were sitting at desks, while more twenty-somethings pointed to computer screens in front of them. 'And here, some of our community are learning how to build their following on social media.'

'I love Instagram,' said Mum. I shook my head in disbelief – was my mother, unbeknown to me, taking photos of her food and posting them for the world to see? 'All that lovely avo on toast.' I made a mental note to see if I could track her down online. 'I've got a hundred followers now, but I'd like more.'

'You could be a micro influencer, Lois,' Fishy Pete said, and she looked really pleased. I didn't know what this was and I'm not sure she did either, but it sounded good.[††††††] 'You could use it to raise awareness of your campaigns.'

'Pete is a peaceful activist in the daily fight against capitalism,' Mum whispered approvingly. 'We talked all about the effects of globalisation when we were last here.'

I eyed him even more suspiciously. 'So, you're part of the yoof team here, Pete?' I asked. 'Do you get free rent?' That was blatant capitalism in action, after all.

'Hey, Calypso, thanks for asking!' Pete bounced brightly along the hall in the direction of the stairs. 'But it's all part of my mission for the community. I love being here with like-minded people. And one of my duties is to show prospective community members round.'

He got free rent, then. 'Do you have an outside job too?' I followed him as he turned the corner to a lift.

'I'm studying the advancement of human kind,' Pete said. 'And hey, Calypso, thanks so much for your interest in me as a member of the community.'

'Look, no more stairs.' Dad nudged me in the ribs as Pete pressed the lift button. I could see that not having to climb stairs was a big bonus for them, but had they worked out

---

[††††††] I now know it means a person of influence on social media. If this person says something is cool on Instagram, for example, then other people will think it is cool and buy the product. I still can't see how this applies to my mum.

that this place had the distinct feeling of a cult? Was Pete about to persuade them to sign up to a dubious religion and hand over all their worldly possessions so that he could buy himself and his fellow cult members several Rolls-Royces? Wasn't that the chosen thing for fake cult leaders to do – buy a shitload of prestige cars? I made a mental note to do some hefty due diligence before my folks went anywhere near the place.

But when we got upstairs to see the accommodation, we were presented with a beautiful, spacious flat, brightly decorated and comfortable, from the shiny kitchen to the upright chairs and large TV. Outside the window, cherry trees wafted in the spring breeze. On a further look, it was clear that the rooms had been converted with the elderly in mind, with hand rails and space for walking frames, but it had been done with discretion and taste. My parents clearly adored it and there wasn't much not to adore.

'You can cook here for yourselves – I bet you're a great cook, Lorca.' Pete winked at my dad and got an approving look from Lois for such an outward display of feminism. 'Or you can join other members of the community downstairs.'

Wow, I'd never have to come home and think about feeding my parents again. I wouldn't have to clean their house every Saturday or worry about what they were up to next. I'd get a bit of my life back. And more importantly, I'd be able to go to Cape Town and see Wilf without worrying about what was going on with my parents.

'It's got a great vibe, hasn't it?' Dad said and grasped Mum's hand. 'You know what, Lois? I think we should give it a go.'

As we drove home, they talked excitedly about the trial period. Pete had given us lots of paperwork and several web addresses to check out 'user reviews from our community'.

'If we don't like it, we're not committed,' Dad said.

That was good, I agreed. 'And Pete, you don't think there's something odd about him?'

'Well, he's just one member,' Mum said. 'He told us he'd never felt more at home anywhere. He didn't have a great family upbringing himself, he said. His parents were negligent capitalists, like many others. That's probably had a formative impact on his politics.'

'He seemed quite upbeat to me for someone who's had a miserable time.'

'You're always so suspicious, Callie. I thought he had an awful lot of positive energy, considering his background.'

I muttered something about a weird smell and she said, 'And all your negativity is not helpful. You'd be better off sorting out your own life, rather than worrying about what we are doing with ours.'

It was brutal, but there was no doubt she was right.

When I got home, I visited the Dutch company's website, where most of the reviews were – surprise – in Dutch. But with a bit of help from Google Translate, I perceived that the old people of the Netherlands felt more alive as a consequence of living alongside the young people of the low countries. This was heartening. There were also a couple of reviews from new inhabitants of Seymour House, talking in gushy tones about the facilities. Well, it looked like a solution with not too many downsides for the folks. Lois and Lorca loved being occupied, they liked young people and needed feeding and looking after.

So Fishy Pete was weird, but loads of the people they liked were weird. And there was nothing I could find on the web about these houses being a secret set-up to get people to join a pernicious cult. In fact, it was quite sensible: remnants of the post-war generation – all beneficiaries of final-salary pensions and property booms – helped to support Generation Rent.

Wilf came wandering into the living room and my heart ached for the day that was coming, when he'd no longer slope around the house, doing not much. I looked up and determined to make life as normal as possible until that day dawned – and be as supportive as I could be in making the change. 'So, did you say you were going to sell your bike?'

'Yeah, I'll have to get another one in Cape Town, so I might as well, Dad says.' *Oh, does he?* 'That guy, Patrick, offered to come round and help me do it, but I think it's just because he wants to see you.' He looked vaguely fascinated at the idea of someone fancying me. 'So, like, I didn't say yes or anything.'

'Oh,' I said and giggled with him at the absurdity.

'Yeah,' said Wilf. 'But maybe you could go out with him and see what he's like.'

'So he'll help clean your bike?'

'No, so you might have some more people to hang out with when I'm gone.'

I got up and held him and he put his face in my shoulder for a minute. Then it was obvious he was about to cry as he quickly ran out of the room.

I FaceTimed Marvin before I went to sleep. He was sitting on his couch wearing his favourite purple silk dressing gown. He looked like Hugh Hefner before he was old. I wondered anew how Marv managed to get so many women to fancy him.

'Hey,' we both said.

'So, I was thinking that I might get in touch with the youth worker that Daisy's hanging out with and find out anything I can do to help Lily get through the exams.' I gave Marv a recap on how her stress levels were now off the scale. 'And she's withdrawing from me. And, maybe, how to support Wilf.'

'Hmmm, and this is the hot guy who just happened to appear in your kitchen?'

'It's got nothing to do with that.'

'But you said you looked like shit when you saw him?'

'He just said to call him if I wanted some support.'

Marvin went quiet for a while, then said, 'And this time you're going to look fantastic?'

I sat up indignantly. 'What are you trying to say?'

Marvin paused. Quite a long pause for someone who talked that much. 'I'm your friend, right? Your oldest friend? Well, along with the AAs.'

I nodded. This sounded ominous. 'Just spit it out.'

'Well, the thing is, you probably need a bit of a makeover. I'm just trying to be kind.'

I looked at Marvin with disgust. 'You think I should be thinking what I look like *now*?'

'I'm only saying it because you've had so much going on that you've stopped taking care of yourself.' Marvin was kind but emphatic.

'Are we talking a quick eyebrow shape?' I looked at the square of the picture of me in the corner of the screen. I looked pale, tired and there was still the remnant of a bruise under my hair. 'OK, more than a quick eyebrow shape. But the cycle guy who knocked me over keeps sending me round food deliveries and texting me flirty messages,' I told Marvin in my defence. 'I can't be that bad.'

'That's good,' said Marvin, who spent quite a lot of time trying to get me to have a love interest in my life.

'But I'm concentrating on the kids and the folks.'

'All work and no play makes you boring,' Marv said. 'Now, what do you say, we go and get a little Botox and fillers?'

OMG, it'd got *that* bad. It wasn't a question of booking a colouring appointment at the hairdresser's or buying a new outfit in my lunch hour. Marv was talking middle-aged overhaul. Had things got this bad that I needed needles in my face?

'No way,' I said. 'I mean, shiny concrete forehead. No one knows whether you're happy or sad. At least now I'm sad people know about it.'

What about the celebrities you saw on the Sidebar of Shame in the *Daily Mail*? I mean, I'm not saying I visited that page very often, ahem, but there was certainly a plethora of women with not just pneumatic chests but weird, meerkat faces. I also went there to laugh at the language. Where else did someone going to the gym 'step out' with their 'beau', 'flaunting their fabulous figure in revealing Lycra' rather than 'go out of their house with their boyfriend wearing exercise kit'? When did anyone else ever 'display their pregnancy'? Fascinating stuff, but also enough to put me off needles in my face forever. Despite knowing Marv didn't share my horror, and also recognising he was thinking about me, it still hurt to suggest I needed it.

'But I was thinking about what you were saying the other night,' Marv went on persuasively. 'You kept going on about being invisible.'

'I had potential concussion,' I said, holding a cushion over my face to suggest that if he couldn't see it, then it couldn't be that bad.

'But then look at how you reacted to the zombie apocalypse game,' Marv argued. 'It's like you're angry with the world for thinking you're ineffectual, and, at the same time, you're not prepared to put your best foot forward.'

'I am not having Botox! And doesn't it hurt? And cost a fortune?'

'Well, here's the thing. I was talking to Abby about you—'

'Cheers for that.' They were all happily talking about my decay while I wasn't there.

'And it turns out she's been having Botox for years. You know the way she always does things like that. Buys all the same clothes so she doesn't have to think about it.'

'And that place she goes in London where you can get your hair blow-dried at the same time as you're having your nails done...'

'Polish and Blow!' Marvin said excitedly. 'Well, it turns out that they also tart up your eyebrows and stick Botox in your head, all in the space of an hour or so. Apparently, she started having it years ago as a preventative measure – everyone in the City does. The amazing part is that she'd got loads of loyalty points. So, we thought we'd take you one night after work. Give you a bit of a boost. Hair, nails, eyebrows and maybe a chat about freezing some fine lines. And it won't cost you more than a few quid because she's their best customer, ever. C'mon, it'll be fun.'

'Hair, nails and eyebrows. Fine. But no way am I having holes in my face. I'd dream about leaking like a colander every time I had a drink.' I tried to smile on but really I was thinking my friends had already decided that I'd lost all my spark, so there was just my dignity to go.

'Then you'll feel a bit more up to fighting Petra and Ralph, and getting on with everything,' said Marvin. 'And you'll be able to nab the hot youth worker. Or the delivery guy. I mean, he must be fit, all that cycling...'

And the conversation continued in this frivolous vein until he'd made me forget for a moment that he'd told me I needed a makeover.

Later, though, with my head on my pillow, I thought about how there'd been actual men I'd dated when the kids were young; how even after Dougie had gone, I hadn't given up on love.

There'd been the six-months romance with a man I'd met on Plenty of Fish. Tucson was American, loud and fond of big impulsive gestures. Unfortunately, this wasn't compatible with having two-year-olds in the house and a full-time job. He'd tried to forgive me when I couldn't find emergency childcare for what sounded like a sexy weekend in Paris, but texted me all day Saturday and Sunday to tell me how lonely it was mooching round Le Marais on his own and it wasn't much fun *tout seul.*

After that, I'd had to suggest that he was probably more suited to someone who didn't have commitments like mine; someone who was free as a bird to fly off on mini-breaks; who when rooting around in their handbag for an emergency condom didn't throw out packets of rice cakes and tubs of Sudocrem before she eventually found one.

There was also a very short-lived thing with a bloke Ajay introduced me to called Paul. I was about thirty or thirty-one then – and it was summer. This was relevant because we went on a couple of dates and they were outdoor, sun-based activities: a beer garden, a couple of glasses of Pimms. He wore shorts, which was appropriate as it was twenty-four degrees or so. But then, the next time we went out, a couple of weeks later, autumn had come, there was a distinct chill in the air, and we went to the cinema. However, when I met him outside, quite excited about a whole grown-up evening out, he was still wearing shorts. I don't mean arse-cheek-gripping short shorts. There was nothing camp or unmanly about his choice of legwear – they came nearly to his knees. But it was less than ten degrees, it was 8 p.m. and we were in a city. In late September. As soon as the movie finished, I told him I had to rush home for the babysitters and nearly ran all the way to my front door, calling Ajay on the way and shouting, 'You set me up with a man who wears shorts to the cinema.'

Ajay – typically – was nonplussed by this. 'Interesting. I must admit that I've only met him in summer, so the inappropriate baring of shins and ankles wasn't obvious.'

'But you've met him in the evening. After dark,' I snapped. Ajay had claimed to have met Paul at an event for techies in London.

'It was in a roof garden, so outside,' Ajay said, as if the lack of a roof made it better. 'Now you can never tell really, what with everyone wearing trainers and jeans everywhere. I mean, even hedge-fund people all dress like they work in Gap. The problem is you're very superficial.' Considering he was one of the most surface-level, lightweight people who'd ever walked the earth, this was rich, and I told him so, but with more swearwords.

Did I want to be her again? Going on dates with unsuitable men? I was more than a decade older now with none of the physical confidence or energy I used to have.

I smiled as I remembered all the time I'd spent having phone sex with someone I never actually met in person but had met on an online dating site. Or *pretending* to have phone sex. I couldn't be bothered and felt a bit embarrassed really about actually masturbating while on the phone to someone in another city, so I just let him assume I was getting it on with myself while he huffed and puffed himself to satisfaction. You'd never get away with it now, what with Skype and FaceTime.

This was the sum total of the men I'd been involved with post-Dougie and pre-Ralph, I worked out as I felt sleep creep up on me. I wasn't exactly going out every night. There were wastelands – big old T. S. Eliot ones – in the middle of all that action.

But, back then, I didn't feel like I did now – as if my sexual currency was worthless, as if I'd disappeared from a world where people fell in love.

14

A few days went by, the way they do, even when it feels time should slow down and be on your side.

With exams creeping up and the situation with Wilf, I felt like I was permanently holding my breath. My parents were busy planning a trial move to Seymour House, Lily stayed in her room working all that weekend and even Daisy pretended to put in some effort, before she said she 'just had to get out and see some peeps before I go f-ing nuts' and bolted out the front door. Wilf came and went as usual, but was quiet. Aside from going round to clean my folks' kitchen, I stayed in all weekend, as if, by being there, I could create the illusion of a perfect, stable family home.

Being back at work on Monday was no distraction. I had to deal with a complaint from a woman who'd encountered one of our HGV drivers – conveniently still wearing a high-vis jacket with the Carter's logo on it next to his lorry in the street in Holloway. It seemed – and why on earth would she make this up? – that he'd wolf-whistled her and then when she'd told him where to get off, he'd accused her of being a lesbian as if it were an insult.

I marched into Eli's office. He was sitting at his desk with his brogue-clad feet on its polished surface, watching motor racing on a huge screen on the wall.

'Ah, Callie,' he sighed when he saw me. He knew that I rarely brought him good news. He was holding a Tupperware box and picking from it in a desultory fashion. 'Now she's got me eating kale.' He was talking about his wife, who he always referred to as 'she'. I ignored him: if he'd wanted to be allowed to carry on eating what he wanted, he should've stayed with his first wife, rather than shagging and running off with a younger version. Then he might have been sexually unfulfilled but at least he wouldn't be permanently starving.

He indicated the chair on the other side of the desk and put his feet back on the floor. 'You look like you've got something to say. Is it about that lunch thing? I did try and have a word with them all and tell them you are an integral part of the senior leadership team.'

I grimaced and sat down on the leather chair. 'It's fine. Well, it's not, but it's not about that.' He looked relieved until I told him about the driver.

'Stupid bastard,' he said. 'Do we know which one he is?'

'Yes,' I said, looking down at the printout of the complaint in my hand. 'He was deluded enough to say, and I quote: "When you get round to men, darlin', the name's Tommy," before he said the remarks.'

'Going to be bad publicity?' This was always Eli's question in the face of complaints. He worried a lot more about what the Internet and papers might say than he did about the effect on the victim.

'She's reported it to Everydaysexism.com,' I said. 'But like she says, what she wants is this bloke fired before he can do it to anyone else. We need to fire him very publicly and *now*,' I said.

'OK,' sighed my boss, as if it were my fault that his workforce terrorised the female population of London. 'Get on with it.' Then he picked up the TV remote control and made the noise of the racing rise, so it sounded like a swarm of virulent flies.

I stomped out. I wasn't going to do his bloody dirty work. I got back to my desk and, while Charles, Greg and Ayesha watched me, picked up my phone while standing up. I rang the manager at the depot and very loudly told him in no uncertain terms to get the driver off the books immediately, P45 to follow, 'and the whole of your depot is now down for sexism training,' I finished. 'You'll all be signed up for an evening session, mandatory attendance.'

'Oh, Cal,' pleaded the site manager. 'That'll really piss off the lads.'

'Should have thought about that before you employed a misogynist arsehole,' I told him. Then I slammed the phone down.

Ayesha looked at me in awe and raised her eyebrows. 'Go you,' she said.

Greg just sighed as if he'd seen it all before.

Charles, though, was wide-eyed and looked at me with new appreciation. 'Oh, Callie,' he said. 'You're so *powerful*.'

And I wanted to tell him that, no, I wasn't. In my real life, everywhere except when firing stupid blokes, I felt truly powerless.

I was wandering along my street from the station, wondering about whether I should go to the mediation session with Ralph and Petra, when Patrick came running down the road from the other end, wearing shorts.

When he saw me, his face lit up in a pleasant smile. 'Callie,' he said enthusiastically and bounded across the street, skidding to a halt beside me. God, the man was sporty and energetic. Another reason not to flirt back with him: I certainly wasn't.

'Hello, Patrick.'

'Umm, sorry, you seem to have mistaken me for someone else. The name's William. Just William.'

I smiled politely. He seemed to get that I didn't want to play, because his face became more serious. 'I wanted to ask you if you minded me talking to your... to Wilf the other day? He wanted to know how to strip his bike and I said I'd ask you if it was OK to show him.'

'I don't see why not,' I said, but suspiciously. 'He's only here for a few weeks now.'

'Yes, he told me about going to Cape Town with his dad.'

Patrick/William didn't appear to be trying to be nosey or to find out more. 'Yes,' I said, moving off. 'Look, if you're sure you've got time.'

'What with having to give up on feeding the lazy people of Seymour Hill, I've got quite a bit. Sorry, shouldn't insult Seymour Hill when I don't come from here. Rule-breaker.'

I supposed he was quite droll. If I'd been in the kind of mood to engage with my neighbour's jokes, I might have laughed.

Lily was in her bedroom as usual, her face buried in a past paper. It was chemistry or physics – the ones she found really difficult. I was passing on the landing, ostensibly putting a pile of towels into the airing cupboard, but really lurking round my teenage children's doors to make sure they were OK.

I heard her cry out as I passed, a stifled gasp, and I ran into her room. She was clutching her chest and seemed to be unable to take in any air. Her face was white and then puce, contorted in an expression of abject fear.

I pulled her up from her chair and she still seemed unable to breathe. 'I... think... I'm... having... a... heart... attack,' she managed in between gasps.

Oh, no, oh, God, oh, no. Aside from holding her by her arms I felt paralysed; it was as if, however hard she breathed, she couldn't manage to find any oxygen. As I held her wrists, I could feel her pulse racing as if her veins and arteries were going to jump out of her body. She fell back onto the bed.

'Don't worry,' I said as calmly as I could. I knew instinctively that it wasn't a heart attack, but – recalling my work mental-health training – it would feel exactly like that to the victim. This was a panic attack: all that anxiety and terror turned into a full body meltdown. And watching it happen to my daughter, rather than hearing about it in a training room, was horrendous.

I shouted to Daisy: 'Come quickly, your sister's having a panic attack.' All I wanted to do was breathe for her. As she writhed on the bed her muscles were twitching uncontrollably. My own heart felt as if it would jump out of my body with fear.

Daisy's head appeared round the doorway. 'Quick, get a paper bag from the kitchen,' I cried. 'Lily, listen to me, it's going to be OK.'

What if I was wrong? What if this wasn't a panic attack but her young body was in real trauma? Should I call an ambulance? From Daisy's face, which went quickly white with distress, I figured we shouldn't waste a moment.

'Wilf,' I shouted. 'Quick, come here!' But there was no sign of him – probably wearing his headphones and impervious to the world.

'Lily, it's all going to be OK,' I said as I heard Daisy race back up the stairs. Lily's eyes were open in real fear and her thin chest heaved back and forwards in her school shirt as if she was pleading with me to make the whole thing go away. I undid her top button. 'I'm not going to hug you as that will only make it worse, now shush, shush…' I grabbed the brown paper bag that Daisy held out and put it to her lips. They looked blue instead of the natural pink colour they should've been.

'I had to empty out onions,' Daisy said. She was stiff with terror. 'Lil, it's all going to be OK.'

'Now breathe into the bag, Lily,' I instructed, still as calm as I could be. I tried to hold it to her face as it moved to create a seal around her mouth as I'd been instructed in first aid. I thanked the gods of HR.

'Ambulance?' Daisy mouthed as she watched her sister try and do as I'd instructed. The bag puffed up like a balloon and then Lily was pulling back in the air from inside it; the air she'd just breathed out. There was a scientific reason concerning oxygen and carbon dioxide that made this the right treatment; I couldn't remember what it was, and, in the moment, I didn't care.

'Yes,' I mouthed back as I held her sister's back with one hand and the paper bag with the other. Daisy raced off – always better in action mode.

I sat beside Lily as she breathed into the paper bag, time after time, first violently in a gasp for any air she could reach, and then, gradually, after torturous minutes that felt like hours, more slowly, in and out, in and out.

My hand was on her back and I could feel her heart rate start to slow too, from the feverish thumps to a still too-fast beat. Her eyes held an expression of terrible fear. All I could do was repeat 'shush' and tell her everything was going to be OK, over and over again.

Daisy came running back. 'They'll be here very soon,' she said in a soothing, but scared voice. 'Oh, she looks a bit better, doesn't she, Mum?'

'Yes, she's getting there now,' I said in as reassuring a voice as I could. 'I think you're having some sort of anxiety attack, Lily. We had training at work about it. They are surprisingly common in times of stress. Still best we let the paramedics check you out.'

Lily burst into tears. This came as a huge relief, as she pushed aside the bag; the weeping came with wailing. I remembered what it was like to hear them both cry all those years ago back in the maternity suite; the acknowledgement that they were *alive*, that they survived that traumatic journey from amniotic sac to fresh air and were both crying at the shock of it all.

I sat down and pulled her to me. 'Lily, you've got yourself into a bit of a state, that's all. There's no reason why this should ever happen again.' Recalling that first-aid session I knew, however, that there was every likelihood it *would* happen again. Victims needed training and techniques in how to cope with stress, and how to avoid it. Mindfulness lessons. Yoga.

She leant into my shoulder and gasped. 'It's physics. I just got a D in a practice paper.'

'Was it last year's paper?' Daisy said in a bright voice. 'Everyone said it's a complete bastard.'

I couldn't be bothered to argue with her about the swearing at that moment, I just felt the benefit of her strength and hoped that by process of osmosis her sister would absorb even a little bit of it. She sat down on the other side of her sister and went on. 'Yeah and loads of famous people have panic attacks and they all get better. I mean, think about Robbie Williams. Or Zayn Malik. I mean, he's seriously, like, a worldwide superstar.'

Lily's sobs started to reduce to an occasional blubber. 'He didn't have to sit a physics exam though.'

'All you have to do is get into the exam room and do your best,' I said as they both looked at me with exasperation. 'And if your best isn't a nine that really doesn't matter. You can sit the exam again or go and do something else.'

'Not if you want to be a doctor,' Lily said. I took an inward breath. It had been Lily's dream to be a hospital doctor since she and Daisy had played as children. Later, obsessed with other people's babies, she'd always said she wanted to be an obstetrician. She watched and rewatched episodes of *Call the Midwife*. It was one of those things we did together. If she was going to succeed she would need to develop a real resistance to this awful anxiety that had crept up on her in adolescence.

Resilience; that word again. I *would* call Sunil, I thought, and see what he recommended. Take her to the GP. And make her stop revising and take some time out. And be there for her. At every moment.

'Sunil says that the more people who talk about mental health, we'll all start to see it as just the same as our physical health,' Daisy said.

'No different from having a broken leg,' I joined in. 'Except for this is nothing serious at all, like having a little sprain.'

Just then we heard the ambulance tear into our street, its flashing light visible through the window, a small screech of tyres as it came to a halt. God bless the NHS; we were getting our taxpayers' money's worth lately.

'I'm going to go down and talk to them,' I said. 'I'm sure they'll want to have a look at you.'

Wilf came out onto the landing as I did, headphones now round his neck. 'What's going on, Cal?' he said, his eyes lit with fear as if he could easily imagine further rocking of his world.

'Lily just had a bit of an anxiety attack,' I said. 'There's no emergency. It's all OK now, they just need to check her out.'

He came downstairs with me and two paramedics stood at the door. I explained quickly what was going on and they pushed past us both and went up the stairs to make sure Lily was OK.

Wilf clasped my hand. 'It's the exams,' I told him. 'She's got herself into a bit of a state.'

All I want is someone to give me reassurance. But it's what everyone needs from me.

Just then, the blue door at number 36 sprang open. And there was Patrick, still in his running shorts, in the yellow arc of the streetlight.

'Callie,' he shouted. 'I saw the ambulance. Is everything OK?'

'It's one of the girls,' I said as he came racing down the pavement. 'She's fine, I think, just very stressed about the exams.'

'Thank God,' he said.

'Hey, Patrick,' said Wilf.

'Hey, Wilf.' They looked genuinely pleased to see each other.

'I'm going to see what the paramedics are saying.' I left them to it.

In Lily's crowded room, one paramedic was taking her blood pressure, while another stood by with an oxygen tank.

'Mum gave her a paper bag,' Daisy was explaining, squashed now up against Lily's dressing table.

'Exactly right,' said the second paramedic with the oxygen tank. 'Now, how old are you, Lily?'

'Sixteen,' Daisy said on her behalf and gave their mutual date of birth.

'Twins always answer for each other.' The paramedic smiled. 'But right now, young lady, we need to be talking to your sister and your mother.' She indicated that she should move outside onto the landing, and she had a point – the room was no bigger than twelve by eight and Lily needed all the air she could get. 'You OK with me talking in front of your mum, Lily?'

She nodded, even while she looked at her arm compressed in the rubber tourniquet. Daisy went reluctantly outside; I heard her go down the stairs.

'Now, Lily,' went on the paramedic. 'Looks like you've had what people call a panic attack. Absolutely nothing to worry about, at all. Your blood pressure is a bit high but that's normal after what's gone on. You'll need to pop with your mum to the GP in the morning, but you'll be all right now. Your mum did exactly the right thing.'

I felt a small flush of pride, but mostly enormous relief.

'Now you need to get some sleep as your body needs to recover,' the paramedic went on.

'But I've got to revise, I've got GCSEs starting,' Lily said, looking as if she was going to start crying again.

'No more tonight,' the paramedic said with authority. 'And you need to make sure you're taking regular rest breaks in the run-up to the exams and through them. Spend a bit of time with your mates.'

Lily looked very doubtful, but I nodded approvingly. The other paramedic unwrapped the tourniquet and got up from the bed. 'Now lie down. And you'll feel a lot better in the morning.'

They indicated to me that we should leave. I was dubious: what if something happened to her again when I wasn't in the room? But the second paramedic made another gesture with her head and I followed her downstairs to the hallway with her colleague behind me with the equipment.

'We see it all the time at the moment,' she said in a whisper when we got there. 'Girls especially. Putting themselves under so much pressure to pass their exams. You've got to make sure she stays as calm as possible, realises it's not the end of the world.'

'I've told her all that, time and time again,' I whispered.

She nodded sympathetically. 'I'm sure you have. Now, just try and make everything as unstressy as possible. Normal life, even though there's exams.'

I could see Wilf and Patrick out on the pavement, where a couple of my other neighbours had come out to find out what was going on. They seemed to be telling them that it was all OK and for a moment I was grateful for Patrick's presence.

The ambulance left and Patrick waved and went back inside his own house.

'He's kind of cool, Cal,' Wilf said as he came through the door. He quickly forgot this though as we went up the stairs to Lily. As he saw her, pale and depleted on the pillows, he sat down beside her and said, 'Hey, Two, sorry I didn't hear you and call the ambulance. I shouldn't have had my headphones on.'

She patted his hand as I quickly told him it wasn't his fault at all.

'Yeah,' said Wilf. 'It's just that, what with going and everything, I'd really like to know you guys are going to be OK.' And he said it as if he was the man of the house, which I supposed, for a while, he had been.

Eventually, Lily slept, and it was only then that I left her, door firmly ajar, and went and lay on my own bed. My limbs wouldn't stay still, and I kept jumping up to go and look at her, colour finally coming back into her face as she slept away the horrible pressures of growing up.

I needed help. This was more than I could cope with alone. I'd take Lily to the GP in the morning, get some time off work to focus on the kids.

But I needed someone now. Not Marvin and the AAs, who meant well but thought the answer lay in the bottom of a bottle of Sauv Blanc or in fixing my decaying face. I got up and padded down to the kitchen and picked up Sunil's card. 'Youth worker' it said, with the logo of Resilient.

I typed the number into my phone and waited to leave a message. I was ringing him out of hours after all, but I hoped we could make a time to meet up.

But he answered, and his voice was lovely and reassuring. 'Hello, this is Sunil, how can I help you?'

'This is Callie, Daisy's Mum,' I said nervously. 'I'm sorry to call you so late and…'

'Oh, hello, I was hoping you'd call,' he said warmly. 'I sensed there was quite a lot going on.' I felt like a drowning person who was being thrown a very thin lifeline. He'd been hoping I'd call. He wanted to help me.

In a rush, I gave him a rundown of what had happened to Lily. He occasionally gave a soothing and concerned, 'I see,' but let me talk until breathless, until I finished with: 'and it's all on top of what's been going on with Wilf and…

you talked about resilience. I think we could all do with some of that right now.'

'Look, it's my job, but, much more than that, I'd really like to help you. Daisy is a top kid and I'm sure the others – all of you – are going to get through this. I want to do what I can.'

My overwhelming feeling as I promised to meet him at the youth centre at 11 a.m. for a coffee, on Friday, when the children would be at school for study revision, was that I no longer felt quite so alone. I'd tell Eli I needed some time off. Get Greg to step up to the plate. Misogynistic arsehole drivers seemed very irrelevant right now.

It'd never really occurred to me to feel lonely and I was very rarely by myself. There were the kids, my folks, Marv and the AAs, colleagues, other friends. But as I clicked 'off' on the phone, I realised quite how alone I'd really been feeling. And for quite a while now, even before this all happened.

It was a chilly place, full of responsibility and a need to hold it all together.

15

I woke up from a frenzied sleep and texted Eli that I had some personal problems to deal with, simply getting a curt response:

OK, you'd better get those bozos you work with going then

No 'hope it all works out', no bunch of sympathy flowers; he was just concerned with making sure the job got done. So, I emailed Greg, Ayesha and Charles with a series of instructions about making sure no one cheated on the pay-roll run and so on. Ayesha sent the predictable email about handing in her notice and a possible racial and sexual discrimination claim but, while I felt sorry for her, I had to put her off and tell her I'd deal with it on my return.

Then I battled the phone system for the local GP. This meant calling exactly as the clock on my iPhone turned to 8 a.m. to immediately get held in a queue telling me that thirty people were ahead of me, and wailing, 'How is that even possible?' before listening to piped music and information about smoking cessation clinics for half an hour. When I finally got through to a receptionist, she said all today's appointments were gone. I told her it was an emergency and unless she let my teenage daughter see a doctor that morning, I would personally stage a one-woman sit-in of the surgery. Then I waved Daisy off to study group and tucked in Wilf's school shirt before he went off on his bike, his blue and white scarf wrapped round his neck. I wondered what state of dishevelment he normally went to school in, in my absence, and felt a massive spike in mother guilt. Maybe Ralph was right – Wilf would get much more attention in Cape Town with full-time support from his father.

Putting that aside, I gently coaxed Lily from her bed – 'Will you stop asking me if I'm all right?' – her face wan and pale, and drove her to the GP. We saw a locum in the end, who looked as if he couldn't have passed his A levels let alone got to medical school; he asked her a series of gentle questions.

'Do you want to talk to me without Mum?' he said after she mumbled a few answers about being fine, just a bit worried about the exams.

'No, it's all right, Mum's cool,' Lily said and smiled sadly at me. 'I just feel like she's got enough to deal with at the moment without me being a nightmare.'

Oh, the guilt again. 'I'm absolutely fine,' I reassured her, taking her hand in front of the doctor.

'It sounds like your mum did exactly the right thing last night,' the very young GP said, and proceeded to give Lily instructions about carrying a paper bag with her at all times and scheduling rest periods. 'You will perform better in the exams if you do,' he said. Then as he typed into the computer, kindly: 'What do you want to do in the end?'

'I want to be a doctor,' Lily told him.

He appraised her as if she were completely nuts, obviously remembering recent ninety-seven-hour-a-week shifts, but only said, 'Well, then, you know you need to look after your mental health.'

He went on to say he wasn't going to give her drugs, because the side effects could be worse than managing any further attacks during the exam period, but told her to come back at any time she needed.

As we left, and I dropped her outside school, I kept asking her whether she wouldn't rather study at home that day. 'Or go to bed and have another rest?'

Lily shook her head and said she needed to ask the teacher about some of the formulae she couldn't remember, and went off into the glass and concrete of the old school building, looking fragile in the spring breeze.

It was as I turned the ignition on to drive away that I spied a Mini with a very naff number plate come into the school car park, a blonde steering the car. My blood became instant boiling lava in my arteries. Petra! What the hell was she doing at the school?

I turned the car off. This was my turf. My kids. The school where I turned up time after time to go through the shenanigans of parents' evening. The school she'd never set foot in until very recently.

Before I had time to think about what I was doing, I'd jumped out of the car and, as she got out of hers, neatening a red scarf round her teensy, tiny neck, I found myself blocking her path. We were between a shiny blue Astra and her own car; there was nowhere for her to go unless I got out of the way.

'Oh, gosh, Calypso.' She jumped in surprise as I towered over her.

'And you are here, at *my* children's school, why?' I hissed.

She sighed and put her hands on her little hips, clad in another colour-block trouser suit. 'Well, that is none of your business, really, Calypso, is it?' She managed to sound calm and collected in the same moment as I sounded desperate and dogged. 'And while the girls might be yours, you've already understood the law as it relates to Wilf.' Her eyebrows were pitched in a perfect arch and she was talking with none of the tact she'd engineered into her tone when Ralph was by her side. Before I could speak she continued, spitting out the words now: 'And that's something you need to get your head round, *sweetheart.*'

Could a word be more laden with sarcasm? My hands clenched by my sides. 'But at the moment Wilf lives with me and has been my responsibility for the last eight years. Why can't you respect that?'

She took a step back and appraised me with the same false solicitude. 'Oh, Calypso.' Her sleek blonde head cocked to one side. 'The thing is, we've been very patient, my *husband* and I, especially when I've been so dying to have Wilf under our roof and to develop my relationship with him as his *stepmother.*'

Despite knowing that she was deliberately trying to hurt me, I was still winded by the words. 'And for the sake of a few weeks, we thought it worth letting Wilf stay with you, but we might have to rethink that plan in the face of your obvious hostility towards his legal parents and guardians.'

I didn't understand what she was saying for a brief moment. Then it hit me, like a punch in the abdomen. 'Oh, you wouldn't...' was all I could manage.

'Ignoring our request for mediation? Showing a lack of care for Wilf's future happiness? Refusing to put his welfare ahead of your own? I think we have every right to suggest that Wilf immediately relocates to our home.'

She wanted to take Wilf now. Not in a few weeks' time. To have him live across town with them and get on his bike every day and go to school and return there instead. My sense of loss was as if it had already happened. Would I see him in the high street, pedalling past? Be lucky enough if he decided to come round to our house once a week for a brief, awkward visit? Oh, that hurt.

'Ralph would never be so mean,' I managed, but given what he'd already said 'yes' to, was I that certain that he would stand up to her?

'And I think, once we pointed out that there have been two ambulances attending your family in the last week...' How the hell did she know about Lily? I groaned and thought that Wilf must have texted his father about his sister last night. '... and the obvious strain that exams and this situation is putting on you all, it might be better if Wilf packed up his belongings and I helped him move immediately, don't you?'

'Don't be so ridiculous,' I seethed at her. 'He would never agree.' And he wouldn't. I knew that. He'd say, 'Cheers, Dad, but I think I'll just stay with Cal for the rest of the time.' *He doesn't even like you – he thinks you've sucked out his dad's soul.* That was what I wanted to say but, of course, I didn't.

'I think, as we've found out, the law is pretty clear about parental will in the case of minors of Wilf's age.' Petra's voice dripped with false pity. 'And you are clearly in no fit state to parent effectively.'

'How dare you? I've looked after Wilf since he was little! I've been there when his father wasn't! When Ralph – I mean, I know he was very depressed and in grief but sometimes he was little better than a drunken—'

'He is 394 days sober,' Petra interrupted. 'He attends AA meetings regularly and conducts himself in a way akin with a healthy lifestyle. I don't think anyone could call my husband a drunk any more, do you, Calypso? Unlike when he was living with you.'

'What don't you get? I couldn't care less about Ralph, aside from that he is now a better dad and I'm glad he's recovered. The person I care about is Wilf; that's it. And my girls.' I felt a desperate urge to grab her and pull her hair, as if we were kids back in the playground, but instead put my clenched fists in anguish to my face.

Petra looked impatient. 'I suggest, if you care about him so much, then you move out of my way, Calypso, and allow me to continue into the school so I can arrange his departure and onward education.' She flicked the key fob and her Mini locked itself. 'I am here to undertake the necessary formalities. Now, please, step aside.'

I was beaten. I found myself turning from her and walking back towards my car as she walked jauntily into the school to decide Wilf's future.

Later, after spending the rest of the day wondering how to exact revenge on Petra and looking up voodoo dolls on Amazon, I came down from checking on the girls in their rooms and wandered into the kitchen to see Patrick in my scrubby back garden. He and Wilf were standing and talking about Wilf's bike, which was upended in front of them. I gave the universal sign for a cup of tea and he grinned broadly and mouthed 'yes'.

I took it out to him. Bodger took a step back and looked approvingly at me as I handed Patrick the mug.

'It could do with a new chain,' he said, nodding at the bike. 'But aside from that, just a bit of oil, air in the tyres and a rub-down.'

A bit like Marv's plan to refurb me. 'Pat says he'll help me.' Wilf got up from the ground where he'd been crouching.

'You know you're supposed to call me William,' Patrick hissed and they both laughed. Bodger seemed to join in, giving one of his occasional grins. 'Let's get cracking, then.' He started pulling cans of oil and puncture repair kits from a bag at his feet and Wilf's face lit in delight.

Later, when dinner was ready, they were still out there in the fading light. I hovered, thinking I'd have to ask him to eat with us, he was being so kind to Wilf. Plus, most of the food on our table recently had had something to do with him. I was hoping that Daisy was at least a pescatarian today because we were having fish pie, Lily's favourite.

Pat accepted with alacrity and washed his oily hands at the sink with Wilf. He was enjoying himself; they both were. I wondered how much he minded having time off from teaching – and whether he had any kids of his own.

Daisy raised her eyebrows when she saw him at the table. Lily said nothing but promised me she'd had lots of rest breaks during the day.

'Patrick would know about that,' I said. 'He's a teacher.'

'Please,' he said, his fork heavy with mashed potato, 'call me William.'

The twins looked confused; Wilf looked really pleased to be in on the joke and then explained it to them. Daisy raised her eyebrows at me again and I ignored her, so she started talking about *Riverdale* and Patrick leapt in: 'That's such a cool series.'

And they were off – all why this character did this to that character in episode three series two, until Lily said, 'Have you got kids of your own, William?'

Patrick looked a little bit more sober, but then said in his frank way, 'No, wasn't lucky enough. My girlfriend and I tried for years but it wasn't to be.'

The kids nodded. 'Did you try adoption and stuff?' Wilf asked.

'Wilf,' I said, 'Patrick – sorry, William – might not want to talk about that to people he's just met.'

But Patrick held up his hand. 'Amazing fish pie, by the way. I'm happy to talk about it. Yes, Wilf, we decided in the end to try adoption, but it's a really intense process and that made my girlfriend and I realise that, while we wanted a baby very much, we probably wanted that more than each other. So, we split up and I was miserable for a while and then I got a new job here, in newly trendy Seymour Hill.'

He was factual and honest, and the kids nodded, appreciating it. I ate some broccoli and thought: *We all have our stories by the time we get to our age and this is his.*

Daisy wanted the focus back on her, so she said, 'And do you know what you're letting yourself in for at Whitebury?' They all then competed to tell him stories of how heinous the kids who went to the school were. Patrick joined in, matching them with outrageous, probably made-up tales from schools he'd taught in and it was clear they all quite liked our new neighbour. I quite liked him too and he was certainly helpful. It was just that if you were going to have a man sitting round your dining table, it would be great if he was noble, beautiful Sunil.

Patrick hung around after they disappeared, offering to help me load the dishwasher and asking about the kids – how Lily was doing after last night and when her exams were starting. Then he asked me about their dads, and I filled him in on Dougie and Ralph in a light-hearted way, and then, much more seriously, on the current situation with Wilf. 'So, you see, when you thought I was a nutjob the other day, there's been quite a lot going on,' I finished. He'd been frank with all of us, and it felt right to be candid in return.

'Sounds like you've got enough on to be completely certifiable.'

Bodger yawned as if all this talking was highly boring to dogs. There was a natural pause in the conversation and I waited for him to say he was going. Instead he said, 'What with having banned me from delivering food to you, would you come out for dinner with me one night instead?'

I wasn't used to men asking me out; the last time had probably been when fossils were forming, so it did feel very strange. In addition, he was standing in my kitchen. He cocked his head to the side, looking a bit like Bodger when he was desperate for the bone from a roast. It was cute, but I didn't need cute.

'Oh, thanks lots but, you know… ummm… no, I can't.' It came out more harshly and louder than I'd anticipated, and he stopped looking cute and looked startled instead. I added, 'That came out wrong,' but he just stood and raised his eyebrows. 'Anyway, I know you only said it to be nice to me.'

'I didn't, actually,' he said, looking straight at me until I blushed. 'But happy to postpone the invite. Keep it on ice. Maybe you'll wake up one day and just be really starving and say, "Oh, there was that nice bloke down the road who asked me to go out to dinner with him. Now, what with being really hungry, I might go out with him after all."'

'No,' I said, horribly embarrassed now and wanting him out of my kitchen.

He seemed quite laid-back about the whole thing though. 'Is it because I was a humble delivery driver?' He hung his head in mock shame.

'There are several reasons, actually, but that's not one of them.' Again, my voice seemed unnecessarily officious.

'Perhaps madam would be so kind, then, as to give the evidence for the prosecution.' He smiled on, folding his arms and standing with his back to the kitchen cabinet, blue eyes twinkling.

I refused to be charmed. 'Reason one is that I have far too much going on at the moment with the kids. As I've just told you.'

'May I put the evidence for the defence?'

'I suppose so,' I said.

'The defence humbly suggests that sometimes it is good to have a distraction from one's day-to-day difficulties. Sometimes it's good to have some time out from them, or, alternatively, have someone to discuss them with.'

'Humph,' I said and put my hands on my hips. 'Reason number two, however, is that we are neighbours and likely to remain so.' I'd taken on his tone of a sham courtroom. 'Anyway, I can't bump into you in the street all the time if it works out that the date is a disaster.'

'May the defence humbly suggest that, as grown adults, we may be able to deal with such an occurrence in a mature manner that would not affect the freedom of our residential status?' He raised his eyebrows and it was very difficult not to laugh, despite myself. However, he might be a mature adult about stuff like that – I wasn't sure *I* was.

'Reason number three, however,' I almost barked, 'is that I'm not in a fit state to go out on a date with *anyone*. I mean, it's ages since I went out with someone. I'm concentrating on my kids and my parents and, I mean…'

I was becoming agitated.

'Hey, no worries,' he said however, very simply. 'I get it. No room for a man in your life. I understand, and I won't hassle you any more.' His face took on an empathetic look. 'But maybe we can be friends, huh? I've still got quite a lot of bike fixing to do.' His eyes started twinkling again.

Phew, the difficult conversation was over. 'Friends is fine – and thanks for helping Wilf.'

'He's a great kid; they all are.' As he went out of the back door, telling me again how awesome my fish pie was, it was difficult not to remember the look of sadness in his eyes as he'd explained how he hadn't got any of his own.

I went upstairs then, and made Lily put her books down. 'Fancy a couple of episodes of *Casualty* or *Call the Midwife*?' We sat on the sofa together, cuddled up and she eventually fell asleep.

16

Sunil was like tomato soup after a long cold walk. Like honey and whiskey when you had the flu. Like cold water in the driest desert. He was all these things, but the sexy version.

The parquet-floored entrance hall of the charity centre had a musty smell; corkboards filled with flyers advertised rallies. A corridor led to what was probably once a church hall. Chairs were stacked around the wall and old red curtains hung from the windows, frayed and flapping in the breeze.

I wandered in, only briefly remembering that I still looked like shit and was about to meet a highly attractive man. It didn't seem the most relevant detail after everything that had been happening; what I needed was his help.

Sunil was in a small room at the back of the hall. He must have heard my footsteps because as I raised my hand to knock on the door, he opened it and a smile of warm greeting appeared on his (seriously quite gorgeous) face.

'Callie. I'm so glad you could come.' He ushered me through the door and into a book-lined office, where there were a couple of chairs facing each other. His desk was stacked with piles of paper round a large Apple Mac screen. Old mugs of coffee were spread across the surface. The impression was that he had lots to tackle out there in the big bad world, and no time to concentrate on the minutiae of daily life – like cleaning. 'Sit down. Sorry about the chaos – there's been a lot going on.'

'Thank you so much for making the time to meet me,' I said, sitting down and feeling flustered, despite everything, to be in such close proximity to such a very beautiful man.

'Hey, like I said, if there is any advice I can give you, or help or... It's what we're all about here. Young people's causes. Fighting their fight alongside them.'

Here was someone who was on my side. I relaxed a little.

'Would you like a cup of coffee?' Sunil continued, looking around him as if this was going to be a bit of a big ask.

'I'm fine, thank you,' I said. 'I took Lily to see the GP and she's been at school but with the exams starting on Monday, I'm feeling really worried.'

Sunil sat down on his own chair and peered at me from under his thatch of thick hair. He was wearing a dark blue T-shirt, above jeans. 'I see an awful lot of kids at the moment who are facing into unjustifiable pressure. And Lily – I don't know her yet, remember – might be one of those children who are unable to accept less than perfection. It's the system they've been brought up in; and the government, bringing in much harder GCSEs, and changing the syllabus all the time, hasn't helped.'

I nodded eagerly. He knew *exactly* what my children had been going through.

'But at the same time, they've starved our schools of resources to help our children stay strong in the face of all this pressure. The kind of episode that happened to Lily is something we see more and more of.'

I was no longer alone.

'She'll be worried that if she doesn't spend every hour of every day working on her exams, then if she gets less than a perfect score, she'll be to blame.'

'The GP told her to prioritise rest breaks.'

'Yes, it's about learning when to switch off as well as when to switch on. We have some sessions scheduled for next week on just that, if you could get her to come along?'

'Oh, I'll try really hard. Maybe if Daisy comes too?' I thought my chances of getting Lily to the centre to build her mental strength were probably a lot higher after the shock of the attack.

'Daisy's one hell of a kid,' Sunil said. 'Born activist.' I smiled with the pleasure that all parents got when their kids were praised. 'And now tell me about your – stepson? Is he your stepson?'

I described how Wilf wasn't and how that affected what was going on.

Sunil started scrolling through his phone. 'We've got some good pro bono lawyers we can call on, just to get a second opinion? I'll give one a call later and see if there are any other angles they can think of.'

I nodded gratefully, pulling a tissue from the bottom of my bag. 'I have got a friendly lawyer if I need one, but he said don't hold out too much hope,' I said.

'Sounds like you've been really, really strong, Callie.' Sunil put out a big arm and just for a moment touched mine, letting his hand rest on my wrist in a gesture of comfort. I felt the warmth of his skin on mine and... then I pulled myself together. I was sitting here because I had teenagers in trouble and his job was to help them.

He wasn't wearing a wedding ring though; I noticed that.

'Have you got kids of your own?' I asked.

'Ha! No, unfortunately. Married to the job, I'm afraid.'

Single, then? It was hard to stop the thought even as I put it to one side and focused on why I was there. As he leant away, though, there was a smell of him, manly and big and caring... with a hint of soap. There must be a queue of younger women trying to be the one who landed Sunil.

'You've been so wonderful, listening to me.' I got up and pulled my bag onto my shoulder.

'Hey, I really want to help if I can,' Sunil said with the same warm smile. 'I can tell you have a very special family, Callie. Look, I'll make these calls and then maybe I could call in on my way home? Nine-ish? Maybe we could have a beer or something?'

OH. Of course, he was just being friendly. He didn't mean any more than to come round and have a chat to a mother of one of the kids he was involved with. This was just the way woke blokes in their mid-thirties acted. My next thought was that I didn't have any beer. And should it be Becks or one of those fruity ones with names that suggested sunshine?

I tried to look as if this were a very run-of-the-mill event indeed, thank you. I moved quickly to the door. 'Great, see you later,' I squeaked.

I scuttled off across the hall. I was having a beer with a man because he was helping me. The kids were what I needed to be focused on, just as I'd told Patrick. I was a stupid, deluded woman, who was so unused to male company that I didn't know how to act any more around men.

But I'd be lying if I said there wasn't a small smile on my face.

17

That evening, I felt a sudden need to do some body maintenance as well as wanting to stalk my kids round the house, checking they were OK every minute. Cooking wasn't high on my priorities.

Particularly not high on that list was cooking for my folks as well as my kids, but Lois and Lorca appeared at 6.30 p.m., simply shuffling into their places at the table. Wilf came in just after that – he'd been with them on another recce trip to Yoof and a Roof, ready for their trial, and walked his bike back alongside the old people.

'It's cool, you know, Cal,' he said enthusiastically. 'Pete's got some decks so we all played a few tunes.'

'Choooooooo-ooooons,' chorused my parents, and fell about laughing. 'Not tunes, Cal, but chooooons.'

'That's what Pete called them,' Wilf said. 'I'm going back to have another go with him tomorrow when Lois and Lorca move in.' Ah, yes, the joy of moving my folks into a home – that was what the weekend comprised.

I carried on rootling around at the back of the freezer, wondering what the hell everyone could eat that would take the least amount of time. My frozen hand eventually alighted on two plastic tubs of pre-cooked bolognese sauce – well, that was what it said on the sticker in my own handwriting. I couldn't remember when I'd had this fabulously fortuitous Nigella-like moment, but I figured they'd still be good to eat. I put them in a massive pan to gently defrost and then heat.

'I'm going to check on Lily and have a shower before dinner.' Mum, Dad and Wilf all looked aghast at me, as if the idea of having to wait for half an hour for food was a complete disaster. Bodger joined in, like a mimic dog.

I ignored them, and they went back to talking about mixing desks and how inspiring Pete was. I decided not to ask if no one else had detected a tang of dead seafood emanating from this veritable guru.

Lily was sitting at her desk but looked at me when I put my head round the door and said, 'I've just had a power nap for twenty minutes. I'm going to do another thirty then have another break.'

'Dinner will be ready then,' I said, relieved, and went into the bathroom. There I attacked my armpits, the worst of my bikini line and my legs with a Bic razor. I'd never been a particularly hairy person but, after so many months of neglect, this felt like deforesting the Amazon jungle. It had probably been the previous summer, when I was last wearing shorts and a vest, that I'd bothered with any of it.

I washed my hair and combed conditioner through it. Then I exfoliated my face, emerging feeling like a raw, smaller, smoother version of myself. Definitely not with the makeover Marv had prescribed, but better. I put jeans on, a stripy top and Converse, not daring to put make-up on as the kids would accuse me of 'grafting' on Sunil.

Dinner that night was good – no one seemed to notice that the bolognese was from an uncertain date in the past; Lily joined in with the conversation; Wilf seemed to have put his departure to one side and, if Petra had said something about him moving to her house before they emigrated, he didn't mention it. Daisy and Mum had a lively debate about the Labour party – I say debate as they both agreed with one another but couldn't stop arguing for long enough to realise it. I ate a few spoonfuls of spaghetti, my stomach small and unwelcoming in the face of all the worry of the last few days and the fact that there was an attractive, soulful, younger man coming round for a beer in a couple of hours.

After we cleared up, Wilf said he was going to walk round to my folks' house with them. My dad had been going on about having an old record player somewhere and Wilf wanted to see if he could get it going. As he went out of the door ahead of her, I could see Mum's face looking haunted by the idea of losing him. Just for a moment she looked up and her eyes met mine – I tried to signal that I knew exactly how she felt.

Daisy said she was going to her friend's house in the next street to revise. Then Lily surprised me by saying, 'Aiden texted me – he said it might be cool to have the night off and watch a movie. What do you think?'

'It's a great idea,' I said. 'The doctor said you need to be chilling out as much as possible.' Aiden lived a few streets away and I knew his parents would also keep an eye out for Lily. 'Make sure you're back not too late.'

As the girls left together in the light spring night, it occurred to me that there were no kids to comment on whether I put on mascara and lipstick before Sunil came round – or changed my very casual top into one that was a little more feminine and attractive...

I spent the next hour yanking hair from my eyebrows and experimenting with contouring, which the girls had assured me was just clever use of highlighter and bronzer. Despite copying tips from a YouTube video, narrated by a nasal-voiced woman, I just ended up looking stripy. I washed it all off again, carefully checking my neck for stray brown blobs.

I also put on a floral shirt, which, tucked into my jeans and with boots rather than Converse, I convinced myself should be the sort of look a woman of my age would wear, while pottering picturesquely round her own kitchen. I stood on my bed and peered into the mirror to check whether I looked like, as Marv would say, 'mutton dressed as mutton' (bad – meaning a middle-aged woman who dressed her age) or 'mutton dressed as beef' (also bad – a middle-aged woman who was dressed aggressively, say in punky or gothic clothes) or 'mutton dressed as sheep' (also bad – too many jumpers on) or the more usual 'mutton dressed as lamb' (also bad but, in Marv's book, the most forgivable because at least you were fighting the natural condition of ageing).

The house was eerily quiet. I texted all three kids to make sure they were OK. Both Daisy and Lily sent back slightly bored affirmatives with Lily adding:

stop worrying!

Wilf frequently didn't answer his phone anyway.

Sunil would either cancel or be late, I told myself as I wandered around the ground floor, picking up shoes and jumpers and books – the daily mess of family life. But at 8.55 p.m., five minutes ahead of when he'd said he'd be there, there was a rap at the back door.

It was very helpful that I was a trained professional. I mean, if I hadn't had quite a lot of experience in how to maintain composure in all circumstances, the moment I saw Sunil, it would have been really easy to be jolted by the spark of pure desire and leap straight into his arms, turning the spark into a fire of never-ending lust…

But, of course, he was here to talk about building resilience in children, not to rip off my clothes, push me up against the kitchen counter and kiss me into nothingness. Despite everything that was going on, the glorious, beautiful sight of him, his hair dark and shiny above his face, which smiled at me so warmly, was enough to turn me – a grown woman who hadn't thought about sex for months or years probably – into jelly: the melty kind that had already been out of the fridge too long.

Anyway, I welcomed him in, took his jacket, asked him in an embarrassed voice what kind of beer he wanted, gave him a bottle of Becks, found the bottle opener, opened one for me too and invited him to sit down.

Sunil surprised me, though, then. Instead of sitting down at the kitchen table, he seemed to take my invitation to 'sit down', with a waft of my arm, as a gesture that meant: 'go through to the sitting room and sit on the sofa'. He started in the direction of the door and, before I knew it, was seated in one corner. I followed tentatively.

It seemed so *intimate*.

'So lovely to be in a real family home,' he said, sinking back into the cushions and slurping his beer appreciatively. I sat balanced on the edge of the sofa at the other end. 'Ah, that's great, I needed a beer.'

'It's so kind of you to come,' I said, but it came out in a kind of stifled whisper. I added, 'Very kind,' but that came out in a loud squawk. He didn't seem to mind, just carried on smiling at me.

But then he looked serious. 'I'm sorry, but I don't have good news from the lawyer I spoke to…' he started, his voice thick with concern. I nodded resignedly. I hadn't expected anything else. 'He said you were welcome to contact him direct, but he said the way he understood the legal position was the same as you'd already been advised.'

'I don't have a leg to stand on,' I said.

He nodded, grimacing. 'He said it was an unusual situation and the best hope you had was to appeal to the father. Or try to get the kid a voice.'

'I can't ask him to stand up to his father like that,' I said.

'Not everyone would put the child first – it's very brave,' Sunil said and reached out a hand towards me. It was as if he wanted to place it on my arm in a comforting way, but the gap on the sofa between us was quite large. I moved a little bit closer with a small laugh.

'The most he's said is why does he have to go? Which I think is reasonable,' I said.

'I think you're being incredible.' Sunil looked at me with admiration. I felt myself blossom under his gaze. He'd called me *incredible*. It felt like quite a long time since I'd been called anything like that.

I giggled but quickly returned to despair. 'Oh, I don't know what to do.'

'It sounds like trying to reopen a dialogue with Wilf's dad is the best answer,' Sunil said. 'Sorry there isn't anything more I can suggest.'

'I'll go to the mediation session,' I said resignedly.

Sunil reached out his arm again and this time it met my upper arm. I instinctively tensed it so that, if he could feel the shape of it through my shirt, it would be more Michelle Obama than Bat Wing Betty. I hoped he couldn't feel my blood speeding round my veins like haemoglobin in a racing car.

As his warm hand left my arm, he looked down at his beer – it was almost empty. I leapt to my feet and said, 'Let me get you another one,' rushing into the kitchen before he could say, 'No, I've got to go.'

He didn't seem as if he was going anywhere though. He grinned agreement – oh, the beauty of his lovely mouth – and seemed to settle another few inches into the cushions.

'So,' he said, when I'd come back with another Becks. 'How's Lily?'

I registered that with all the kids he had to keep an eye out for, he'd remembered the names of mine, and then told him about how she'd been better after school and had gone to her boyfriend's house for the evening.

He nodded approvingly. 'That's just what she needs now – normality and chill-out time. But do get her to come along to the resilience workshop.'

'I'll try. Maybe the attack was a bit of a wake-up call.' I shuddered at the thought of any more of them.

'She's lucky to have a mum like you,' Sunil said. I turned warmly to him and started to ask him questions about his work. He became animated and passionate about improving the lives and chances of young people. There was always more to do to get the funding required, pressure the government to put adolescents and young people at the heart of its agenda.

I nodded. God, he was so *principled*. He made me – a person who contributed precisely nothing of a positive political nature to the world – seem very inadequate.

Oh, the intensity though, when he talked. It was so enthralling to be in the presence of such *goodness* and such *energy*. And it was emanating from someone of considerable physical gorgeousness. I felt myself lulled by his voice and let my eyes roam a little over the width of his torso in its blue shirt, still crisp despite it being the end of the day. As he talked there was a nine o'clock shadow on his chin, but it just made him look more rugged. How fabulous would this man look in the morning, stretching on the pillow beside me in the dawn sunshine?

I gave myself a metaphorical slap. There was absolutely no way that this piece of delicious XY chromosome-ness was ever going to end up in my bed. He'd have a string of gorgeous, young, socially noble women waiting to contribute politically as well as sexually with him. And I should be listening rapt to his conversation instead of staring at him with hidden lust. I tuned in again.

'And with austerity for so many years, we're only creating an even worse childhood legacy to come,' Sunil was saying.

I slurped my beer and realised that he'd again finished his. 'Do you want another…?'

But just then, there was the noise of the back door clanking open. It was like a bright electric shock into the calm of our evening together. I jumped, and Sunil sat back from where he'd been leaning towards me.

Wilf came quickly through the kitchen and appeared in the doorway. 'Oh!' he said as he saw us sitting on the sofa together. 'Sorry, didn't know you had friends round.'

'Hey, man.' Sunil got up, went towards Wilf and put out his fist. Wilf awkwardly put up his too for a small bump. 'I'm from Resilient, you know, the youth group Daisy goes to. Great to meet you, man.'

Wilf looked at him suspiciously and Bodger looked up from where, until now, he'd been sleeping peacefully beside the sofa, and joined in.

'Hey,' he mumbled.

'I was just hanging with Cal here and talking about youth resilience,' Sunil went on smoothly.

'Right.'

'We're having a session next Tuesday, if you fancy coming along?'

'Yeah, maybe.' Wilf nodded, but he didn't smile.

'Got to go now,' Sunil said. 'Maybe see you soon then, Cal?'

'I will be there.' I nodded, smiling hard at him.

I saw him to the front door. Bodger followed, slowly sniffing the air behind him. 'So great to hang out with you.'

I smiled about as broadly as it was possible to grin. He gave me a big smile back and went off into the night. I did a little jig in the hallway as the door closed.

But behind me, in my reflection as I spun round, there was Wilf, his face pale and undecided.

'Did you find the record player?' I asked immediately.

'Yeah,' he mumbled and headed for the stairs. I heard his bedroom door slam.

18

Saturday: Wilf got up and seemed to be wearing his headphones as a barrier against the world. Or maybe it was just me. He gave me a sad smile while he spooned cornflakes into his mouth.

'Hey,' I said, indicating that he should lift up an earphone, so I could talk to him. 'What are you up to, today?'

'Going to see Dad,' he said, in a small voice, 'then I'm going to hang with Pete. Aren't Lois and Lorca moving in today?'

'Yes,' I said. 'But only for the trial.' I hated the idea of him sitting around with Ralph and Petra plotting the future, but what could I do?

Wilf got up and put his bowl in the dishwasher without even being asked and put out his hand to open the door. 'See you later then, prob,' he said and was gone with a swish of his bike. He was clear that he didn't want to spend any time with me. Bodger looked at me disapprovingly.

'I don't see why I'm subject to your judgement, dog,' I said. 'All I did was have a beer with a man.' Did everyone else have dogs that acted as their conscience or was it just me? I was sure whatever weird freak-out Wilf was having was a by-product of his anger about moving to South Africa. Why, then, had he chosen to go to Ralph's house again?

I told Lily to take regular rest breaks. 'I'll be back as soon as I can, and we'll go to Nando's. No argument. Aiden can come,' I banged on Daisy's door. 'Out of bed, madam.' She grunted but I'm pretty sure rolled over and went straight back to sleep.

As I came out of the house to walk Bodger to the park, Patrick appeared, very nonchalantly, from number 36. 'Hi, Callie,' he called in a neighbourly way, and looked as if him coming out of his door at exactly the same time as me was a complete surprise.

'Hello.' Bodger looked very pleased to see him and wagged his runty tail enthusiastically.

'How are you doing?'

'Good, thanks. Just hanging on in until the exams.'

He propped himself against his fence post in a conversational way. I slowed down, just to be polite, remembering that I'd agreed to be friends with him.

'You know that once she's done one it won't seem so terrifying,' Patrick said. I suppose he was a teacher. Today he looked more like one, but a weekend version, in jeans and a plain red jumper. It wasn't a bad look.

I needed to get on with the day. 'Come on, Bodger, we need to get you walked if we are going to move Nan and

Grandad today.' I realised I was talking like a person who thought humans were actually biologically related to dogs.

'Can I help with that?' Patrick leapt in. 'Moving boxes and stuff? I mean, I *am* quite strong.' He flexed his muscles in a way that made him look, despite the fact that he was obviously quite fit, really weedy. It was difficult not to laugh. He persisted. 'You know what it's like when you move somewhere new – you want to spend your weekends doing usual stuff. And now we're friends...' he winked '... that's the sort of normal thing friends help with.'

'There is nothing normal about my parents or their moving.' I tried to put him off. Bodger sat down again – he'd never been less keen on going for a walk. I gave Patrick a precis of the idiosyncrasies of both my folks and their chosen new home.

He laughed along. 'Sounds great. What time?' he said. 'I'm free all day.'

Patrick certainly made it easier. Lois and Lorca were over-excited and no use whatsoever. As soon as we delivered them to Seymour House, they were whisked away by Pete. 'I am so glad to welcome you two very special people,' he gushed as they arrived, bouncing around on the doorstep.

He wasn't quite so welcoming to me. 'Hello, Callie. We'll leave you to move the stuff while your parents join in some really exciting activities.'

'Who's *that*?' Patrick whispered as we went to start moving the suitcases and boxes that were in the boot of my car.

'Just some pseudo class warrior who's happily benefitting from capitalism.'

'Is it me?' he asked a little later as we were unloading the second load. 'Or does he have a strange smell?'

As I sniggered, Wilf arrived on his bike and gave Patrick a big grin. 'Hey, neighbour.'

'Hey,' said Patrick. 'Come to see the grandparents already?'

'Pete's got some cool decks,' Wilf explained. 'But yeah, Lois and Lorca too.'

'Was he always called Lorca?' Patrick asked.

'He changed it from Lawrence when I was about twenty,' I said. 'Lorca was a poet in Spain who helped bring surrealism into the mainstream. Hung out with Dali, that kind of stuff.'

'Interesting.' Patrick looked confused nonetheless.

'He had a thing about him for a while,' I went on, heaving a box. 'Quoted him in Spanish, got a lobster phone, you know. I think of it as his surrealist phase.'

Wilf propped his bike against the wall and came to take the box from me.

'But then Lorca was in *Star Trek*,' he told Patrick, as if this made it all better.

'Boldly going where no man has gone before,' Patrick said as we went back into the house. 'In every sense of the word.'

Later, I parked the car in our mutual street. 'Thanks so much for all your help,' I said.

He smiled. 'Got time for a drink, friend?'

I shook my head but did feel very ungrateful. 'I'm going to spend this evening making sure Lily is OK. Try and take her to Nando's maybe.'

Patrick nodded. 'It was fun to hang out with you today. I guess your folks being in that place is one less thing to worry about.' Earlier he'd tried to disguise his look of amazement at the state of their house or the fact that Mum had bellowed, 'Lorca! Cal's here with a man,' at the top of her voice as we'd arrived in the kitchen.

'I'm her neighbour, come to give a hand,' Patrick had said, going forward and speaking at a normal volume.

'I can't hear a word you're saying,' she'd shouted. Patrick had tried to look as if all this were completely normal and hadn't confused anyone with jokes about being called William.

'I hope so,' I said now as we stood in the street. 'They're probably learning grime moves as we speak.'

Lily, Aiden, Daisy, Wilf and I were in Nando's. Lily was tense, but the others had a competition as to who could eat three extra-strong wings in a row without turning into a fiery-mouthed dragon. I sat and watched them all teasing each other, tucking into less hot wings, rice, coleslaw and chips.

'Daisy was supposed to be grounded,' Lily pointed out.

'I've done my f-ing time,' said Daisy, gulping down a glass of water but refusing to acknowledge that her tongue was the temperature of a furnace.

I shot her a glance. 'No abbreviated swearing either,' I said.

'FFS,' they all immediately chorused back at me. Then Daisy started to tell a story about school, dipping chips in ketchup and waving them around as she talked. 'So, I'm in the dining hall and my friend Georgia says, "I have something DMC^{‡‡‡‡‡‡} to say." And so, we all shut up and then she says, "What I want to say is I think I'm a 'they'."'

I looked completely confused but Lily and Aiden nodded as if this was quite cool. Wilf said, 'Is that like being gender fluid? When you're not a boy or a girl?'

Daisy looked at him scornfully, but I was glad he'd asked the question; I didn't have a clue what she was talking about either.

'Yeah, and so we all talked about being defined by our gender,' Daisy went on. 'And how it was such a, like, outdated way of looking at yourself.'

'Like, I'm all man though,' said Aiden with a big grin at Lily. She smiled back at him and it was good to see her mind on something else, even if their conversation was making me feel about as old as an Egyptian mummy that had decayed into bandage dust in its pyramid.

'Yeah right,' scoffed Daisy. I thought about her legs, endlessly on display, and how very female that made her look, but just concentrated on eating my coleslaw instead.

'So, I said, "What pronouns do you want to use? He, she or they?"' Those who were gender fluid could choose how they were addressed, she explained patiently to Wilf and me. I raised my eyebrows but determined on a neutral face to match the conversation.

'Well, there's Ze or Zer,' Lily said.

---

‡‡‡‡‡‡ Deep and Meaningful Conversation. Teenagers have a lot of these.

'What difference really if you just change the "h" to a "z", though?' Daisy went on in her best woke voice. 'I mean, if you're truly fluid, that's kind of defining too.'

I nodded as if I understood, while they moved on to a discussion of omnisexuality. As far as I could work out, it meant if you were a kid today, you could pretty much have sex with everyone, which sounded at least non-judgmental, if completely bewildering.

Wilf was obviously as confused as I was. He caught my eye for a moment and rolled his; I stuffed another wing into my mouth so that I didn't laugh. But then, quickly, he looked away and I felt the same pang of hurt as that morning. *I still have some time left with you. Please don't turn away from me before you have to go.*

He'd been the youngest; my baby, even while the girls grew up and got all sophisticated. And now he was going before I'd had time to help him learn to fly the nest.

The next morning, Sunil pulled up outside our house in a blue car with a huge Resilient logo on its side. Daisy was poised in the front window – having claimed that she'd done all the revision she could possibly do for GCSEs and *had* to go to the rally – wearing a long Resilient T-shirt as a dress, with red DMs. She immediately rushed outside. I wondered if I'd have refused to let her go if it hadn't been with Sunil. I'd spent a little more time than was usual on getting dressed and painting my own face that morning, and I tried to look as if I weren't waiting eagerly to see him. Wilf looked up at me though, as I stood up and went down the garden path.

Sunil opened the car door for Daisy. He looked almost picture perfect in the May sunshine and it was hard not to blush. 'Hello, Cal, we're really excited about the rally today.' He looked directly at me. 'It's going to give us great profile. Maybe we'll be on the telly later.'

His life was so glamorous. I tried to look supportive, but my voice came out in a simpering squeak. 'I'll keep an eye out for the news.'

Daisy looked appraisingly at me and mouthed the word 'grafting' as she climbed into the car. There were a couple of her mates already in the back.

'I'll try hard to get some screen time, then,' said Sunil, smiling back at me.

Just then, three doors down, Patrick came out of his front door, wearing running gear. He waved and unplugged his earbuds, heading over to where we were talking on the pavement.

'Hey, neighbour and some of her multiple offspring.' He grinned as he arrived. Sunil stopped talking mid-sentence and looked at him appraisingly.

This is helpful of Patrick. Just when I'm having five minutes with the focus of all my recent sexual fantasies, he turns up.

'How's the folks today?' he carried on blithely.

'Mum messaged on her new WhatsApp to say it's all cool,' I told him, then, turning to Sunil, I said, 'Sunil, this is Patrick, my neighbour. He helped move my folks into a home yesterday.'

'Mate,' they both said in that awkward way that blokes did when they instinctively didn't like each other. You could almost feel them sizing each other up.

'Sunil's taking Daisy and some other kids to a rally in London,' I said. Daisy banged on the window just then and pointed at her phone to indicate the time.

'What's it for?' Patrick asked.

'It's about campaigning for more resources to counter the negativity peak that's traumatising our young,' said Sunil. Even to me it sounded slightly pretentious, but I supposed in his job you had to be serious about the issues.

Patrick looked for a moment as if he was going to laugh but then he said, 'Negativity peak? That's a new term.'

'It started on the street in Detroit, I believe.' Sunil nodded. 'But now is in fairly extensive use when we're talking about the future of the young.' It wasn't clear whether he meant to sound superior when he said it, but he did.

'Woah, going to have to try that one in class.' Patrick plugged his earbuds back in and sped off down the road without looking back.

'He's a teacher,' I told Sunil.

'Not always up on the latest thinking,' he said dismissively before smiling. 'Really look forward to hanging out with you again on Tuesday.' He got back into his car.

I skipped inside and went to help Lily with last-minute chemistry. But it was hard to sit and not think that there was definitely some sort of reaction going on with Sunil too. Later, when I'd got her to have a break and take Bodger out with Aiden for an hour, I went to look for Wilf but he was getting ready to go out again. 'Going back to Seymour House,' he told me. 'I've got a really good vibe going with Pete and I need to make the most of it.'

'Umm, Wilf, is there something the matter? I mean, not the South Africa thing, but something between you and me?' He looked up but wouldn't meet my eyes, just wrapped his scarf more tightly round his neck. 'Because I would hate that.'

Did he want me to more visibly fight for him to stay? Was he trying to protect himself by withdrawing from me before he had to? Did he think that me having a drink with Sunil was me moving on from him already? All I wished were that he would tell me.

But Wilf just looked up sadly. I guessed it was a combination of these things.

'Look, I really don't want you to go to South Africa, you know,' I blurted out then into the noise of him zipping up his jacket.

'Yeah,' said Wilf, as if he wasn't really listening or interested.

'And I'm only trying to hold it together because I think that's the right thing to do for you,' I carried on.

If only kids came with a health warning: 'Avoid if you don't want to experience extreme hurt as well as complete joy'.

'Yeah, I know,' he mumbled, but still looked as if he wanted nothing better than to get out of the hallway and away from me.

'And me having a drink with Sunil was just about trying to help Lily.'

At this he looked up and said, 'Yeah, you can go out with who you like, though, yeah?'

'I'm not going out with him,' I pleaded weakly. 'And I thought you wanted me to go out with someone – like Patrick.'

'That's different,' he said.

'Why?' I was bewildered.

'It just is,' he said and then he was past me, down the steps, already unlocking his bike from the lamp post.

I don't think he heard me start to cry.

In the early evening, Lily had another panic attack. It wasn't nearly as bad as the first one, but it was still very frightening, for her and for me. This time, I gave her the paper bag immediately and she started to breathe into it, her eyes wide with questioning fear. After ten minutes, she was calmer, but curled into my arms, gently crying.

'It'll be OK,' I said, over and over again. I hoped that Patrick was right and getting the first exam out of the way took the fear out of the rest. I shushed her and comforted her the best I could, but there was nothing I could change about them starting in a few hours.

In the end, with Daisy back, breathless about how brilliant the rally had been and how amazing Sunil was, I made all the kids sit on the sofa, eat pizza and watch TV. I wanted to create calm; then I intended to make both girls have a warm bath and go early to bed. Wilf said that Lois and Lorca seemed really happy at Seymour House. Daisy showed me an Instagram post from Mum – a photo of Dad twerking captioned: 'Good vibes in our #newhome #lifeintheoldmanyet'. I tried to feel relieved. Pete (@ peteforfreedom) had already liked the post.

Sunil was quite a big chunk of the Channel 4 news, although he got a lot less airtime on the other channels. He was pictured on a large stage in Trafalgar Square, in front of a huge crowd of mostly young people, pounding the air with his fist as he demanded, in politically charged tones, that 'Government took the voice of the next generation seriously' to generally rapturous applause.

Marv texted to wish the girls luck with the exams, adding,

That bloke you fancy is on the telly. Nice wallpaper.

I ignored him and went to bed, full of trepidation for the twins. But yep, Marv had got that one right.

Lily seemed to have more fortitude if not more colour in her face the next morning. I kept up a cheerful monologue about anything other than chemistry, while trying to make sure she'd eaten enough. Daisy had lost her scientific calculator and both of us running around the house lifting up cushions and looking for it did slightly destroy the illusion of calm I was looking for, but at least it was a distraction. When she'd found it, in her school bag all along, I drove them to school, thanking my foresight in making sure that I'd booked the day off as holiday a few months back.

Lily held her head high as she walked into the school; it was as if, in the end, with the exams here rather than anticipated, she'd found some extra strength. Daisy tried to look as if it were just an ordinary day.

'Good luck,' I shouted.

'Thanks, Mum,' they said in unison, looking back over their shoulders.

It was difficult not to remember them going into their first day at nursery like that, side by side. It felt like such a short time ago.

When Lily came out of school two hours later, blinking in the light, I jumped out of my car and ran towards her. 'How was it?' I asked.

'OK,' she said slowly, her face one of relief rather than one of panic. 'It was better than I hoped.' I hugged her hard. She let me hold her for a minute and then said, 'Better get on with studying for physics tomorrow now.'

Daisy, however, looked shell-shocked when she appeared. 'There were bits of it we hadn't even studied,' she said in disbelief. 'There were whole questions I didn't even know were on the syllabus. Fuck, I'd better get on with some revision for the others.'

I decided to halt my campaign against her swearing until the exams were over. Still, if the fright of the first one made her spend more time at her desk that wouldn't be a bad thing.

19

At work the next day, still with half my head in the exam room with the kids, Ayesha was telling me about how she couldn't work in such a sexist, racist environment. I felt weary but also completely sympathetic. There was no denying that she hadn't just been the victim of unconscious prejudice: some of it was pretty conscious too.

'I'm in the kitchen making tea and Eli comes in and asks me if I have to wear my hijab as I probably have really pretty hair.'

I could see that he probably thought he was being complimentary but, hey, what was he doing in all those awareness courses I sent him on? Dreaming about a world where women used to be less confusing, I suspect.

'Then, one of the site blokes says, "Why don't you marry me, Ayesha, so I can get my paperwork."'

This sounded a bit desperate.

'But then, Charles, I mean, good God, why should I have to put up with him, ummm, asking me out every five minutes just because he's got nothing else to do?'

'Asking you out?'

'It's a bit more than that,' she said, tears coming into her eyes. Then I had the benefit of reading the messages that Charles had been sending Ayesha, pretty much twice a day, over the last fortnight and even me, with ten years of prejudicial comments under my belt, was shocked. 'My tawny owl,' one of them read, and I groaned. 'Let's twit-twoo together'. Others were a bit more straightforward but equally offensive: 'Please go out with me. I look forward to unwrapping you.' She'd asked him to stop; he hadn't.

'Fuck his posh arse,' I said under my breath.

When I swiftly fired that posh arse ten minutes later, he looked aghast. 'Do you mean I'm not an asset to your team? Everyone keeps saying how great it is that I'm going to be the next Uncle Eli.'

'You're deeply racist and sexist, I'm afraid,' I told him. 'And I'll be having words with Uncle Eli.'

When he was gone, still muttering about having 'given it 120 per cent' I indicated to Ayesha that she should resume her seat at her desk. She looked relieved; I felt it.

'Onwards,' was all I could manage.

Greg muttered from the other desk to Ayesha, 'This is a fuckwit place to work.'

I said nothing, just turned to my PC.

He did have a point.

Patrick was completely right about Lily gaining confidence once the exams started. She'd come home from physics saying that she thought she'd answered 90 per cent of the questions correctly.

Daisy, meanwhile, had looked paler than usual when she came out of a geography paper, and, with French up next, said she was going round to her friend Clare's to practise for her oral exam with Françoise, Clare's conveniently French mother. Maybe she was learning that she couldn't just wing it swearing through life.

Wilf still seemed distant from me after his reaction to Sunil, polite enough but as if he was already trying to create artificial distance between us. It was hurtful and confusing, but all I could do was keep trying to spend any of the dwindling days left with him. I'd tried to talk to him again but got a worse brush-off than before.

I dropped into Seymour House on my way home and there he was, sitting with his grandparents in their new flat, alongside a very comfy-looking Pete. Mum and Dad looked a bit dazed and confused but Wilf was nodding enthusiastically.

'Ah, here's capitalism in action,' Pete said when he saw me, 'back from the daily grind.'

I wanted to tell him to get his idealistic arse out of my parents' lives but instead I said, 'Hey, guys, how are you doing?'

'I'm exhausted,' shouted Mum.

'We've completed a lot of activities and had a lot of discussion,' Dad added.

Pete got up but said as he passed me, 'Best to let them acclimatise without too much visiting in the first few days.' I gave him a big glare but my folks and Wilf all started immediately talking about how inspiring he was, so I figured it must just be me that thought he was a freeloading numpty.

They'd been spending time dancing, playing cards and learning new online skills as well as mixing, I heard. 'Do you think you might be overdoing it?'

'Enough time to rest when we're dead,' Dad said cheerfully. Mum was, however, now asleep in her chair.

'Do you want to come to the Resilient session?' I asked Wilf. 'It might help when you move.'

'Is it with that guy Sunil?' I nodded and Wilf shook his head. 'I think I'll stay here for a bit instead.'

A meeting of Resilient was like being at a Billy Graham concert but with no Billy and a lot more Sunil. So, lots of clapping and cheering but no mid-western Christianity; instead lots of criticising the establishment. The hall of the youth centre was full of Sunil-worshipping teenagers. He came on stage, gave pretty much the same speech as he had on TV to much cheering, and then everyone took part in a training session to build resilience. Lily joined in guardedly alongside Aiden, who'd come along with her.

'It's goals to be Zen,' he'd said when I'd invited him.

'Oh, hun,' Lily had said adoringly, giving him a big kiss in the kitchen.

'Ewwww, PDAs are so 2017,' Daisy had said in disgust. 'Get a room.'

'Are you coming to the session?' I'd asked.

'No, my only goals right now are revision,' she'd added, her face uncharacteristically worried. 'And no grafting on Sunil, even though he is peng.'§§§§§

---

§§§§§ Gorgeous. Nope, no idea where it comes from or why.

Aiden joined in with the breathing exercises, clutching Lily's hand while they inhaled and exhaled, but much more interestingly, from my vantage point at the back of the hall, I could feast my eyes on Sunil, who was leading the session with gorgeous gusto. He even looked fanciable when he was slow breathing.

'It's a huge task,' Sunil told me as he came to find me at the end. 'We're looking at nothing less than a crisis in teenage confidence.'

I tried really hard to think of something intelligent to say. 'You're doing great work,' I managed, and he gave me one of his devastating smiles. I needed to concentrate on my breathing, just as the kids had learned, just to manage any semblance of normality.

'Will you come to another session on Friday?' he asked softly.

'I... we'd... love to,' I managed.

'I was wondering if you'd come out for a drink with me afterwards, Callie? I really enjoy being with you.'

A million OMGs. A billion 'woohoooos'. A trillion 'can this really be happening?'s... but it really, really *was*.

'I'd love to.' It was difficult not to grin like the Cheshire Cat.

'It's a date.' Sunil smiled back.

A date. *A date.* And not just any old date in my loveless life but a date with unbelievably gorgeous Sunil. I was back on the horse. Back in the room.

I sang loudly along to the radio as I drove Lily and Aiden home, my face one big smile. 'Don't be afraid to catch fish, ha...'

Lily immediately started laughing really loudly. 'Oh, Mum!' and Aiden joined in.

'What?' I knew I wasn't Aretha Franklin but my singing wasn't that bad.

'It's "catch *feels*",' she snorted from the passenger seat.

'What? Not fish?'

'No, *feels*. You know, like emotions! Everyone knows that.'

'I've been singing fish for years and now you tell me?'

They both laughed like drains while I felt like a dinosaur from the other side of an ice age.

'And, Callie?' Aiden piped up from the back.

'What?' I smarted under their ridicule.

'That other song, "Another one in the basket", isn't about online shopping either.'

I felt like I'd emerged from a chrysalis and was fluttering about on early spring flowers, like a tentative butterfly the next day. I bounced around the office until Greg started going on about Prozac in my breakfast cereal; then after work listened eagerly while my folks, Wilf and Fishy Pete played me an impenetrable demo of electronic squawks; and smiled appreciatively at the kids as they let me cook them a meal with little or no thanks. After dinner, Wilf worked on his bike with Patrick.

He was easy to have around, squatting beside the upside-down bicycle outside the back door and discussing chain oil and tyre pressure with Wilf. I went out with a mug of tea and he took it with a 'Cheers, mate,' but, aside from that, he resisted too many other jokes.

Instead, he sat at the kitchen table after the bike-fixing session with another mug of tea in his hand and talked about how he missed kids and couldn't wait to go back to work in September.

'Did you always want to be a teacher?'

'No, I wanted to be a pro footballer like every other kid. Then a pro cyclist.'

I smiled. 'If it makes you feel any better, I really, really wanted to be an HR person in the automotive industry.'

'But when I wasn't good enough, I worked out it's pretty cool working with kids who still have that dream,' he said. 'Bugger, I sound like someone off the *X Factor*.'

'To do that, you'd have to be on *a journey*,' Daisy piped up from behind her laptop.

'Aren't you supposed to be revising?' I asked.

'Yeah. Hey, Pat-the-Teach, are you any good at French?'

'*Bien sûr, je suis* an expert,' said Patrick in perfect Franglaise with no effort at an accent. '*Je m'appelle* Pat-the-Teach.' If I'd made that kind of joke, Daisy would've rolled her eyes in disgust, but with him, she sniggered and went out of the room.

He was so easy with kids it was difficult not to think back to when he was talking about not being able to have any. 'You don't talk about your old life much,' I said in a leading conversational tone, which made him smile.

'Nothing to see here,' he said. 'Very boring person, me.'

I ignored him. 'So where did you grow up?'

'Village on the south coast, m'lud, near Southampton, called Wittering. Yes, really. One sister named Mandy, also a teacher. Now married. Two parents, still living – in said village on south coast. Now retired. Also teachers. Everyone is a teacher. It's what we do. No one knows why but no one has the key to break the curse.' He said this last sentence in the gravelly tones of a film trailer voice-over artist.

'So you went to uni?'

'Roehampton,' he confirmed.

'Then what?'

'Signed up as – guess what? – a teacher. Stayed in south London aside from "gap yahs" and travelling.'

'Never got married?'

'Yes. Did get married.' I raised my eyebrow: this was new news. Bodger also looked up expectantly. 'To a woman named Saffy. She was American. The marriage didn't last because we were both young – and, frankly, I was probably a bit of an arsehole at the time.'

'What kind of arsehole?'

'Your standard kind of arsehole. Kind of married to her but still running round the world with a backpack as if I wasn't – and not taking her with me, that kind of arsehole. Anyway, it was what you call a "starter marriage" – no kids, split up after two years when we were both twenty-eight, she went back to America. Sometimes we still talk on Skype.'

I nodded. 'Go on, please.'

'Cor blimey, m'lud, all right. So, then I eventually got on with being an actual teacher and lived for several years, in Clapham this time, in a shared house with some other teachers.'

'Other male teachers with frequent visitors of female teachers?' I asked.

'Well, one of us was gay.'

'All right, you know what I mean.' I was impatient.

'And then when everyone else had got married and all that stuff, I met Louise, and, after a couple of years, we decided to try to have a family – and then there were about five years in which we tried and failed to do that and then we eventually split up and sold our flat.' He spoke quickly at the end, as if he wanted to get the sentences out and over with.

'How long ago was that?'

'A year now. It was horrible and then it was less horrible. But I also wanted a promotion and the one at Whitebury came up.'

'Not too many applicants, huh? Do they pay you danger money?'

He laughed. 'And it's newly trendy here, in case you hadn't noticed. And so, I gave up work at Christmas, did another bunch of backpacking – South America this time – and then decided to come to Seymour Hill and settle in.'

'Which so far means hanging out fixing bikes?'

'And some supply teaching,' he said. 'And some running. And fixing up my flat. And making friends with my neighbour and her multiple offspring.' He pretend-doffed his cap to me, I smiled, and he got up, putting his mug in the sink.

'They're great kids,' Patrick added as he got to the door. 'I can totally see why you haven't got time to go out with men right now.'

I felt a bit guilty when he said that. But it was true when I was explaining it to him and, I reasoned, that was before Sunil asked me out. Sunil didn't really count as *men*, did he? When someone like him asked you out, then the usual rules went out of the window. Who wouldn't make time in their life for him?

.

Marv was beside himself at the thought of me going on a date with a hot, younger guy and immediately insisted on me going to Polish and Blow with him after work the day before, to spend Abby's loyalty points. There was no way I was having Botox, I told him again – 'What if I end up with a face like a bag of Birds Eye peas for my date?' – but, yes, an eyebrow shape and a bit of waxing wouldn't hurt.

Polish and Blow was minimal-but-tasteful. As we arrived I glanced round me at the other clients, and tried to guess how many of them were going to have their faces injected with paralysing agents or filled with foreign bodies. We sat down in the waiting room. It was hard to ignore the screen above the fake marble fireplace, with the 'before' and 'after' videos.

'She's got no make-up on in the first one and full-on Kardashian in the second. First one a track suit and the after shot, she's dressed up like she's going to a wedding,' I hissed under my breath to Marv, after one particularly duck-to-swan photo set, featuring Julia, a lawyer from Milton Keynes.

'It's not even the same woman,' Marv said and we both started snorting.

The next video was for tooth-whitening. Models turned and 'tinged' their newly snowy gnashers to me on screen.

'Not just white, but Daz bluey-white,' said Marv, just as I was called in to be waxed, scrubbed and plucked all over, like a turkey ready for the Christmas dinner table.

'All in a good cause,' Marv said afterwards when I moaned about the extreme pain that went with being a beautiful person. 'Making you visible – very visible – to Sunil.'

'I'm pretty sure they've ripped hair out of bits of me that should never be visible to anyone.' But all Marvin did was smirk.

20

It was finally Friday. Daisy, who'd walked around all week saying: 'Je voudrais deux baguettes, s'il vous plâit' and similar under her breath, had managed to smile when she came out of French but said she was off round to Clare's to get some more help for the next exam on Monday. She was going to chill with her mates afterwards – 'no parties, I promise' and I believed her for once – and stay the night with Clare.

Wilf was down at the centre with his grandparents. I'd dropped in to find him and Pete sitting in a corner of my folks' flat; Mum and Dad were both fast asleep. I made a mental note to check up on whether they needed to do quite so many activities every day.

'We're going to another Resilient session tonight, Wilf,' I said as he held a headphone to the side of his face and rocked from side to side. 'Do you want to come along?'

He blushed in a way I didn't quite understand and then said, 'I thought if you were going out, I might go round to

Dad's and sleep there. Petra says it's good to get used to it and she said she'll make some food like they have in South Africa. With meat even though she doesn't eat it.'

I felt immediate rage at Petra. What happened to her food tasting like polystyrene? But as I opened my mouth to say something, I could see Pete standing back, one blond eyebrow raised, as if he was waiting for my reaction. I took a breath, determined to stay calm for Wilf and make all this as easy as possible for him.

'OK,' I said slowly. 'But if you want to come home you know where we are.'

Wilf nodded and bent down to the decks again.

'Tell these guys to chill a bit,' I said to cover my hurt, indicating my snoring parents.

'Their tiredness just reflects engaged brains, Callie,' sang Pete. I stomped off down the corridor, telling myself that it was natural for Wilf to make baby steps towards his new family, but it was very, very hard to watch it happen.

Getting ready to go out with Sunil was a big distraction. Telling myself there was nothing wrong with spending money on new clothes for myself in my quest to be the best version I could be of me, I'd bought a new camisole-style top from Zara on the way back from Polish and Blow. I felt quite naked in it, as if I were going out in my underwear, but Marvin assured me that it was on trend and very flattering. Now, I pulled a jacket on top of it and surveyed myself in the mirror. I still looked like a forty-three-year-old woman in jeans and a nice top, but I was a shinier, more upbeat version. I shivered with apprehension and anticipation. What if it went really well with Sunil, he whisked me home for a nightcap and got to see the newly waxed bits of my body? I shivered again.

The session was about how to understand the impact of negative online images. 'Beauty comes in all sorts of forms,' Sunil told the group, who stared up at him adoringly. I just hoped my sort of form, especially after all this effort, was the kind he'd approve of.

Afterwards, Aiden came over, holding Lily's hand. 'I was wondering if Lil can come back to mine as it's Saturday tomorrow and she hasn't got any exams?'

It was a clever ploy – getting Aiden to ask me for a sleepover in a public place, rather than Lily asking at home.

Hmmm. I wanted Lily close to me to make sure no harm came to her; I also *really* wanted to be able to go out for a drink with Sunil without having to worry about any of the kids. 'OK, this once,' I said. 'You sure your folks are OK with it?'

'They invited me, Mum,' Lily said. 'And I feel so much better.'

'And we'll practise our breathing exercises round at mine,' Aiden went on.

I bet you will, although it might be deeper and faster breathing than was recommended. Still, most of all I wanted Lily to be happy.

'All right,' I said. 'But make sure you get an early night.' They looked at each other with glee and disappeared out of the door.

It suddenly occurred to me that I was about to go out with a man, *a gorgeous man*, and there were NO KIDS AT HOME. That didn't mean anything, of course... but it did add a *frisson* of possibility.

A huge frisson.

★

We went to a pub and I listened to Sunil talking about his campaigns and how he'd been so dedicated to his 'mission' that he'd found it hard to develop a close relationship with a woman. Actually, I didn't listen much, just sipped three gin and tonics while he talked and gazed at his beautiful face.

He grinned. 'It's great being with you, though, Callie – you understand me.'

I didn't know whether I did but that seemed quite irrelevant.

'Shall I walk you home?' he offered eventually. I'm sorry to say that the first thought that came into my head was my empty house. It felt as if the gods had aligned to make this happen on exactly the same night as I was out on a date with a man for the first time in years. And not just any man, but Sunil.

As we got to the gate, I gave a quick glance round to make sure that there was no sign of Patrick, and then invited Sunil in, trying to remember how to do a seductive smile.

He looked at me and grinned.

'The kids are all out,' I said, and I guess, from then, we both knew what was going to happen. Certainly, I had one thought on my mind – the same thought I'd had from the moment I saw him.

I parked him on the sofa with a beer and nipped to the loo. Peering in the mirror, I looked flushed and excited with a heightened colour. I pushed back a strand of hair and took a deep breath.

By the time we'd finished the beer and Sunil had told me some quite serious stories about his run-ins with 'the establishment', I felt intoxicated. We had clinked bottles and were now quite close on the sofa.

It was then that he said, 'Callie, I… well, I just wanted you to know, that I think you're great.' Subconsciously, I waited for the 'but'. It was very difficult to believe that this activist Adonis really liked me.

'That's sweet of you,' I said.

He paused. 'I don't want to say anything that's going to make you uncomfortable…' He edged a little closer. 'I mean, I respect exactly how you feel, and you would tell me if…' And he came closer still.

He wanted to kiss me. It hit me hard with a jolt of ridiculous fabulousness. For a moment I worried about my not-very-fit stomach but figured I'd try and lie down where everything looked so much better than when I was standing up.

It took me a while to splutter, 'No, I mean yes, I mean…' and he looked questioningly at me, so there was nothing really else to do except lean towards him.

My expectation, as a person who hadn't kissed anyone for a very long time indeed, was that it would be both discombobulating and very, very exciting. My first feeling unfortunately was: ewww *wet*. It was *unexpected*. I adjusted my head and decided I was just out of practice.

He became passionate quickly, sliding his arms round me, and pulling me closer to him, kissing me harder and more breathlessly. I tried to join in enthusiastically.

'Shit, I fancied you the moment I saw you,' Sunil gasped, and I found his hands on the front of my new camisole top, roaming over my chest, my breasts responding as if they'd never been touched before. In fairness, they hadn't for a while.

'Of course, I wanted to help you too...' he went on in a voice that told me that I shouldn't doubt his motives. God, did he have to be quite so noble all the time? At that point I couldn't give a shit about his motives. I'd fancied his very bones from the moment I first saw him and couldn't quite believe he fancied me – *me* – back. And I'd get used to all this physical stuff quite quickly and it would be mind-blowing.

That was when he said into my hair, 'Would you be comfortable going upstairs?'

I wondered if he always seduced people with this much sensitivity, but realised that, what with being really woke and at the frontline of youth gender politics, he probably had to get a triple-opt-in for sex from anyone. It was terribly polite though, compared to my previous experience.

It did also seem a bit rushed – from a kiss and a bit of a fumble straight to going to bed – but the whole thing felt very new, a bit like the first time but for the second time. I was very old-fashioned and this was how people did it now.

'I'd love to,' I said, standing up and holding out my hand. He came towards me and kissed me for a long time again, before I ran up the stairs, two at a time, with him behind me. As we fell onto my bed, he was kissing me again, his body moving against mine; I writhed back and felt him quickly lifting the camisole over my head and unzipping his jeans and mine. Extended foreplay was obviously for a previous generation, although he couldn't be more than eight or ten years younger than me. It would just take some getting used to – having sex again after so long.

Eventually, we were both naked, apart from one sock that was stuck to my left foot. I had a moment to congratulate myself, as he pulled off his jeans and looked down at me appreciatively, that all that pain in the beauty clinic had been *so* worth it. Still, I instinctively pulled the duvet towards me as I whipped off my remaining sock and waited with my head on my pillow. I wasn't sure he needed to have such a panoramic view of my unloved body.

He seemed to like what he had seen though, coming down to lie next to me and then newly exploring every single bit of me. I tried hard to relax, thinking that he would definitely have a condom.

All the rest of the world was shut out.

But that was when the door opened, and the world rushed back in, very fast and furious indeed.

21

'I forgot my mouth guard, Cal.' That's what I heard, in the sweet, innocent voice.

Then I saw Wilf's face and it was white. Aghast. Stricken. He stood as if anchored to the carpet in the doorway, his hand still on the knob, his body still coming halfway round the door. His eyes were wide with what seemed to be a slow dawning realisation of what he was seeing.

All I knew was horror.

Oh, no. Oh, no. Oh, no.

Sunil didn't seem to understand what was happening. His back was to the door, he was half on top of me and half beside me, quietly moaning with pleasure, his hands still roaming across my lower half.

Then, I screamed. It was potent: a chilling mix of panic and pressure topped by overwhelming guilt.

First there was the shock, the incredible shock of realising that Wilf, vulnerable Wilf, had caught me in bed with a relatively strange man, then I was pushing Sunil off me. He turned to see where my frightened eyes were looking and then shouted himself, 'Oh my God,' and pulled the duvet over his bare arse.

'Wilf, Wilf,' I cried as he turned, another long second later; my eyes met his and I saw only betrayal. I pushed Sunil further away as Wilf turned and ran, his big feet clomping down the stairs. How had I not heard him come up them?

'Oh, shit.' I grabbed my dressing gown, pulled it round me and gave chase.

But as I leapt down the stairs, all I could see was that the front door was wide open and there was the sight of his bike, being pedalled away from me into the night.

22

'I thought they were away for the night,' I told Sunil, my dressing gown wrapped round me tightly. I sat at the head of my bed, watching him hurriedly pull on his boxers, jeans and shirt. All the sexual chemistry had evaporated like a fast-burning compound over a Bunsen burner. In its place was his face – a picture of guilt and horror — his body, rushing to get out of my bedroom as quickly as possible, and me: a vassal of shame.

How could I have been so selfish and stupid? When Wilf needed me most, he'd had to see me, naked and ridiculous, focused not on him, but entirely on someone else. The betrayal was evident. All he needed right now was to know that I loved him with all of my being – and instead, he had to have this permanent picture in his mind of me. It was hard to imagine how alone he must be feeling.

The shame! I'd all this worry about the children in my life and all I'd been doing was thinking about my own wants and desires.

'I'm so sorry, Cal, this is all my fault,' Sunil said, taking the blame.

This made me impatient. 'Of course, it isn't,' I almost snapped, then I said: 'He said he was staying round at his dad's. But he forgot his mouth guard. He'd need it for football in the morning.' It sounded so normal and domestic in the face of what had nearly just happened.

And I remembered what I'd said earlier: 'If you want to come home you know where we are.'

The point was, it didn't matter what had made him want to come home – he had, and when he'd got here, he'd found me in a position I'd hoped he'd never have to see. The guilt doused me from all angles as if I were in a petrol-station car wash.

Sunil nodded grimly. 'I knew your life was complicated; I should have stayed away.'

I knew rationally that we were two grown adults that had every right to have met each other and then jumped into bed together. It was modern and right and spontaneous. It was acting on our desires. But it wasn't that simple when there were teenagers involved.

'It's not *that* complicated,' I said. 'Well, not normally, it's just now and…'

'I should have known that and respected it,' Sunil went on as if he was telling himself off.

'It's *my* fault,' I said. *I should have all the kids here with me instead of being in bed with you.* My daughters were in other places in the middle of their GCSEs; Wilf would undoubtedly be thinking that right when he needed me, my focus was on a man instead. And one whom he'd made no secret of disliking.

Sunil gave me a brief kiss on my cheek. 'I'd better go before he comes back,' he said.

Good. What was important now was explaining to Wilf that I still loved him and hadn't forgotten him before he'd even gone. I followed Sunil down the stairs and he went out of the front door. I looked anxiously around for the sight of a bike light coming down the near-dark street, but there was nothing.

'Goodbye and I'm sorry,' Sunil said. 'I'll... I mean, I'll check in with you and...'

I let him kiss me again briefly but didn't watch him go down the path.

Instead I went back inside to phone Wilf and beg him to come back and talk to me.

I rang Wilf's phone repeatedly. He rarely answered it anyway, but now he was angry and upset, so I didn't panic, although I hoped that as soon as we could communicate he'd understand that me having a shack-up with a man didn't mean I wasn't there for him. I had to explain to him that he didn't need to resent me because he was having to leave us; he could go and I would still love him and he could still love me. I would just force him to sit and listen.

When the phone rang and rang with no opportunity to leave a voicemail, I gave up and rang my parents. It seemed most likely that he'd have gone to them. God knew what he'd told them: 'Cal's having a shag, so I thought I ought to come and see you.'

I FaceTimed them, knowing that I'd set the volume to very loud on Mum's iPad when she wasn't looking. There was a moment before she appeared, a blur of mad white hair on a stripy pillow case. She didn't have her hearing aid on as she immediately shouted, 'Calypso? Lorca, it's Calypso.'

There was a noise of Dad sitting up and shouting, 'Where? Where is she?'

'On the FaceTime; she's on the FaceTime,' shouted Mum.

'Is Wilf with you?'

'No need to shout all the time,' said Dad. 'It's all very well for your mother but it's going to make me go deaf too at this rate.' He grabbed the iPad and peered into it. 'Very good picture quality, very good indeed.'

I sighed and repeated more quietly, 'Is Wilf with you, Dad?'

'He was, wasn't he?' Dad looked flustered, as if he was trying to remember what had happened that evening before he went to bed. 'He was here, wasn't he, Lois?'

'You've not got IT yet, you old fool,' Mum shouted. 'Your father's constantly questioning his memory, as if he *wants* to have dementia.'

'I don't want it, I just want to test I haven't got it,' Dad muttered.

'Never mind that. Is Wilf with you now or not?'

'He went, didn't he?' Dad asked Mum. 'He was here earlier but then he said he was going to see his dad.'

'But has he come back again after that?'

'Did you hear him come back?' Dad asked Mum, then muttered, 'Stupid question.'

'What I don't understand is why he would come back here,' Mum said.

'We had a…' I struggled hard. How did you tell your folks you'd been caught in flagrante? I decided not to give them a reason to worry.

He must have gone back to Ralph's, which felt like a new level of parenting failure. What if he was there now, telling Petra what he'd seen? I put my head in my hands as I imagined her face lit from ear to ear with sanctimony.

I let out a low moan and rang Wilf's mobile again. This time it was switched off, but voicemail kicked in, so I left a message: 'Wilf, please, I'm so sorry about what happened, but you need to call me as soon as possible, please, and let me know you are OK, please, Wilf.'

How long did I leave it before I contacted Ralph? I paced round the kitchen. Then, through the door of the sitting room I could see the empty bottles of San Miguel on the coffee table and I grabbed them and shoved them right to the bottom of the recycling bin as if they were proof of my dissolute lifestyle.

Perhaps I'd wake up in a minute and this would all be some terrible dream? I'd dreamt about sex because I hadn't had any for so long. And I'd dreamt about Wilf leaving because I was so worried about him actually leaving and I would wake up in a minute and shake my head and get up and...

I looked at my phone, which now said 10.58. I was definitely awake, and this was no troubled dream – it was a very real nightmare.

Still I put off calling Ralph. I'd text Wilf's friends instead – Jowan and Miguel.

Hey boys, if Wilf is with you? Get him to message me if so?

I was trying to be casual, not sound like I was panicking, but I could feel the bile rising at the back of my throat.

I flicked the switch on the kettle, aiming for a cup of calming camomile, then went and peered out of the back door, more in hope of hearing a bike being locked up on the path than seeing anything. Aside from the gentle sound of traffic coming from the main road to the station, there was nothing. I went to the front door and yanked that open again and did the same thing. Our street was empty. Just for a moment, I thought about waking up Patrick and asking him to come and help me, but I knew I was overreacting.

Back at the kitchen table, I decided that Marvin might be the most sympathetic. I FaceTimed him just as a text arrived back from Jowan.

No not here.

They were fabulously expressive, teenagers – told you loads with *so* much additional information. Miguel would probably be asleep. I wondered what either of their parents would say if Wilf turned up – they'd put it down to adolescent behaviour, the fact that all kids had rows with their folks as they grew up. But I knew they would insist that Wilf contacted me as soon as possible.

The screen eventually lit up with Marv's face. He was in bed and in one corner of the screen, from another pillow, I could see a long strand of blonde hair. Not alone, then, but also either pre- or post-shag as he'd made time to answer the phone. He looked ruffled and happy. Post-shag, then.

I didn't bother to enquire, just started, 'Oh, Marv, Wilf's gone.'

'What do you mean, "gone"?'

'He caught me in...' I realised I was about to update the other occupant of Marv's bed – almost certainly a total stranger – on my eventful evening. 'Wait, I don't want to be rude but the person you're with...'

'It's just Debbie.' Marv smiled affectionately in the direction of the other pillow and swirled the camera so that it showed a glorious tousled blonde, rolling what looked like a joint; she put down the large paper in her hand and gave a lazy wave. 'What do you mean, *gone*?'

'He left about thirty minutes ago and he's not at my parents' – there was a scene.'

'Does Wilf do scenes?'

'No, he just ran out of the door. He caught me with—'

'With who? With what?'

'Let me speak,' I snapped. 'He caught me in bed with Sunil.'

'Oh, my God, you went to *bed* with him?' Marv looked highly amused. 'Oh, my God, Cal,' and carried on chuckling. There seemed to be a splutter from Debbie on the other pillow too.

'That's not the point,' I went on, trying to get him to understand the bigger issue. 'Wilf came in, unexpectedly, right in the middle.' I gave Marv a quick precis of what had happened. 'And I'm terrified I've sent him straight to Ralph and Petra and...'

Marv's face grew grave as I talked through the consequences of my shag. 'It sounds likely he went back there. It's going to be a real shock to him, as he would never have thought that *you'd* be at home getting laid and—'

'I'll call Ralph,' I said.

'Let me know when he's back,' Marv said, and his face disappeared from the screen.

I put aside my pride and called Ralph.

You weren't doing anything wrong. Wilf was supposed to be out. I told myself this as I hoped, despite all the embarrassment, that Ralph would tell me he was safely tucked up in a beige bedroom at his and Petra's executive home. It took a while for him to pick up.

I wasted no time: 'Wilf is with you, isn't he?'

Ralph yawned and said sleepily, 'What do you mean? He was earlier, but he said he forgot his mouth guard for football or something, so he went back.'

'Oh, God.' My voice slumped. What if he'd been kidnapped? Or had an accident on his bike? Or…

'Callie, what's going on?' Ralph sounded frightened.

I told him that Wilf had run off. 'He'd have come back here,' Ralph said. 'Where do you think he might be?'

'I don't know,' I groaned, tears springing from my eyes, like warm water from geysers. 'I mean, he's bound to turn up in a minute or…'

Ralph sounded as if he was getting out of bed. 'I'll go downstairs and see if I can see him in the street.'

He put his hand over the microphone as the sound became muffled and busy, then there was a brief terse exchange with Petra, ending in, 'Go back to sleep, babe,' then I could hear him going down the stairs. There was a click on a couple of light switches. I wiped my face on my pyjama sleeve.

'What happened anyway?' Ralph asked.

I took a deep breath. Why did I feel embarrassed explaining to Ralph that I'd been to bed with someone else? It was a very long time since we'd been in bed together – and he was married again. I could go to bed with whoever I liked. '... a bloke round and Wilf came barging into my bedroom and caught me, us...'

'Oh, that can't have been good for him.' Ralph whistled.

I shook with outrage. 'And telling him he's moving from everything he's known in his life to an entirely different country away from his family is?'

'I just mean it's a shock, you know.' Everyone seemed to think that me going to bed with someone was highly unexpected. Even Ralph, who I used to have quite good sex with back in the day, now thought it was unlikely that I would ever be having sex with anyone else. 'We need to think about where he might be, not argue,' Ralph said down the phone.

We went through a roster of kids' clubs or activities that Wilf had belonged to or currently belonged to. We had a few parents' numbers but decided it was over the top to call them when it wasn't even midnight.

'Can't you go out in a car and look for him?'

'Drive to the school, round the market, that kind of thing?'

'Yes, do that,' I said.

Ralph rang off and I paced the kitchen. Should I go and drive around too? Better that I waited until I heard the click of the door and his return.

I tried calling him again.

How long was it appropriate to wait before you phoned the police? Surely it had to be more than two hours? Especially for a fourteen-year-old boy who would just be at one of his friends' houses. But I'd sent Ralph on a tour of those over the last half an hour – or all the ones I could think of – and there was no sign of Wilf's bike outside. I'd also stalked his FB page – absolutely nothing posted for the last twelve months and, before that, just a picture of him and Lois and Lorca; FB was no longer cool for kids. His Twitter account had 326 followers but was set to private. His Instagram posts were about his band and music. He had 943 followers there. I had no idea how you accessed his Snapchat.

He could easily have gone to find one of his sisters? Perhaps he'd gone to find Lily at Aiden's – he knew Aiden well and Lily was his comfort blanket.

I hated worrying her, but there was no other option. She picked up on the first ring, her instinct of imminent doom as keen as ever. 'What is it?'

'Do you know where Wilf is?'

'No – isn't he with Ralph?' Her voice was fighting sleep. I could hear Aiden from beside her: 'What is it?'

'He came home and there was a bit of a scene and he ran off. I was hoping he'd come to find you.' I tried to keep my tone as light as I could.

'Oh, no,' Lily said. 'I'm coming straight home.' There was another noise of Aiden sleepily asking her where she was going, and it sounded as if he was volunteering to walk the couple of streets with her.

The anticipation of her arriving was some solace: in my distress I wanted my family around me; people who knew Wilf as much as me and would care as much as me that he was gone.

I rang Daisy too. 'What's going down?' she whispered, when the phone had rung a good few times.

I explained quickly. 'Fucking weird of Bro,' she concluded with much less panic than her sister. 'I'll get Aiden and Lily to come round for me on the way back.'

While I waited, I texted a few parents with a brief:

Hi, I know really unlikely but if you see or hear from Wilf, please let me know. Prob nothing to be worried about. Kid thing.

Jowan's mum was the only one who texted back – all the other parents would be sensibly asleep. But she had young children as well as Jowan and slept erratically, if ever.

Is everything OK?

Wilf and I had a row and he's gone off. Am sure he will be back soon.

The problem was, as the clock ticked forward, I was less and less certain that this was right.

The kids came running down the street ten minutes later, Aiden between the girls wearing what looked very much like pyjamas under his hoodie. Lily's face was puce, her jaw rigid and she was out of breath. I grabbed her to me on the doorstep, then her sister.

'Right, it'll be nothing and he'll be home soon but thanks for coming back,' I gabbled.

'You go back to bed, Aiden,' said Lily. 'I'll call you in the morning.'

'I'll stay and help...'

'No, this is just us now,' Lily said firmly, and he sloped off down the street, making 'call me' signs back at her in the half-light of the street lamps.

Daisy just asked, 'What happened to make Wilf leave like that?'

'I think it all just got too much,' I said.

I was pale, powered only by coffee and fear, my eyes aching from lack of sleep exacerbated by crying.

'It's OK, Ma,' they both said in unison. 'It'll be OK,' and I wondered just for a minute when they'd grown up so much that it was their job to comfort me now.

23

In the end, Ralph went to every house all of us could think of and woke up Wilf's school mates and their parents. They answered, according to him, with general wrath at being woken up, but all quickly felt the panic of a parent with a missing child and, after saying that Wilf wasn't there, offered their help. By now it was 3 a.m. – tortured hours of waiting had gone by – but we still thought he would come home soon.

'It was just a bit of a scene,' was all I could manage to tell the twins. I guessed it would come out quickly enough – my role in Wilf's disappearance – but I couldn't bring myself to tell them yet, terrified of their judgement. Instead, the kids circled Ralph warily and looked at him accusingly under their lashes. Then they took to thinking of anywhere else that Wilf would have gone and fired up their laptops to start looking online for any signs.

Trying to stay calm, I rang the police, attempting to keep the panic out of my voice. The officer on the other end was soothing and helpful. She took my address, listened to me confirm that I had every reason to suspect he'd run away following a 'family scene' and told me she would put his description out to all current patrolling cars. An officer would be round to see us shortly. Yes, we should keep following up any ideas. Statistically, she added kindly, it was highly likely he would be found or return shortly.

By 4.30 a.m., when we were almost mad with worry, there was a whoosh of a car outside. My first thought was that the police had found Wilf and were bringing him back, but as we all rushed to the door it was clear the two PCs on the path were alone. In the dark of the early morning we stepped back to let them in.

'PC Warren, and this is PC Moshulu,' the female one said. I motioned to the girls to stay in the sitting room and sat down with them and Ralph at the kitchen table. Quickly, feeling there was no time to waste, I made tea and told them the basics of what had happened.

'He might be upset though,' Ralph said, his face a pale shade of grey.

'Why would that be?'

Ralph avoided my eyes and then said, 'We – his stepmother and I, no, not Callie here, but my wife...' I realised he wasn't about to tell the police what Wilf had seen. Instead he gave the police a rundown on our relationship, referring to me as 'the woman he considers his stepmum'. Then he carried on, 'The thing is my wife and I are relocating to South Africa with Wilf and so it's a big change.'

PC Warren looked at us with sympathy. 'So potentially a little emotional distress, then?'

I coloured. This wasn't the only emotional distress. 'He also saw... I mean he saw... I mean, Wilf came back unexpectedly...' PC Moshulu smiled at me encouragingly. 'He came home unexpectedly, and I was in... bed... with someone.' The PCs looked unfazed. 'Unexpected... wasn't expecting anyone here...' and then, looking through the deep crimson blush that was now my face at the police, I said, 'Doesn't usually happen...'

'But you're saying that Wilf catching you... might have been a bit of a shock to him?'

'Well, on top of finding out that he's moving away from us.'

PC Moshulu nodded. 'Right now, the best thing to do is sit tight, try and get some sleep if you can...' I looked at him amazed: sleep? He handed me a card. 'Ring us the moment you hear from him. In the meantime, all our patrol cars have his details. We'll go and check the school grounds – kids go there sometimes; it's a place they feel at home – and we'll have a good look in the parks.'

7.30 a.m. A gathering of the clan. The extended clan. This included Lois and Lorca, who'd arrived in a taxi when they'd found out he hadn't returned, Ralph, Daisy, Lily and me. Marvin was on his way.

I'd warned Ralph about Lily's anxious state, although without any sleep, her jaw rigid, she was now one of the calmest people in the room.

'Yeah, Wilf said there was an ambulance round,' he mumbled. 'She always was a bit more... sensitive than the others.' There was a moment when it was nice to share an understanding of what was going on with someone who actually knew my children.

He went out into the back garden and I could see him rolling a fag while he talked on his mobile to someone – probably Petra. She hadn't managed to make him give up all his vices, then.

Ralph came back into the sitting room and everyone pointedly ignored him.

'Look, we need to work together to work out where Wilf is,' I implored my parents, my ex-partner and my children.

Dad sniffed. Mum raised her eyebrows. Daisy, fuelled by an audience, spat at Ralph, 'I just want you to know that none of this would have happened if it wasn't for you.'

He looked shell-shocked but didn't answer her directly. 'I've been to all his mates' we could think of, the sound-engineering centre at school, the market, the square. The police are keeping an eye out too.'

'And no sign of him at Seymour House,' Dad said. 'I mean, why didn't he come to us?'

'Nothing on his social,' said Daisy, who'd been furiously tapping on her laptop and phone all night. 'He might turn up at football?'

'Good thinking, Daisy,' barked Dad. 'We need more factual thinking like that.'

'I'll go and look at 9.30,' said Ralph. 'But I guess he still hasn't got his mouth guard.' I was silent but Daisy looked at me with more suspicion.

'Who has he been talking to in the last few weeks?' I asked, to move the conversation on. 'Is there anyone new in his life? Anyone he's mentioned?'

'Only the food-delivery guy,' Lily said.

'Patrick?'

'With his bike and stuff,' Lily went on. 'He did say that.'

'That man who helped us move,' shouted Mum. 'Wilf seemed to like him.'

'Well, I'm sure he won't know anything, but it's definitely worth asking him if he's seen him.' I pulled out my mobile and searched for 'Bloke in Lycra'.

'Who?' Ralph looked blank.

'Mum got mowed down by a Deliveroo dude,' Daisy said, as if it were Ralph's fault that I'd been sprayed with Thai green curry a few weeks ago.

'Yeah, Wilf said about that.' Ralph ignored her malevolent tone.

'You guys carry on thinking,' I ordered and went into the kitchen.

Patrick didn't sound surprised to hear from me at such an early hour of the morning. In fact, he sounded really pleased – and it was like an unexpected salve to my soul to hear his voice. He was always so *helpful*.

'Great!' he said when he answered the phone, instead of 'hello'.

'Umm, it's not that great, actually,' I said. 'Look, sorry to ring you so early… You haven't heard from Wilf, have you?'

'Umm, no. Why?'

I burst into tears. 'He went out last night… after a bit of a scene… and he hasn't come back all night,' I managed in between blubs.

'Oh, shit,' Patrick said. 'I'll be round as soon as I'm dressed.'

He arrived at the same time as the two PCs, who'd come to talk me through a plan of action before they finished their shifts. The sun was now high in the sky; Daisy and Lily were still pinned to a laptop; my parents had both gone to sleep again in their armchairs. I'd urged them to go home but they insisted on staying. Bodger walked round the house, his face in an expression of extreme concern, peering up the stairs, as if he knew someone was missing.

PC Warren had a sympathetic smile on her face. 'We'll find him, Ms Brown. He can't have gone far.'

Patrick, in jeans and a bright red jumper, just waved at me to go ahead but gave me a nod to say he was ready and waiting. I indicated the sitting room – he could join the mêlée.

I could hear Ralph on the phone. 'Babe, no, you stay there in case he comes back.' I raised my eyebrows at him, and we all sat down in the kitchen. 'Look, I know it's a hassle, but kids just aren't predictable.'

How was she going to cope with a teenager she didn't understand when he was under her roof in another country? I thought viciously, but then shook myself. Hating Petra wasn't going to get Wilf back.

'Now, we suggest the following in these circumstances,' PC Warren said. There was something heartening about realising that they had a 'usual' plan of action. 'Kids do this all the time. So, the first thing is that he just turns up again. It's quite likely he's been staying with a friend.'

'Should we put something on Facebook?'

'Well, we advise holding off on the social media until at least a few more hours have passed,' said PC Warren. 'It's because it's highly likely that he'll return – and that sort of thing causes quite a lot of embarrassment at his age. We make a distinction between "missing", which means he could be in danger, or "absent", which means he is probably somewhere close but not at risk.'

I shuddered at the words 'danger' and 'at risk'. 'Absent, then,' I confirmed.

'Now, has it occurred to you that Wilf might have a girlfriend or a boyfriend?' PC Moshulu asked. 'Not unusual at his age.'

'I think I'd know,' Ralph said. 'I'm sure I would.'

PC Warren smiled as if she knew better. 'We don't always tell our parents everything.'

'True but…'

'Some colleagues will be in touch either as soon as we hear anything, or later in the day.' PC Moshulu got up and PC Warren followed. I told them how grateful I was for all their help and Ralph and I stood in the doorway, as if we were still a couple, watching them get back into their patrol car.

'Who's the guy in the sitting room?' he asked as we turned back inside. 'Is he the guy from…?'

'No! Don't be ridiculous,' I said. 'He's the guy who knocked me over – lives down the road. He's become a friend. He's a teacher. Starts new term in September.'

Patrick was sitting with the twins in the sitting room discussing what they knew. 'You look absolutely exhausted,' he said.

I grimaced. 'It's been a long night. Look, thanks for coming.' He got up and looked as if he wanted to hug me. He held out his hands instead but then returned them to his side. 'This is Wilf's dad, Ralph. This is my friend, Patrick.'

Patrick looked momentarily pleased and briefly shook Ralph's hand.

Mum woke up then and shouted, 'Men, bloody everywhere.'

Patrick smiled at her and said, 'I'm here to help.'

'She needs a rest,' shouted Mum, glaring at Ralph, as if the lack of sleep was his fault too. It was really.

'Yes, you should see if you can get some kip,' Patrick said. 'I can wait here. You guys must be knackered.'

Ralph took on a proprietorial air. 'It's fine, mate,' he said. 'Cheers but...' My mum humphed loudly and Dad woke up.

'Is he back?' he said immediately and having to say 'no' made me cry again.

Patrick came forward and awkwardly rubbed my back. 'I'll go and look round the town, then,' and went off.

'Are you going to ask Sunil to help?' Daisy asked, wide-eyed.

'Ummm...' I said, colouring. 'I'll definitely ask him for any ideas about what to do,' I wanted to add, 'when he messages me,' because surely he'd do that first thing to check that Wilf was OK.

Wilf didn't just turn up. Ralph had gone to the football club and waited there to find no sign of him, asked his friends to keep an eye out and then gone home to wait there. I sat shaking in my kitchen with my parents, Patrick and Marvin. It was an unlikely rescue party: Marv was wearing striped harem pants and sandals; my mother had her eyes shut. Patrick looked quite bewildered but was politely listening to my dad.

'What we need to do is gather all the evidence,' he was saying in his best professor voice. 'Map out the facts.

Ensure absolute objectivity through an entirely empirical approach.'

'Good suggestion,' Patrick said. 'The trouble with kids though – I'm a teacher—' Dad grunted something about 'fellow professional' while Patrick carried on '—is that their emotions during adolescence mean that we can't guarantee that it won't be a random outcome.'

'Random outcome, eh?' Dad prodded Mum, who opened one eye. 'This bloke might be a bit more with it than Callie's usual sort.'

'Not that there's been many lately,' she barked. I blushed – little did she know. I also couldn't be bothered to clarify that Patrick wasn't my boyfriend. Patrick smiled over at me though.

He continued, 'But, Mr Brown…'

'Please, call me Lorca,' Dad said.

'Lorca… we should start with your approach. Write down everywhere and everyone that Wilf has had contact with in the last few days and make a plan. I suggest that I go out and drive around again to some of the places you might expect Wilf to go in the day – parks, Maccy D's, that kind of thing; Marvin, you help Callie's folks with the plan, as you've described, and, Cal, well, you need to get a couple of hours' kip. Then you'll be better able to help later.'

'I'll never sleep,' I said, but with little resistance.

'We'll wake you up as soon as we hear anything,' Patrick said and pushed me gently in the direction of the door. It struck me anew how calm and together he was when he stopped trying to be funny; I was glad he was there. This might have shown in my knackered face because Marv raised his eyebrows theatrically at me. I ignored him.

Upstairs, I went into Wilf's room, which had the usual stench of used football socks, and breathed it in, cursing myself for all the times I'd made him put all his shoes outside the back door so that we weren't overwhelmed by their toxicity. I shut my eyes and willed him back into the fug.

His sheets were unmade; the desk was a muddle of screens and wires. It was the room of a boy who intended very much to come back. For a start, he didn't have his beloved Mac, which was in the centre of the desk. Beside it was *The Rough Guide to South Africa* – I supposed a present from Petra to get him acclimatised.

I looked amongst the piles of clothes and school books on the floor for a clue and spoke to him out loud, but softly. 'I'm *so* sorry, Wilf, please come home.'

Then I went into my own room to be faced with the evidence of my role in his running away. There on my dressing table was my make-up, spewed across the surface, as I'd painted my face in anticipation of going out with Sunil. I felt a new tang of shame: my infatuation with him had been sudden, physical and, in retrospect, foolish and ridiculous. The bed clothes were a tangle from the tussle of two bodies underneath them; my top was thrown into the corner where Sunil had ripped it off. What the hell had I thought I was doing?

Then, as I sat on the bed and, without bothering to take off my clothes, collapsed backwards, it occurred to me that the one person who'd not come rushing back this morning, or even rung up or messaged to find out if we – Wilf and I – were OK, was Sunil.

I then fell instantly into a troubled, restless sleep where I dreamed I was chasing Wilf across a desert: I could see him at all times in the distance, but I couldn't catch him up.

24

I woke by myself at 1 p.m. and immediately knew that this didn't mean good news. If Wilf had come back, someone would definitely have woken me up. As I went to pull on a jumper, I realised my fingers were crossed – and probably had been for hours.

The doorbell went as I got to the stairs. A different PC stood on the doorstep; he was young, and his face crumpled immediately into an expression of empathy without good news. 'We have yet to locate Wilf, I'm afraid, Ms Brown, but we wanted to talk you through next steps.'

He followed me into the kitchen to see Daisy typing onto her keyboard, my folks now looking even more weary and scared. The young PC said hello and stood while I hit the button on the kettle. He wouldn't have a coffee, thank you.

All the occupants of the table looked up in expectation. My mother even voluntarily switched the knob behind her ear.

'So, if we don't hear from Wilf by about 5 p.m. then we need to kick into action on social media,' the PC said. Daisy looked up expectantly and he didn't disappoint her. 'That will be led by you, I assume?'

'On it,' said Daisy.

'Then the next thing will be that we'll want your voice...' he looked at me '... on the local radio station in the morning, Ms Brown, along with his dad.'

'What if he's gone to London or something?' Daisy asked, and I shuddered. Sure, Wilf had grown up in a commuter town and could navigate the Tube from all his visits to London, but I hated to think of him being preyed on by the underbelly of the capital.

'It's a possibility,' the PC said and consulted his notebook. 'We see that Wilf's big passion is music, so he might have gone in search of something to do with that, but, for now, we're going to assume that at fourteen, with little or no money in his pocket—' this was a good point: how far could he get with no money? '—he is somewhere in this area, probably with access to someone who is giving him food.'

'We've mapped all that this morning.' Dad looked dismissively at the young PC. 'Our friend, Marvin, and that other man...'

'Patrick,' said Mum in a voice that indicated she was still suspicious of his existence.

'... yes, that other young man, Patrick, are off visiting all the places we identified now. I've asked them to capture the results in a spreadsheet format.'

The PC looked momentarily nonplussed but then recovered. 'That sounds very thorough.'

'What about that kid from Yoof and a Roof?' It suddenly occurred to me that out of all the people Wilf had been hanging out with lately, the newest addition was Fishy Pete. I explained to the policeman. 'My parents are part of a community and Wilf has been there quite a bit lately.'

'Oh, Pete was top of the list,' Dad said airily. 'After we went through a process of deduction.' More raised policeman eyebrows. 'He's the first person Marv will speak to, but I have no doubt he will be as worried as the rest of us.'

Marv rang just as the policeman had gone and said that he and Patrick had been to Seymour House and spoken to Pete and some of the other young residents. No one had seen him, they were very worried and promised to put all their social media nous to the fore the moment we started appealing on social media.

'Pat's being an angel,' Marv said in his camp way. 'So helpful and patient.'

'Great,' I said.

'He doesn't seem to know about what actually was going on...'

'You mean about Sunil? He doesn't need to know that. It's none of his business.' I didn't want him to know for all sorts of reasons, but I'd think about that later.

'Lips sealed here. We're going to the school next, just in case he's gone there.' It was a good thing that Patrick was with Marvin, who couldn't really hang outside a school on his own, dressed in stripy harem pants and a fur coat, even if it was a Saturday.

'Just find him,' I begged. 'Please find him.'

★

It was 2.00 p.m. The girls had gone for a nap now. Desperate, I messaged Sunil, and not because I wanted him to rush round for a repeat performance.

> Hi Sunil, Wilf has not come home since last night. Police involved. I just wondered whether with your experience, you have any ideas? Thanks Callie.

I accept that this was a little formal given what had gone down, let alone what had *nearly* gone down. But surely if he had been as upset about the situation as he'd said he was, he'd have messaged me?

Ralph turned up next. He'd been to sleep but had had no word from Wilf. 'I'm going out of my head with worry,' he said, flicking the kettle on as if he still lived in my house. 'And so's Petra. She's going to come and help.'

'Callie will not want that woman in her house,' snarled my mother, then, smiling sweetly at Ralph, 'Gosh, sorry, I thought I was talking to myself. Damn ear thing.'

If it hadn't been for the circumstances we were in, I might have laughed.

A text back from Sunil:

> That is worrying. The circumstances were unforgivable. Please believe you have my support. I will call later.

It was hardly full of unfulfilled lust. Or even a hint of it. And I thought 'unforgivable' was a bit strong.

Marv and Patrick came back at 4 p.m. and while he indicated no news with a shake of his head, Patrick smiled at me. 'He must be somewhere where he's getting food, that's for certain. Kids of his age are always starving.'

But what if that was someone who was doing unspeakable things to him? I didn't say this out loud.

'So now we kick off the social campaign,' Daisy told everyone from her vantage point of the kitchen counter. She liked action. I went and got two photos of Wilf – one in his school uniform and one dressed as he would at weekends: slouchy jeans and a T-shirt with an obscure DJ's name on the front, blue and white striped scarf round his neck. It almost broke me to hand them to her.

Daisy pressed on. 'And the post will read: "Missing since 10.45 p.m. on May fifteenth, Wilf Colesdown, aged fourteen. He may be riding a bike and should be wearing a black T-shirt, blue jeans and a black bomber jacket, with a stripy scarf. He has messy brown hair..."'

'Do you need the bit about messy?' Marv asked. 'Bit descriptive.'

Daisy deleted the word. '"... brown eyes and is one metre seventy cms."'

'Probably need it in feet and inches too for the parents,' Patrick pointed out. He stirred his tea.

Ralph gave no input, just nodded. 'Let's get it out there. Someone must know where he is.'

*

'Are you OK?' Patrick came towards me. I was hiding behind the old pear tree in our scrubby back garden, leaning against its gnarly trunk and gently sobbing.

I smiled. 'No, not really. Thanks so much for your help.'

'Shit, you have some stuff go down in your fam. Think about when it'll just be one of the stories you all tell at the kitchen table.'

'The one where Wilf ran away,' I said.

'What? Say that again? The one where...' It was a pretty accurate impression of my mother with her hearing aid off and I couldn't help but smile.

'That's nice to see,' Patrick said, cocking his face to the side. 'You with a smile on your gob. Want a hug?'

I hesitated for the moment. *He wouldn't want to hug me if he knew what I'd been doing last night to make Wilf run away.* But I stepped into his embrace. He even smelled capable; it was the first moment of calm I'd felt.

'I'll do anything to help,' he said into my hair.

I was crying into his shoulder, the relief of being held by someone so strong in such desperate circumstances overwhelming me. The tears rolled and great judders came from my stomach, up through my mouth and into the warmth of his shoulder. And Patrick stood strong and tall and not moving, just providing arms that wrapped round me as I wept.

Eventually he whispered in my ear, without letting go, 'Just let it out.'

I looked up, taking a gasp for breath, and tried to smile at him. And that was when, if something could go more wrong, it did.

Suddenly I was aware of how close my face was to his. How reassuring he felt. How small I was in his arms.

It was me who did it. I was the one who moved my mouth closer to his, pressed my head up so he was clear that I wanted to kiss him, offered him my lips with my eyes. And for a second, I saw his eyes flicker with a question and then his mouth briefly came down on mine.

It was a moment of madness. I knew that even as it happened. But for those brief seconds, it felt like the sanest thing I'd done in a long time. He was warm and solid, and his kiss was those things too. It lasted seconds.

But then, with a sudden snap, I leapt back. 'Oh, God, I didn't... I mean, not the right time and...' I was really going mad now. It was intense worry, lack of sleep, emotional overload and an absence of judgement and... this was the second man I'd kissed in twenty-four hours.

Patrick held onto one of my hands and smiled. 'We'll talk when this is all over.' Then he offered me the sleeve of his jumper to wipe my face with.

Oh, what had I done now? But I didn't have time to think about it then. We were needed back in the house.

In the kitchen, Lily, awake again, looked pale and haunted. *Please don't have another panic attack,* I pleaded with her silently, feeling awash with guilt now about leaving her for a few minutes – a few very confusing minutes. 'Shouldn't you guys be getting on with some revision?' I asked, but the twins looked as if I was crazy. But then, I'd proven I probably was.

They were busy starting to share all the social media posts that Daisy had made on Insta, Twitter and Snapchat. 'I've even reactivated FB and posted it to the local noticeboards,' Daisy told Lily. 'I'd forgotten just how Year 7 it was and how many parents are on it.'

'Just so 2015,' Lily agreed with a shudder.

Ralph had gone to search through Wilf's room for any clues as to where he might be. I wondered if he would sit, as I had, in the middle of Wilf's bed, sniffing the air and longing for the smell of the real him. But he'd only gone up a few stairs when the doorbell started ringing, loud and insistent.

I could see no one through the glass of the door, but when I pulled it open that just turned out to be because Petra was so small. She stood, in her weekend uniform of cashmere jumper and jeans, and faced me off.

'I'm here to help in the search for Wilf,' she hissed, 'and, from what I hear, it's you and your despicable behaviour that he's run away from.'

I sucked my lip but refused to retort. *But fuck you, Ralph, for telling your poisonous dwarf of a wife about Wilf catching me in the act.* I turned and glared at him as he hovered on the stairs.

'Just let her in, Cal,' he said eventually. I stood back, and she raced into the hallway and threw herself at Ralph as if he'd been the one who was missing.

'Oh, babe,' they both said in unison. It was as puke-making as it sounds.

My mother came out into the hall at that point and looked at the pair of them with undisguised disgust. 'This is Lois,' Ralph mumbled. 'Lois, this is Petra.'

'His wife,' Petra added, ignoring Mum's unsmiling face and holding out her hand. 'You must be Calypso's mother. Pleased to meet you.'

'What an extraordinarily high-pitched voice you have,' Mum said airily. 'I'll have to adjust my hearing aid.' Petra's outstretched hand went limp as my mother turned on her arthritic hip, clicked behind her ear, with a gesture that incorporated a million 'fuck you's' and hobbled off back to the sitting room.

As my eyes followed her down the hallway, there was Patrick, a grin dancing round his mouth. It was clear that he'd quite enjoyed seeing my mother in action.

I couldn't stand being in the same space as Petra, so I told the rest of the assembled kitchen that I was going to take Mum and Dad back.

'The kids at the centre have all said they'd help,' Marv said.

'What about Sunil? Isn't he going to help too?' Daisy asked. 'He's the expert.' I pretended not to hear her and shuffled my parents into the car.

'I'll go and get some food for dinner and snacks and stuff sorted,' Patrick said.

I heard Daisy mutter under her breath: 'At least he knows where all the takeaways are,' and gave her a glare. I didn't think Patrick heard her.

'Hey you don't have to stick around and help us,' I said.

'But I see it as my job to feed you now,' Patrick said. I smiled, remembered what had happened and then firmly put it to one side.

★

Seymour House was the usual: like the warm-up scenes in the movie *Fame*, except starring old people and without leg warmers. There was a disco-based fitness event being held in the main room to the right. Lots of octogenarians seemed to be doing 'the floss', following the directions of a very fit girl in a tight Lycra outfit in neon pink at the front of the room.

Along the corridor, in the online room, were a group of people moving mice around mats with enthusiasm.

Pete was with them. 'Lois! Lorca! We missed you every minute!' They smiled back. Why couldn't they see through his fake gushiness? 'Has Wilf come back?'

'No, he hasn't,' I said. 'Did he say anything to you – anything at all – that might be a clue as to where he is?'

Pete paused and then said, 'I'm aware only that he felt as if his family unit was… changing.' He said it in a voice that suggested that Wilf had trusted him with confidences. I eyed him.

Mum leapt in. 'Pete will do everything he can to help, won't you?'

'You have the support of everyone at Yoof and a Roof – the entire community is behind you in your search.' Pete turned his bogus voice back on. It was hard to ignore the almost langoustine-like aroma that came from him as he waved his arms around. 'The digital class here is on it like a car bonnet!'

My mobile rang then, and I grabbed it and punched 'answer'. It was the day-shift PC who was passing back to the team from the night before, confirming that he'd put out an appeal on their social media.

'I've got as many people sharing it as possible,' I said.

'Good. Now, we'd like to provisionally schedule tomorrow morning at 10 a.m. to record an appeal from you and Wilf's father.'

'OK,' I said. It had never occurred to me that I would end up as one of those exhausted, desperate parents on a TV appeal for a lost child.

'But we have every confidence that he will be home before that. Now, just to confirm, he had no money on him that you know about and no access to any?'

'He's got a bank card,' I said. 'But there's never any money in his account as he spends it all on EDM.' This policeman was so young that he didn't need to ask me what EDM was.

I put down the phone and Pete looked at me without smiling. 'On it, Callie, like a Shakespearean sonnet!'

Back at the house, the kitchen was crowded and busy: the AAs had arrived; Patrick was unpacking food onto the counter; Marv was at the table, huddled with the girls. There was, however, no sign of Ralph and Petra.

'Where are they?' I whispered to Marv.

He gestured over his shoulder at the door to the hall, which was closed. 'Last heard having a bit of a barney in the hallway.'

'Ooh,' I said, although I couldn't care less about the state of their marital relations.

'I could hear her call him a "spineless twat",' Marv said with relish. 'In that weird voice of hers. And get this.' He lowered his voice to a whisper. 'She said that taking him with them was all his idea in the first place and when she'd got married she didn't expect to be saddled with a teenage runaway. And then he told her to fuck off and leave him and his son alone.'

'I knew she didn't want him really.' I burst into tears. The sheer injustice of the situation floored me.

'Then Ralph said, "You can fix him now and lord it over him for life too", or something like that. And she stamped her foot and he called her a "fake fucking nun". I liked that one. It was a bit like the old Ralph.'

'What an absolute cow,' chorused Ajay and Abby, both hugging me. I hugged them both back. Abby got slightly uncomfortable about this after a couple of seconds.

'We met Patrick,' Ajay said, and glanced approvingly over at him as he unloaded plates from the kitchen cupboard. Patrick gave me a quick grin and I blushed.

'I got pizza,' he said.

'Like I said...' Ajay smiled on '... we met Patrick.' I was too tired to explain to Patrick how much Ajay liked food.

'Great,' I said, and he started to move towards the table with the pizza boxes. 'Got a pepperoni and a veggie one and one for the freaks that like pineapple...' Everyone was smiling at him, standing in the heart of my kitchen as if he belonged there. For a moment I thought he might.

It was then, though, that Sunil appeared at the back door.

Into the cold of my tiredness and fear, it still felt as if the world froze for a moment. I was back in the previous evening, desired and desiring. Then Wilf's voice, all innocent, talking about his mouth guard; then his face – horror-struck. Sunil, running out of the house as if his boxer shorts were on fire. Then nothing, all this long, long day.

He looked tired and apprehensive. His gorgeousness wasn't immediately apparent. But he came striding forward and grabbed my hands. 'Cal, we're going to sort this.' He said it with absolute conviction and looked into my eyes until I felt a blush rush up my face. Then he smiled round at everyone else, kept holding my hands and said, 'Sunil. From the youth charity, Resilient, and Cal's friend.'

'Hey, Sunil,' everyone said.

Marv was clearly fascinated. He made his 'OMG whooo-oooops' face. I glowered at him.

Patrick said, 'Hey, Sunil,' along with everyone else, but he took a step backwards. I remembered him seeing me simpering to Sunil in the street and how Sunil had made some sort of superior remark. It felt like weeks ago.

Oh, God, what had I done? Kissing him when I had just got *involved* with Sunil. I stepped forward. 'Sunil, you remember my friend Patrick,' I said, then introduced Marv, Ajay and Abby.

'Nice to see you again, mate,' Patrick said with a broad but stiff grin.

Sunil didn't seem to notice any atmosphere, but Marv and the AAs all raised their eyebrows.

It was then that Ralph and Petra came through the door from the hallway. At the sight of so many people gathered in my small kitchen, they froze. Petra looked tiny next to Ralph.

'This is Wilf's dad, Ralph, and his wife, Petra,' I said flatly.

'I'm *so* pleased to meet you all but wish it were not in such worrying circumstances,' Petra squeaked.

Abby was incapable of not saying the right thing in the right social circumstances, so she introduced everyone, ending with, 'Patrick, a friend of Callie's – and Sunil, also a friend, but also, did I hear that right? A local youth worker?'

'That's right,' Sunil said.

Perhaps Ralph was too tired to not say the first thing that came into his head. Perhaps he was just too worried. Or just too wrapped up in his own world.

'Sunil?' Ralph said. 'So, you were here last night when…'

'Last night?' Lily asked, bewildered. 'What? After the meeting?'

I was standing next to Patrick, who was close to the back door. I felt him freeze.

Marv looked both fascinated and horrified.

'You were one of the last people, other than Callie, to see Wilf?' Ralph was grasping at straws, desperate for information. Of course, at the same time he was also telling the rest of the room – including Patrick – that I'd been with Sunil last night when Wilf had done a runner.

'Umm, yes, but…' Sunil started.

Daisy looked with horror at her sister, who was mouthing, 'What, Mum…?'

Patrick took a step backwards to the doorway.

'Oh?' That was when Petra realised quite what was going on and her face shone with spite. 'So, you haven't told your friends quite what happened? Calypso? Is this true? None of you know the reason why Wilf ran away from this house?'

'Shut up,' Ralph muttered as my face went the colour of an aubergine.

'What's going on, Mum?' Daisy asked.

'N-nothing,' I stuttered. 'Wilf came back unexpectedly last night, when I was having a drink with Sunil...'

It was hard to miss the sharp intake of breath from Patrick, although Ajay did quite a good job of covering it up by also gasping in abject surprise.

Sunil looked worried. 'I was providing your mother with some support,' he started, but Daisy's face gradually went through disbelief to horror.

'You mean...?' Lily's face went through the same emotions a few second later.

'Yup,' Daisy confirmed her sister's thought process.

'But I don't get why,' Lily went on very quietly, 'that would...' She meant drive Wilf away.

'I'll talk to you about it later,' I said.

But there was no stopping Petra. She even seemed to grow a couple of inches as she started to speak. 'I think everyone needs to know the truth now, don't they, Calypso?'

'No.' Ralph.

'I think this is a private matter.' Sunil.

'Fuck.' Marvin.

'That Wilf ran away because he found you *in bed* with Sunil...'

Collective gasp. Everyone.

'You're out of order.' Patrick quietly and firmly in the direction of Petra. He didn't look at me.

'You were having *sex* with a man you *had just met*...' she hissed as if she were accusing me of whoring my arse on the corner of the street in broad daylight.

'That's not true—' Sunil started.

'To be fair, Wilf wasn't supposed to be coming home,' Marv leapt in. 'And Callie's hardly promiscuous.'

'Never gets any,' Ajay added. 'Ever.'

'What's her sexual history got to do with anything?' Daisy shouted. 'Men are always trying to slut-shame women. And—' looking directly at Petra '—you're a stupid cow.'

'Daisy!' I shrieked in horror.

'She called me a stupid cow, babe,' Petra said petulantly, as if she expected Ralph to do something to protect her honour.

'Don't call my wife a stupid cow, eh, Daisy?' Ralph mumbled.

'It's all your fault,' Daisy continued to both of them. 'Making Wilf go and live in another country and breaking up our family…'

Then everyone started shouting at once and, in the middle of it, Lily's eyes met mine. 'Look, it just happened, and Wilf came back and caught us, and he ran off,' I pleaded.

She said, into the mad chorus of voices, 'Did he think that you weren't around for him?'

'I think so, but that wasn't it at all…' I said. 'It was just a terrible accident of timing.'

'Yeah, it's not like you're off shagging every day, Ma,' Daisy said, before turning round and laying into Petra again. She was giving Daisy as good as she got, while Marvin threw in the odd jibe and Ralph stood back, his face a picture of horror.

Sunil was also glued to the kitchen cupboards, every now and then saying weakly to Daisy, 'Think peace and resolution, Daisy, peace and resolution.' I thought I heard him say something about Mandela.

That was when someone banged something really hard – a wooden surface, a door or a table – and said, 'Will you all just shut up, please?'

*

It was Patrick. His face was the colour of a terracotta stone, a pulse going in his forehead. We all turned and faced him and suddenly the noise died, aside from the lone, shrill voice that was Petra, who was saying, 'It's time a good example was given to my stepson—'

'Will you please be quiet?' Patrick said with absolute authority and, though her mouth went up and down like a fish in an aquarium, she did fall silent. 'Now, none of this is going to help get Wilf found, is it? I suggest you all stop arguing with each other and start behaving like worried responsible adults.'

'Quite right,' Sunil said. 'Well said, man.'

'We need a new plan,' Marv came in.

I walked towards Patrick, trying to express simultaneously thanks at what he'd done and horror at what he'd found out I'd done, with my eyes. *I'm sorry.*

But it was much more than wanting him to understand and forgive me. In this chaos, I needed him. I pleaded silently but his face was stuck in an expression of sad resolve.

'Right, I'll leave you to it if there's nothing we can do tonight,' he said though. 'I'm a few doors away if you need me.' And he was gone.

Sunil called, 'Cheers for your input to the cause, brother,' after him and Marv and the AAs raised their eyebrows again.

I felt beaten and moved back towards Lily, who was white. 'Oh, when will Wilf be home?' she wailed quietly to herself.

I went and put my arms round her and took her up the stairs; Daisy followed with pizza.

I pulled almost all of my lower lip into my mouth and bit hard, while I stared at the floor waiting for their judgement. I couldn't work out whether Daisy was going to go apoplectic or Lily have another attack.

But then Daisy started laughing in amazement: 'OMG, Ma, that is JOKES! Seriously, like Sunil? *You* and Sunil?'

'I wasn't doing anything wrong,' I said stiffly. It was hard enough talking to my daughters about the sex they were having or not having, let alone the sex I was having myself.

'I mean, most of the girls think he's a DILF, but people also thought he was gay and...' Daisy was going on in wonder. 'But we never thought... I mean, not that there's anything wrong with you, but remember what you say to us about getting to know a man first and all that?'

I nodded. Yes, I did say that. And both Daisy and Lily could do a fairly accurate impression of me saying, 'Only sleep with men you love,' when I'd had too much wine and became, as they put it, 'lecturey'. 'I've had two meetings with him since then,' I said weakly. 'And it was a bit of an attraction and...'

'I *said* you were grafting on him the other day,' Daisy continued with satisfaction. She still looked shocked though, as if it was just occurring to her that her ancient mother might still have an actual libido.

'The point is that it was awful when Wilf walked in – right into my bedroom,' I told her.

'Like ewwwww. That was a bit gross.' Daisy visibly shuddered.

'Like ewwwww,' Lily echoed.

'Do you think he thought I might not have time for him any more? That I've moved on? What do you think?' I was desperate for any answer that might make me understand his state of mind when he'd gone.

Lily came closer. 'Just in shock, I suppose'. She paused though and was thoughtful. 'But Wilf run away? It's just so unlike him.'

We sat together for a while on her bed, all of us holding each other, but with none of us having any answers.

25

Encouraging Lily to get some sleep, her sister and I went back to the kitchen where Daisy immediately said, 'All right, Sunil?' in a lurid tone designed to make him blush. It did.

Bodger got up lazily from under the table and circled him, then looked back at me as if to say, 'It's a crying shame,' but I was used to my dog being my guilty conscience.

Daisy continued her social media monitoring. 'It's had 3300 views on FB; loads of comments wishing him well; sixty-seven shares,' she said. 'The police mainly seem to be on Twitter. The guys at Seymour House are really going for it on Snapchat.'

Ralph and Petra stood by the side of the kitchen bench, some distance between them. Petra stared resolutely forward, silent and seething.

'Right,' said Sunil and, in the absence of Patrick, we all looked at him for guidance. 'I'm going to get as many people as I can together for tomorrow morning. We'll have a rally and an organised search. Get some media attention.'

'The police want Ralph and I to record an appeal at ten,' I told him.

'*I'm* his stepmother,' Petra spat, and Ralph rounded on her.

'Enough,' he said with more firmness than I'd heard in years. She looked at him aghast.

Marv said, 'I'll stick with Daisy on getting the message out there on social – it's my day job.'

'Shall I make a banner?' Abby asked.

Sunil looked at her appreciatively. 'A banner would be just great.' No wonder people would pick Abby over me in the face of a zombie apocalypse.

He directed his next sentence at me. 'So, we'll gather at the youth centre and then we'll march to the places that Wilf normally visits. We'll give out flyers with his picture on it.'

'I'll make those too,' Abby volunteered. 'Ajay and I will do it now.'

Sunil clapped his hands at her efficiency. 'Now, the most important thing is that you get some sleep.' It was the first caring thing he'd said to me. I tried to argue but the whole room – with the exception of Petra – chorused their approval.

'We're all going to take it in turns to stay up and keep an eye on the social media alerts,' Marvin said, and the AAs nodded. 'As soon as something happens, or we get even a twitch, we'll wake you up.'

'Where will you all sleep?' I asked.

'Sofa? Wilf's bed? In with you? Don't worry about us, we'll make ourselves at home,' Marv said.

'And the police are on it?' Sunil asked.

I momentarily wished for Patrick's cheerful lack of ego. Would I ever see him again, beyond a polite I'm so glad you got Wilf back text or a nod in the street while I put out the bins? He certainly wouldn't pretend it was an accident to come out of his house at exactly the same time as I walked Bodger. I minded more than I'd thought I would.

'I'll call the police and then see if I can pass out.'

'We'll go back home.' Petra stamped her foot as she spoke. Bodger growled at her as she went to the door and waited for Ralph to join her.

'Hey you go,' he said, with a distinct lack of 'babe'. 'I'm staying here and joining in the rota until we find my son.'

The police reassured me that they were doing everything they could to find Wilf and we should stick to the plan. I told them about Sunil's idea of holding a rally the following morning.

'We hope to have found him by then,' the PC said. 'But it can't do any harm. Organised by that new bloke at the youth centre, you say?'

'Sunil, yes.'

'Good at getting himself on telly, him.' The PC sniffed. 'Well, if it helps to find the boy, it can't do any harm.'

I confirmed I'd be at the station in the morning with Ralph and clicked off. Then I lay on my side, the phone beside me, and willed my brain to quiet.

When I woke a few hours later, my first feeling was that I was still exhausted. It was still dark outside – the middle of the night, then. And Wilf, where was Wilf in this darkness? Tears started to wash down my face before I could stop them, and I let them continue until my pillow was soggy and a chorus of birds welcoming the early summer dawn could be heard from the garden.

At 7 a.m. I texted Sunil confirming we would be at the centre after the police interview.

He texted back:

Media all lined up and ready to go. I still feel terrible about what happened.

I decided I was not interested in how he felt.
Then I texted Patrick.

Rally planned for later if you can join us.

I paused and then added:

I would love your support. Thanks for everything.

The reply was immediate, but it certainly didn't have the friendliness of his previous messages.

Fingers crossed that this will lead us to him quickly. I'll be there later.

I knew that once Wilf was found this would hurt. But right now, all I could think about was him.

★

Ralph was arguing down the phone in the garden while I got ready to go to the police station, eventually clicking 'end call' and leaning against the pear tree, where I'd lost it with Patrick yesterday, sighing and rolling a fag.

'Perhaps he's worked out quite who he's married,' Marv said, clicking the kettle for another coffee.

'Cow. Total cow,' Ajay and Abby chorused from the sofa.

Ralph, grubby from lack of sleep and the same clothes, had started to take on more of the air of the man I'd lived with – a bit less shiny; a bit more hobo. I supposed I looked just as tired although Marv made me have a shower, put on a clean shirt and wear make-up. 'It's a good thing you've lost weight lately,' he commented when I was ready. 'Video puts a stone on, apparently.'

The young day-shift PC was waiting for us at the station and quickly showed us into a small room, which was set up with a camera and sound-recording equipment. We sat behind a table side by side but apart, and an even younger PC gave us simple instructions about talking slowly and clearly.

Ralph spoke first – a plea from the heart. 'Wilf, we know you might hear this or see it online and all we want to say is come home, son. Please come home.'

I kept it simple too. 'Wilf, we love you, all of us – Daisy, Lily and me too – we are so worried about you and we would love it if you got in touch.'

'And if anyone else is watching this who knows where Wilf is, please, please contact the police and tell them anything you know,' Ralph added desperately. 'Please come home, Wilf.'

He doesn't know where home is any more, Ralph. That's the problem. I pleaded with my eyes and, finally, there was a flicker of understanding in his face.

There was a long pause and then he added quietly, 'And home is wherever you choose it to be, Wilf.'

The policeman behind the camera looked up as if he was unsure whether to stop filming but Ralph stumbled on. 'We need to talk about everything.' The PC looked very confused. 'And if you don't want to go to Cape Town,' Ralph eventually whispered straight into the camera, 'then we'll stay here, son.'

Afterwards, out on the pavement, Ralph leant against a wall and concentrated on opening a packet of Golden Virginia and pulling out a Rizla.

I'd slumped in my chair as I'd heard him finally say that he wouldn't take his son away, with a mixture of disbelief, exhaustion and relief. Ralph had refused to look at me, but when the camera had been switched off, he'd grasped my hand for a second. Then he'd let go and sunk back in his chair.

'I think we'll cut it at the bit where you say we need to talk about everything,' the PC said. 'Keep the bit about Cape Town for any follow-up we need to do. Now we'll get on with this and put out a short clip on our social media feeds later.'

Now I said to Ralph as he dexterously made a rollie, 'Did you mean that? About not making him move?'

He gave me a short smile. 'I think he needs to know he has a choice.'

I grimaced. 'It's right that he's with you though. Now you're better and all that.'

Ralph looked up and gave a hollow laugh. 'I've been a really crap dad, haven't I?'

'Not lately. You and Wilf seemed to be getting on really well in the last few months.'

'But it was you who looked after him when I was incapable of even *being* a parent.' He looked as if he wanted to rip out his soul, throw it on the floor and stamp on it. 'And I expect I never really told you how grateful I am about that. You're an amazing woman, Cal.'

I nodded. He'd made a couple of half-arsed attempts to thank me in the past for being there for Wilf, but this was heartfelt. 'Thank you.'

'And I was shit to you too,' he said. 'The funny thing is that I would have said that to various counsellors and so on when I was getting better, but I probably never said sorry directly to you.'

I hadn't really wanted him to apologise to me for me, but I had wanted him to recover for his son. I'd known for a long time that Ralph and I were done, our story complete.

'And Petra, you know, she came along—'

'She came along at a time when you needed someone like her to lean on,' I interrupted. He put the fag in his mouth and lit it. I leaned against the wall next to him. 'Come on, she's a nightmare, but she *has* turned you into a sober, solvent adult. And she gets off on that.'

'I thought Cape Town would be a new start for me, for Wilf, without all the memories…'

'The memories of Sylvia, you mean?'

He nodded slowly and tried in his bumbling way to say something about all the memories we'd created too, but both of us knew that it was what had come before us that was most powerful.

The truth was that Sylvia and Wilf had been Ralph's real family. Both his parents were dead by the time he'd finished uni; he'd met Sylvia there and they'd been together until she'd died. Over the years it had become clear that Sylvia had mothered Ralph in the same way as I'd ended up doing, but his heart had always belonged with her.

I remembered exactly when he'd told me about what had happened to her. It was right at the start of us getting to know each other, at a barbecue at the school to raise money for a new playground. All the children were racing around, high on Haribo, and we were eating the sort of burgers that made you think immediately of salmonella.

'You know Wilf's mum died of a brain tumour, right?' Ralph said in a straightforward way that made me look straight into his eyes. I must have looked a bit surprised at his frank tone as he blushed. 'Sorry,' he said. 'I've got this thing where it's easier to just come out and say it to people rather than watch them dancing around the subject or having to answer lots of questions about being a single dad.'

'We're not that great talking about death, are we?' I said. 'Just "I'm sorry for your loss" and "let me know if there is anything I can do".'

'And casseroles,' Ralph said. 'I got a lot of casseroles.'

He took a bite of his burger and I smiled at his attempt to lighten the conversation.

'How's Wilf settling in?'

He gestured in the direction of Wilf, who was at the top of the slide with a queue of small boys behind him. 'He's mostly fine, much better since we moved. But it still hits him hard sometimes and he loves talking about her – I try really hard to keep her memory alive. He was only two and a half when she died so I think he only has a hazy picture of her now.'

He said it in a way that suggested he was betraying her by not keeping her memory crystal clear and sharp for Wilf. I felt very sorry for him, but he seemed stoic, if sad; making the best of the situation, while accepting the shit life had thrown at him.

It was only much later – when he had what could loosely be called his breakdown but was really a gradual descent into alcoholism – that I understood. In those early years right after Sylvia died, when Wilf was a tiny child with so many needs – all of which needed to be provided by his dad – Ralph had no choice but to function. He changed his job to a freelance role to give him more flexibility; moved his son from the north London flat he'd shared with Sylvia to our smaller town in the countryside; delivered him to and collected him from his new school every day and then played with his son, fed, bathed and read to him. Then when Wilf was asleep, he'd do a bit more work and eventually allow himself to open the black box that held all his memories of his dead wife. He told me once that he always cried quietly then, so as not to wake Wilf, and I imagined him, a can of beer in his hand on his old couch, his shoulders shaking from his loss, no sound escaping.

Once he and I had been together for a few years – the good, early years – and Wilf was safe, the black box opened up without invitation, coaxing him in. There was a time at the beginning of his downward trajectory when he seemed haunted, as if there were a shadow following him around; eventually the shadow was evident in his face, and, after that, we had the terrible times when he seemed to give up on everything and all of us.

So, when Ralph said now, 'I'm sorry, really sorry. I wanted a new start where Wilf wouldn't think of me as some useless drunk,' I nodded slowly.

'He hates thinking of you like that,' I said. 'Never discusses it, won't talk about it.'

'Exactly. So, I thought if we moved with Petra, then he'd never have to think about it again. When she wanted to go back to South Africa, it was me who insisted we took him with us – I couldn't leave him, you know that. I honestly don't think it occurred to her until then. But after that, she kicked into action and wasn't going to let anything stand in her way.'

'I just wish she didn't see it as a competition with me.' I sighed. 'Like in order to be a good mother she's got to prove I'm a bad one.'

'And lately, it's like she wanted to be there between us all the time – managing how I got on with my own son.'

'Yeah, Wilf said it was a bit... overwhelming. Look, I'm really sorry that he caught me... you know...'

'He wasn't supposed to be there,' Ralph said. 'Cal, you want to go to bed with someone you should be able to, without thinking of whether my kid is going to walk through the door.'

It still sounded so crass and bald somehow – 'go to bed with someone'. I blushed while Ralph carried on. 'And you deserve some fun. It's time you started putting yourself first.' He stubbed out his rollie on the pavement and kicked it towards a drain. 'I've been a shit dad.'

'You're still his dad.'

'And you're the closest thing he's ever had to a mum.'

God, what a mess modern families could be. It went much deeper than DNA. But if Ralph had been my family – and, maybe in a small way, still was – then this conversation, deep in our shared worry, was a bit like having the old him back again for a while.

'Cape Town will still be there in a couple of years when Wilf's grown up a bit and finished school.' Ralph shook his head as if he was practising the arguments he would use on Petra. I still didn't believe that he'd have the strength of character to stand up to her. 'Right, come on, let's get to this rally and see if your mate—' he had the grace to wink at me '—is going to be any help getting Wilf back.'

Sunil had a small crowd gathered round him outside the youth centre. Daisy and Lily – her hand tucked into Aiden's bulging arm – were there; Marv and the AAs stood back a little. There were a few of Wilf's friends and their parents. Petra was bouncing up and down at the front, tiny and glossy. Her blonde hair fell over her shoulders as she raced towards Ralph and threw her arms round his neck, shouting, 'Babe! Oh, babe.' He cautiously patted her on the back in return.

I stepped aside and looked round for Patrick, but there was no sign of him.

As we approached Sunil waved impatiently at us. There were two enormous banners – certainly not the much smaller ones that Abby had made overnight on my kitchen table – erected across the front of the GenZ centre. One read: 'Our young are our future', the other: 'The government needs to protect our children'.

They *were* definitely the future and the government *certainly* had a role in protecting them, but this didn't seem that relevant to me, when what we were supposed to be doing was drawing attention to the fact that Wilf was missing.

I looked in a questioning way at Sunil, but he was busy welcoming a reporter and a cameraman from the local TV station, who pulled up at that moment. They clambered out of a small van, clapping Sunil on the back in a way that implied they knew him well, and the cameraman quickly slung a camera on his shoulder.

Sunil climbed onto a chair and indicated that Ralph and I should come and stand on either side of him, like courtiers at each side of the king. Petra pushed herself right in front of him so that she was definitely part of the shot.

'What's with the banners? Where's Abby's banner with Wilf's picture on it?' I shouted up at Sunil over the noise of the crowd, but he was busy holding up a megaphone.

'Ready when you are, Sunil,' shouted the reporter.

And he was off. 'People, we are gathered here today because of the great tragedy of what is happening to our young people...'

Were we? This didn't sound specific to Wilf at all. 'Wilf!' I shouted up at him.

'And because a valued member of our local community, a young man named Wilfred Colesdown...'

'His name is Wilf, not Wilfred,' called Jowan, who was leaning against a lamp post with his bike. I looked over approvingly at him, but Sunil carried on as if he hadn't been heckled.

'… has seen fit to disappear… DISAPPEAR… in the face of the continued neglect shown by the government to our young people, the DISINTEREST that the Tory government has spearheaded, so that we raise a generation of children who have NO ACCESS to VITAL RESOURCES…'

'What the hell has this got to do with Wilf?'

The voice came in my ear and I turned, doused with relief, to find the solid shape of Patrick behind me. I wanted to hurl myself into his arms there and then, but I knew I couldn't. So instead I said, 'I'm so glad you're here.'

'About time someone put an end to this bullshit,' he said, pushing me aside.

Sunil was still ranting into the megaphone to the confused crowd. 'Wilfred had NO ACCESS to VITAL SERVICES, which help our young develop RESILIENCE…'

By now Patrick was in front of the chair on which Sunil was standing, and the cameraman from the local news was gesticulating at him furiously to get out of the way. 'Aren't we supposed to be talking about Wilf?'

Sunil stumbled for a while and looked confused, but quickly pressed on. 'So today we are calling for the government of this country to BACK OUR YOUNG…'

'Hear, hear,' shouted Petra.

'NO!' and Patrick reached up and grabbed the megaphone from Sunil's hands, in a way that made him wobble on the chair.

'Hey!' Sunil cried.

'Sorry, mate.' Patrick turned round and tried to pass the megaphone to me instead. Sunil clambered off the chair and there was an unsightly tussle while he tried to get it back from Patrick, who moved and dodged him.

'Give that man back his property,' screamed Petra. By her side, Ralph flapped – his natural inclination in this kind of scenario was to run, fast. The cameraman looked confused but kept rolling while the two men wrangled over the megaphone.

'This is supposed to be about getting Wilf back,' Patrick shouted, and the small crowd started to cheer.

'I was coming to that,' Sunil snarled. 'Back me up here, Callie!'

'Just let her talk instead,' shouted Marv.

'We need to get on with it,' Lily joined in. 'My brother has been missing now for thirty-six hours and we really, really want him home.' She burst into tears and Aiden wrapped her thin body in his over-exercised arms.

I went to her side. 'What she said.'

'But I know what I'm doing,' Sunil went on, direct to me. 'You need to have faith in my approach, Callie.'

'No, she doesn't,' Patrick said, sizing up to him, Deliveroo rider to buff activist, but somehow seeming bigger in every way.

'Let's get our grandson back,' shouted a new voice – Mum, arriving round the corner with Dad, ahead of a small pack of very slow-moving older people, accompanied by a couple of the youth members of Seymour House, including Pete, dressed as usual like a reject from a particularly naff circus.

'What she said!' the crowd roared, as if in unison.

The reporter was jumping around with excitement. 'Keep rolling,' he told the cameraman.

Marvin and the AAs came rushing forward and formed a small human wall between the chair and Sunil. He continued to dodge and dance on the spot.

Patrick thrust the megaphone into my hand and, holding my other arm, urged me onto the chair. I wobbled for a while but put the metal cone in front of my face.

'Right,' I said, staring out across the small crowd of friends and family, and trying to ignore the camera, which was now pointed straight into my face.

'We're here, not for any political reasons, but because our boy...' I glanced down at Ralph, who nodded in agreement '... Wilf...' my voice caught for a while '... is missing and someone must know where he is.' My voice gathered strength as I spoke and suddenly I was transported, my words coming with no effort from me, as if they were being pulled from my heart. 'And we love him so much, all of us—' I indicated towards Ralph and Petra, then Mum and Dad, Daisy and Lily and to the whole crowd '—and please, please, Wilf, come home to us. We are so desperate to know you are OK.

'And I'm sorry your family isn't perfect and that we've got things wrong.' Daisy and Lily glared at Sunil. 'But you know what? We *are* your family and you belong with us.'

Marv wiped a tear dramatically. Mum and Dad cried in unison, 'Come home, Wilf!'

I pressed on, needing to tell him, as directly as I could, that he didn't have to run away from home because he was confused about what that home was any more. 'Your dad says that we all need to sit down and talk about things, Wilf.'

Petra looked furious. But Ralph nodded agreement to what I was saying. 'Home is where YOU choose it to be,

Wilf. We'll always be here for you and your dad will always be where you are.'

Petra understood what it could mean. She turned on her heel and glared at Ralph, her mouth open but no words coming out.

I started to cry then – great big sobs of grief and a torrent of tears that shook my body and came out as a series of painful groans into the megaphone. Patrick leapt up and, putting his hands under my arms, picked me up and dropped me to the ground next to him. There was a collective 'aaah' from the crowd.

Holding me to one side, he took the megaphone from me. 'Right, we're all here to help find Wilf. So, I suggest we split up into smaller groups and go to the major centres in the town…'

'Leaflets here.' Abby bounced into view, holding a bundle of A5 printouts with Wilf's photo on the front. 'Banners, anyone? Come on, let's get organised.' I'd give her the role in the zombie apocalypse too, frankly. Lily and Daisy came in to hug me, Lily crying alongside me. Patrick and Abby quickly shuffled people into three groups and agreed where they would head.

'That was amazing, great for the lunchtime news,' the reporter said. 'That really came from the heart.'

Sunil started remonstrating with him. 'Come on, you must have *some* footage you can use of my speech… We need to get the big issues in.'

'I think the story is about the missing kid, don't you?' The cameraman turned to focus on a group, including my parents, that was shuffling back up the street.

Petra, having been shaken off by Ralph, chased after the camera and joined the back of that group. 'I'm the boy's stepmother,' she said.

Daisy was unusually quiet. Then she said in my ear, 'Sunil was a bit of a twat then, wasn't he?'

I put my arm round her too, so that we stood, the three of us, in a line and started to move forward. 'Yup,' I said. 'Come on, let's see if we can find Wilf.'

Patrick didn't leave my side all that long morning, but he wouldn't meet my eyes and stood at least a foot away from me. We banged on the doors of the houses in the streets near where we lived and handed over a leaflet each time, pleading with whoever answered the door to keep their eyes peeled. Our numbers grew as more and more people joined the search, but by 1 p.m., when my friends and family decided to go into my house to go to the loo and drink some water, there was still no sign of him.

I didn't know whether we were doing any good, but at least it was action.

'I'll have a check online while we're here,' Daisy said. She hadn't said any more about Sunil, but 'twat' was pretty accurate from where I was standing. I felt only shame at how in thrall I'd been to someone who obviously always put himself first.

Patrick clicked on the kettle and said, 'Good idea,' to Daisy. She sat down at the table and he turned his attention to Lily. 'You OK over there?'

'I will be when Wilf's back,' she said vehemently and sat down next to her sister.

'Goals,' said Aiden and shuffled off into the back garden. Bodger followed him enquiringly.

Mum and Dad came in slowly, followed by Marv and the AAs, and everyone sat, exhausted and a little deflated that we still hadn't found him.

'Shall we turn on the telly?' Marv asked. 'It was going to be on the lunchtime news.' He clicked the set into life and there, filling up most of the screen, was an image of me, shouting into a megaphone.

'Wow,' said Marv.

Everyone else shouted, 'Shhhhhhh.'

'Woman's emotional plea for the return of missing teenage boy' ran the headline at the bottom of the screen.

The reporter from earlier appeared then. 'Today, a local woman sent a heartfelt appeal for the child she considers her son, having raised him from the age of six, who has been missing since late Friday evening. Wilf Colesdown is fourteen and has lived in the town most of his life. Calypso Brown was standing beside Wilf's father, Ralph Colesdown, when she said, "Our family may not be perfect, but we are your family and you belong with us."'

There was a collective gasp in the room as the camera cut to me, standing on the flimsy-looking chair, tears streaming.

'Ooh, Mum, you were brilliant,' said Daisy.

'Shhhhhhh,' everyone else howled.

The reporter was on the screen again. 'The police have also put out an appeal on social media where Wilf's father told him they just want him home to talk about everything.' Cut to Ralph's face, wan and pleading in the small room at the police station. 'It is believed that Wilf is still in the area. Anyone with any information is asked to call the police station as soon as possible.' He read out a number that was then featured on the bottom of the screen.

As the news anchor moved to talk about another feature, my sitting room erupted.

'So great – that's sure to get loads of attention.'

'Straight from the heart, Cal!'

'Proud of you – let's hope it gets him back.'

'Not invisible any more,' Marv hissed at me as he came forward and hugged me fiercely.

'You were great,' Patrick said quietly, but then looked away.

'Let's just hope it helps find Wilf,' I muttered.

'Come on, Marv, Lil, let's start on that footage now, get it out everywhere online,' Daisy urged.

I felt flat, exhaustion mixing with the feeling of seeing this desperate image of me out there in the world. I sat for a moment on the sofa arm and tried to find some strength.

It was then that there was a cry from the kitchen.

'Oh, fuck,' Daisy shouted. 'Mum, come quick. I think there's something.'

And as I flew over those few feet to stand behind her at the screen, Marv was saying, 'I really think it might be...'

On the screen was a photograph of Fishy Pete, standing beside mixing decks, with a banner across the middle of it, Snapchat-style. It read:

Shoutout for missing kid Wilf! Share widely.

But more importantly, just visible in the corner of the picture, was a blue and white striped shape.

It was an image I immediately recognised.

It was the stripy scarf that Wilf always wore when he went out on his bike.

26

What happened next could best be described as a hullabaloo.

'It's his scarf. There! Behind Fishy Pete.' I burst into tears.

'Who's Fishy Pete?' Abby.

'What about Pete?' Mum, from the other room.

'There. On the computer.'

Daisy grabbed the laptop and raced it into the sitting room. 'Lois, Lorca, look! This is a Snapchat shoutout that Pete from your centre has put out and just there, in the corner, look, it's Wilf's scarf.'

Mum and Dad peered at the screen. 'That's Pete's room at Seymour House,' said Dad.

I stood in the doorway between the two rooms. 'Do you think Wilf could be there? Do you think Pete has been hiding Wilf all this time?'

'Doesn't make any sense.' Dad shook his head.

Mum looked bewildered. 'But why would he do that?'

'God knows,' Patrick cried, 'but who cares? We need to get down there NOW.'

I rang Ralph from Patrick's car. He sounded as bewildered as everyone else. 'But he said he hadn't heard from Wilf, the kid, Pete. You spoke to him – and so did Marvin,' he said.

The phone was obviously playing on speaker in Petra's car as she joined in. 'I hope you're not getting your hopes up, Calypso. Wilf could just as well have left his scarf there.'

I hated her for being right. In fact, I just hated her generally, but I swallowed my pride and said, 'We're on our way there now. At least we can find out what's going on.'

Patrick ignored the 'we' and put his foot harder on the accelerator. And I'd said it unwittingly, but I'd also meant the wider 'we' – Daisy, Lil and Aiden in the back of the car; my parents following in Marv's and Ajay and Abby behind that in her sports car.

Then I called the station – the phone was picked up by PC Warren. 'We'll meet you there,' she said with muted professional excitement.

As I put the phone down Lily whispered, 'I really, really hope he's there.'

'But why would that stupid twat not have told the truth?' Daisy said. 'I mean, he came on the fucking rally and everything. He's been really active on Snapchat.'

After all this was over, I'd *have* to sort her potty mouth.

'Makes no sense,' Aiden grunted.

'I have no idea,' I said. 'But let's just hope that he's safe.'

Inside the gothic walls of the car park of Seymour House, we sprang out of the car. PCs Moshulu and Warren came speeding in next, a blue light wailing. The other cars followed, including Petra's Mini, Ralph scrambling out before it finally halted.

'Right, we'll take care of this, if you don't mind.' The PC motioned the gathering crowd to stay back.

'You don't think he's dangerous?' I asked.

'We have no reason to believe that,' said PC Warren and they were off inside the centre. As the door swung open we could hear the familiar bubble of music and lively chatter.

'I'm going in with them,' said Ralph and he raced behind them.

'I have no idea why Pete wouldn't mention the scarf,' Dad said, shaking his head.

'Nor do I. Such a lovely boy,' Mum said.

'We've got to wait, so why don't you come and sit on this bench?' Daisy must have known that my parents were about to push everyone else over the edge. I looked at her gratefully as she led them a small distance away.

I crossed all my fingers behind my back. 'Oh, please, please, let him be here and be all right.'

It felt as if a million years passed. Everyone was silent, and then, suddenly, so was the centre.

'Police have shut that party *down*,' Marv said.

'Do you think that means…?' I asked, hope rising like steam in my bones.

But before he could answer, there he was.

Wilf.

Tucked under his father's arm, the blue and white scarf back round his neck, but, aside from that, being led with love and care down the front steps of the centre.

He looked down at the floor but was clearly crying as his skinny shoulders shook. There was a huge, relieved cheer at the sight of him from the rest of the crowd.

Then Wilf looked up and saw me. He gently broke free from his dad and ran into my arms. I hugged him as if I would never let him go again.

27

It was important that Wilf had the time he needed now; everyone else seemed to know that too. His grandparents, sisters and friends took turns, grabbing and hugging him, but leaving the questions for now. He was pale, sobbing now quite freely, his eyes wide with something between shock and relief.

Only Petra said, 'Well, young man, what has been going on here?'

But Ralph shushed her with a glare and a curt: 'Later, leave it.'

All I wanted was him home safe and away from that place forever. I thanked everyone else for all their help, in between tears. 'I'm so glad he's OK, but Wilf needs to rest now. I'll let you all know what's going on later.'

Daisy and Lily hugged him hard. 'Knew you'd be back, Bro,' Daisy said but her twin just looked happy.

One of the policemen came out of the big door next, his hand behind the back of Pete, whose arms were behind his back in handcuffs. His cheery demeanour was gone now, despite the red trousers and the Breton top, his mop of hair was flat and greasy over a face purple with rage. As the officer pushed him into the car, he turned and snarled at us. 'The family is a fucking capitalist construct, man. You choose who you love in life.'

'All right, you'll have your say down the station, sunshine,' the police officer said and put his hand on top of Pete's head to get him into the back seat.

'Do you think that's what made him take Wilf?' Mum asked Dad, super loudly. *'Capitalism?'*

'I have absolutely no idea, but I feel *very* let down,' he replied. Other residents came and stood on the steps as the patrol car drove off and threw questions at my parents.

'We've absolutely no idea,' Mum shouted at them all. Then she turned to Dad and said, 'I think we'd be better off on our own right now, don't you, Lorca?'

'Shall I drop you back at your old house?' Marvin asked.

'Yes,' said Dad. 'That sounds about right for us, now.' I promised to call them later.

Patrick opened the door of his car so that I could get in. 'Do you mind if I sit in the back with Wilf?' I whispered, and he shook his head.

'I'm so glad it's over,' he said, but somehow still grave. Wilf sat holding my hand in silence and Patrick drove us home, without a word.

When he'd parked, he just stiffly raised a hand and said, 'I'll leave you to it, then,' and, after placing a big hand on Wilf's shoulder, was gone towards his door, steps away. As I shouted my thanks at his back, and he turned round to acknowledge them, it felt as if there was a very big distance between us indeed.

'I can roast a chicken,' I said as we came into the hallway.

'Winner, winner,' Wilf whispered – his first real words other than to confirm he was OK.

Ralph came bounding up the steps behind us. 'I'm just so glad to see you, son.'

Petra was lingering outside. I simply turned and shut the front door and Ralph didn't argue.

Wilf looked at his dad, who simply said, 'We'll have a chat, later, yeah? And look, wherever you want to be, I'll be. We don't have to go anywhere.'

Wilf looked for a moment as if he wasn't hearing right. 'You mean… I mean…' and he looked at me for reassurance.

'Your dad means it,' I said gently. 'Now, come on, you'd better have a shower, while I put that chicken in the oven.'

And Wilf walked up the stairs to his bedroom, where he belonged.

'I'm really sorry about what you saw,' I said, catching him as he came back down, clean and having even shaved off the blond bum fluff from his top lip. He had on track-suit bottoms and an old orange T-shirt.

He blushed. 'Sorry for barging in,' he mumbled. 'It was just a shock.'

'Yeah, I mean, ewwww,' added Daisy coming out of the kitchen doorway. 'I mean, who wants to know about their parents getting it on? Like seriously, ewwwww.'

'Daisy...' I warned but she'd made Wilf laugh and the horrible moment go away.

'It didn't mean I didn't have time for you or want you,' I said, because it was important to me that he heard this. 'I will always love you, Wilf.'

'Like, vom,' said Daisy, but he came towards me and let me hug him again.

Ralph was tucking into roast chicken alongside the kids, as if he'd missed my cooking.

'Petra doesn't agree with meat,' he mumbled.

'You can cook your own food, you know,' I grumbled, and Wilf smiled at me.

'Yeah, what about feminism?' Daisy hissed at Ralph. He ignored her and carried on slurping gravy.

'Yum, Bisto,' said Lily and smiled at me. It was so lovely to see her happy and relaxed and taking the mickey out of me, that I just smiled back too.

It felt odd having Ralph there, rejoining our odd little family, albeit temporarily, but it also felt right, after everything that had happened. Eventually he put down his knife and fork and looked over at his son. 'You about ready to tell us what happened?'

Wilf had been spending time with Pete, as we knew, making music, but he'd also been listening in to Pete's conversations with Mum. 'They get pretty deep,' he said. 'And Pete said families weren't real. They were just something that society fed us to keep us controlled.'

'What about DNA and evolution?' Lily asked.

'I don't know.' Wilf flushed. 'He just kept going on about people choosing their families, rather than being born into them. It made a bit of sense, like, well, like Cal not being my real mum, but also just like a real mum, I suppose.'

Ralph nodded slowly.

'Is it because he lives in that centre with what would have been strangers?' Daisy asked.

'Maybe he doesn't like his own family,' added Lily.

'He said his mum didn't love him and stuff like that,' Wilf said. 'But, you know, most of the time we were on the decks.' And where were my parents when this was all going down? Wilf answered without me having to ask. 'Lorca pretended to be really into mixing, but he was mostly asleep, and Lois just talked and then fell asleep too. That place knackered them.'

'And then what happened?'

'Well, I told him all about having to go to Cape Town… I mean, going to Cape Town.'

Ralph nodded but only said, 'Yeah, we'll talk about that.'

'Go on,' I urged.

'And he kept telling me that the only true thing… he used a word: "authentic" …'

'Yeah, authentic,' repeated Daisy.

'Well, authentic thing, was to choose who was in your life. I was just going along with what he said, but when I came back and…'

'Yup, let's skip over that,' I said.

Both girls went, 'I mean, ewwwwwww.'

Ralph looked at me sympathetically.

'Well, I was upset, and I went there, and Pete let me in. He said I should just stay there the night, in his room so I didn't wake up Lois and Lorca, and because it was against the rules to have guests and stuff, and that seemed a good idea.'

'You should have let us know where you were,' I couldn't help saying. Wilf went red.

'You were angry, though, right?' Daisy threw in. I tried to remember he was only fourteen, when new emotions were racing through veins that weren't ready for them.

'Sorry, go on.'

'Anyway, in the morning, he kept going on about how it was a good idea to make people understand what they were doing to kids when they messed with their lives like you guys had... Anyway, he told me loads of stories about his mum never being there for him and sending him away to school and stuff like that.'

'He wants revenge on mothers,' Daisy said.

'He's dangerous,' Ralph cried. 'I mean, he pretty much kidnapped you.'

'No. Not really. I mean, I could have gone any time I wanted, but every time I said I'd better be off, he said that I should really freak you out, teach you a lesson. He doesn't like you much, Cal.'

That'd been pretty obvious whenever I'd visited the centre but, aside from not liking him much either, I hadn't really thought about it.

'He just kept going on about giving it a bit more time and then he locked the door when he wasn't in his flat to make sure no one else came in. He said it was because of the rules of Seymour House. And he said it would teach you a lesson about what was important.'

'Little bastard, didn't he have any idea how worried we were?' Ralph growled.

'And he just let me watch telly and play on the decks – and he bought me food,' Wilf went on. 'So, it was all right for a bit. But in the evening, I knew you'd be really freaking. But my phone was out of battery and there was no charger and…'

'Were you really scared he was going to hurt you or something?' Daisy's eyes were wide. Ralph and I both glared at her, but she carried on. 'Like poison you until Mum and Ralph paid a ransom, or cut off your ear or—'

'Daisy!' I hissed. 'Enough.'

Wilf smiled though. 'No, none of that. It wasn't like being in the movies or anything. It was more like just hanging out with someone who was older and doing cool things.

'Anyway, he said we'd just leave it a bit longer and then I'd just go home the next day. He had to go somewhere in the morning and then he'd come back and sneak me out, so no one knew we'd broken the rules. He said it was about keeping his job and he'd been so nice to me, I didn't want him to get in trouble.'

'So, he came on the rally knowing all the time where you were, the bastard,' Ralph spat.

'Rally?' Wilf looked really confused.

'It doesn't matter.' I put out my hand and touched his. Despite the shower and the warmth of the kitchen and the dinner that was going inside him, he still felt chill to my touch.

'Anyway, I looked at his phone when he went to the bathroom and saw there were loads of Snapchats and stuff about me...' Wilf's eyes filled with tears. 'Then he said it was good, as when I did go back my family would treat me properly. I was pretty freaked out then.'

'He must be mentally ill,' I said.

'He might be nearly dead if I get near him,' raged Ralph.

'He wasn't like obviously crazy or anything to start with and, I'm really sorry...' Wilf started to cry again, not worried now about doing it in front of us.

'It's OK, it's OK.' I patted one shoulder while Ralph grabbed the other. 'You're here now and that's all that matters.'

'Did you wonder if you'd ever get out alive?' Daisy whispered.

'Shut up, Daisy,' Lily hissed.

'It was like he was really enjoying winding you up,' Wilf went on eventually. '"Getting one over on the establishment." That's what he kept going on about. I didn't even know what it was.'

I felt cold with fear but on fire from relief. 'So, he came back and by then I was thinking of all the ways I could escape without getting him into trouble and stuff. Like, because he had nowhere to live but the centre,' Wilf went on. 'But then, he was really, like... hyper... and I didn't know why, and he kept saying he'd really managed to get to you. And he started going back on Snapchat, said I needed to wait a bit longer.'

'Like he was high on seeing the mess he'd caused or something?' said Lily.

'And did you put your scarf in the picture deliberately?' Daisy sounded impressed.

Wilf, though, looked bewildered. 'No, I never thought of that.'

'Would have been fucking great if you had,' his sister said dismissively.

'We're just all so glad you're back,' was all I could manage.

The police came and took a statement from Wilf later that evening. By then, he and Ralph had spent a bit of time alone and decided they were going to put off going to Cape Town until Wilf had completed his GCSEs.

'Petra won't like it.' Ralph looked terrified at the conversation he knew was coming.

No, she wouldn't. But I was so relieved and tired that I couldn't care less.

After she'd taken down Wilf's version of events, PC Warren took Ralph and I to one side. 'Turned out all right, then, really glad,' she said. 'This Pete is no real harm, I don't think. Just got himself into a situation which got really out of hand. He's looking at a trial for kidnapping a minor maybe, but we're also referring him for mental health checks.'

'I want to kill him,' Ralph said under his breath.

'Me too,' I agreed.

'We've got no record of him – so he's got no previous. The company behind Seymour House are checking out his employment references and stuff now, but even they said he was just a bit strange...' She opened her notebook.

'"Suspiciously cheerful" is how one of the managers he worked with put it.'

'Yes, awful,' I said. 'And an unfortunate aroma of fish.'

The PC looked a little startled but carried on. 'Fish? No one's mentioned that. Anyway, he keeps going on about stuff from Karl Marx.'

'Kidnap. Coercive control,' Ralph said. 'Brainwashing a child.'

'I'm just so glad he's back,' I said, all anger gone for the moment and exhaustion flooding through me.

'I'll update you as soon as I know more,' the PC said.

Ralph kissed his son goodbye and went off to face Petra.

I stood over Wilf as he smiled up at me and drifted off into a deep sleep.

He looked just like he had when he was six.

28

I'd always liked the bit at the end of true-life films when all the visual action had stopped, and people were filing out of the cinema. Then, if you hung back for a bit, there'd be white text on a black background, explaining what happened to the people in the movie.

Gertrude lived to be 102 and was still famous for her gin in rural Suffolk. She never married.

Or:

Randy became a fireman in Detroit rising to station manager. He and Ruby were married for forty-seven years and had three children, five grandchildren and one great-grandchild at his death. Ruby died shortly afterwards, it was said of a broken-heart.

You know the sort of thing.

Well, sorry, but what came next didn't provide a neat wrap-up for everyone, including me. It seemed that the true life of my family didn't conform to the cinematic ideal.

'OMG, don't apologise,' Marv said, when I called to update him. 'It's like being in a suburban soap opera.' He said this as if it was one of his goals, and it probably was. 'How's Wilf?'

The best description of Wilf was tired. There were the inevitable police interviews in the days that followed, and these drained him even further. He had to be checked physically by police doctors – luckily there were no effects: he'd been well fed and had slept on Pete's couch the first night, stunned by anger and lulled into sleep by the older man. The second night, he said he'd rolled around, worried about all of us and what we must be thinking. Pete had made no sexual advances towards him – this question made him blush and mumble: 'No. He wasn't like that.' It seemed, from everything that the police were telling us, that Pete's motivation was simply to freak out a family that seemed, on the surface, to offer the things that he hadn't had. This, said PC Moshulu, when he came to update me, 'was all mixed up with stuff that made him angry with the world'.

Peter Robert Spencer had grown up in a small town in Hampshire with a divorced mother, with a successful career leading an international business. The father was some sort of hotshot in utilities. He'd been sent away to school pretty early, following the death of a grandmother who'd looked after him when his parents were at work. 'So, deprived in some way or other, but hardly abandoned by junkies,' PC Moshulu gave his opinion. 'No violins playing yet.' He'd been sent to all sorts of courses and programmes in the holidays and, according to his headmaster, had little contact with his parents, but was very much a smiling boy who liked to please others.

'You don't need to be Freud to work that one out,' went on the PC. 'Privileged but neglected, that's what he'll claim in court.' He sounded as if he wasn't going to waste what sympathy he had on someone like that. 'Anyway, best we can find out, he goes to college, then drops out, no one seems to care less where he is for a few years, he says some sort of commune, but we think more of a squat in Lewisham.'

'But how did Seymour House and all the police checks not pick that up?' I was outraged. 'That's basic HR.'

'Yeah, and she knows,' Ralph said from his side of the kitchen table.

'He has no record so police checks all good. And then, he turns up in Seymour Hill and goes to the college for sound engineering. Life back on track. Lives in a shared flat in town and then applies for the job at Seymour House. Put it this way, the company behind that place are looking long and hard at their processes.'

'Petra says we should sue them,' Ralph said, but wearily.

'Bit early for that, still got a lot of investigating to do.' The PC shut his notebook with a satisfying click and got up.

'All I can think is that he's OK.' I shuddered.

'Yeah, could have been much worse,' he agreed. 'But we don't want to think about that, now, do we?'

No, we didn't. What we wanted to think about was him being back, safe and relatively unharmed. My kitchen was full of people checking in on us. Mum and Dad just came back and sat in their old chairs as if the brief interlude at Seymour House had never happened.

'I feel so terrible about it all,' Mum mumbled, her hearing aid on and all the fight seemingly sucked out of her.

'It was my idea to go there,' Dad said, holding her hand.

'But I like it in our house really.'

'Yeah, and you can always come and hang out here.' Wilf nodded earnestly.

And of course, they should. And be fed regularly without me moaning about it. That was the deal really, and I should be glad to have it.

The GCSEs continued apace: Daisy came out of the French written exam beaming, which made me feel better. Lily managed exam after exam, her confidence building as the days progressed. She had no further panic attacks but that didn't stop me worrying about them.

Daisy told us she was dumping the GenZ centre, one evening as we ate spaghetti carbonara. 'I mean, it's just another institution designed to turn us into snowflakes,' she said dismissively, trying to get more than her fair share of the sauce.

'That's got bacon in it.'

'Yeah, I need meat right now for mind protein, but I'm going to become vegan after the exams.' She nodded and spooned another load into her mouth. 'And you know what, I'm going to be a lot more careful about who I listen to. I mean, Sunil turned out to be a right...' she started on the first sound of making an 'n' and, thinking she was going to say 'knob', I immediately shouted 'Daisy!', at which point she smiled sweetly and said '... narcissist. He turned out to be a right narcissist.'

Smart-arse kid.

'Yeah, so maybe I'll become a Liberal Democrat now...' she went on. And as Dad turned to her to debate the merits of being a third party and Mum, now much quieter about politics, said very little, I let the hubbub of the dinner table go on round me and felt glad they were all there, eating spaghetti I'd cooked, and chatting away.

Sunil, narcissist or otherwise – and he probably was, as well as being a very good seducer of middle-aged women who were a bit down on their luck - came by to say goodbye. He was leaving Seymour Hill, he said, as the opportunities to further his cause (by which I think he meant his career) were limited.

'I wanted to apologise to you, though, Callie,' he said, his beautiful, noble eyes pleading with mine, 'for potentially causing disruption in your life. I wanted you to know that I think you're really amazing.'

He nodded very seriously when he said this. *But not as amazing as what you think you are yourself.* It seemed almost impossible to me that I'd been so head-turned by someone this young and self-obsessed.

Marvin enjoyed debating this point. Over a bottle of a very good New Zealand Marlborough in his kitchen with the AAs, he psychoanalysed me.

'The trouble was that you were so starved of male attention, that when he cast you in his light, you flew into his sun like Icarus,' he said dramatically.

'Icarus was the dude who melted, yeah?' Ajay said from the other side of the table. He was eating more cheese straws, but, this time, Marvin had made a double batch.

'Where were you when the rest of us were getting an education?' Abby asked him.

'Anyway, Callie was in what, in later years, we will call her "Invisible Phase",' Marv went on. 'And she'd forgotten that, actually, she's pretty hot when she bothers. So, when Sunil came along and showed a bit of interest, she fell head over heels in lust, not recognising that he was a bit of an arsehole.'

It was true, but it was also a bit close to the bone.

'What about that other bloke, though?' Ajay said. 'The one with the food?'

'He was cute,' Abby confirmed. 'And quite useful.' This was high praise indeed from her. 'Why didn't she do the whole Icarus meltdown with him?'

'I am here, you know,' I pointed out. 'No longer invisible, people.'

'Not after your TV appearance,' Marvin said proudly. He'd been even more approving when I'd got a call from the TV station to appear on another programme.

'You were so authentic,' said the producer of the show. 'We'd just love it if you could show some of that emotion again, but this time in a pre-recorded studio session.'

I declined. I'd had enough of that kind of visibility.

Marv returned to focus on my love life – or lack of it. 'The problem was, Patrick doesn't have the obvious appeal of a man like Sunil.'

'Not ugly though,' Abby mused. 'Quite attractive in his way.'

'None of that young passion and flair,' Marv went on.

'But, still pretty passionate about what he does. Just doesn't go on about it,' I said.

Marv raised an eyebrow at me, but then carried on talking to the others as if I were an exhibit in a zoo.

'What I'm saying is that he was just too *there*. So in front of her face that she didn't see him.'

'It was him who didn't see me to start with,' I said. 'Remember?'

'And Callie was in her invisible phase, remember? At first, not to be a snob but, anyway, she thought he was a forty-year-old bloke who drove a bike for a living. Then she had all that stuff going on with Wilf and no time to think about a man and that's what she told him. Quite emphatically, if I remember.'

'She wasn't thinking, really, was she?' Ajay slurped from his glass.

'No, Callie wasn't thinking,' Marv continued with wonderful, patronising judgement. 'She wasn't thinking at all.' He turned, mock TV-presenter style, and peered into an imaginary camera. 'Viewers, she certainly wasn't thinking when she, in emotional distress, turned to Patrick, the food-delivery guy, and kissed him in her garden. Is it too late now, do you think, for the revival of this love affair? Watch this space.'

'Of course, it's too late,' I said, more emphatically than I'd anticipated. 'I told him I didn't want to go out with any men at all, and then I KISSED HIM and only then he found out I'd been to bed with Sunil.' Even as I said it, I cringed, mortified about what Patrick must have thought of me.

'We're still impressed about that, by the way.' Ajay patted my hand.

'But it was the night before,' Marv threw in.

'It was a crazy time when Wilf was missing, and emotions were all over the place.' Abby tried to be the voice of reason.

'But I haven't seen him for weeks,' I said. It was about three weeks, actually, but it felt like much longer. All I wanted him to do was come out of his house a few doors down and look as if it was an accident that he'd bumped into me. Patrick was definitely at home – his car was there and sometimes his bike. But there was no sign of him.

Although he hadn't been part of our street and our lives – my life – for very long, he seemed to be missing from it very quickly. Even the kids had remarked on not seeing him. I walked past his door with Bodger very slowly, half hoping that he'd come out so that I could just explain, but his blue door stayed resolutely shut.

I minded much more than I'd thought.

'He turned out to be great,' I went on, finally talking about it with the benefit of a Marv-sized glass of wine. 'But you're right. First of all, he was just there when all the bad stuff was going on. And I liked him, but I didn't have time to think about it. And not immediately like that. And then Sunil came along, and I couldn't believe someone like that fancied me, so I acted like a complete twat. And then I kissed Patrick – the next day. Even more of a twat and then he found out. I mean, he must just think I'm awful.'

My skin crawled every time I thought about it. And while I went to work and came home on the train and cooked food for my extended family and went to sleep, I thought about it quite a lot.

'Not so awful,' Abby said. 'You're just out of practice with men.'

'What with only just having come out of your Invisible Phase.' Marv smiled.

'But saying one thing and then doing something else behind his back,' I went on. 'And then kissing him anyway.'

'It's not that bad…'

'Yeah, you should see how Abby treats the blokes who fancy her.'

'So, what do you think I should do?' I asked more desperately now. We brainstormed the options over another bottle.

'Book Deliveroo every night until it turns out to be him.'

'He's given that up since he knocked her down.'

'Send one of the kids round with some sort of excuse?'

'Bit pathetic, isn't it? Like sending your mate in the playground over, to ask someone out in primary school.'

'Callie could take up running and just run up and down the street in front of his house until he has to come outside.'

'Also, a bit desperate.'

'And she wouldn't look that good with a red face from running.'

'Sweaty, yuck.'

'He's hiding from me,' I said. 'And how's he to know I'm not still going out with Sunil?'

'Good point. The only option is to ring his doorbell and ask him to have a conversation with you, where you explain everything.'

'I couldn't,' I said, wanting the floor to open up and swallow me. 'I think he'd just tell me to forget it.' I wasn't sure I would cope with that humiliation.

'Well, you won't know unless you try, will you?'

But I'd seen the look on his face when he'd found out I hadn't just kissed Sunil, I'd been naked and in bed with him, and I didn't think he would ever look at me the same way again.

.

29

Spring morphed into summer but while the world heated up and seemed more benign, there was still a chill in the air in Patchett Road.

Some of it was caused by what happened between Petra and Ralph, which upset Wilf. It seemed that Pet didn't like being told 'no' when her only true answer was the one she'd chosen. And the idea that, once the Rehabilitation of Ralph was complete, he might have some views of his own obviously hadn't occurred to her. So, when he plucked up the courage to tell her that he and Wilf wanted to wait a while before they moved to South Africa with her, you could probably hear windows shattering from her screams all the way down her executive cul-de-sac.

What we had talked about, though, was a tentative movement towards Wilf making a proper home with his dad. I knew really, after what had happened, that I'd been on borrowed time – or at least borrowing him from Ralph while he recovered – and the right thing to do was restore father and son to under the same roof. Then Ralph would accept that his mistakes were in the past and Wilf would know that he had a home with his father as well as with us.

So, Wilf said, for example, that he'd like to stay at Ralph's for a few days each week to check it out. But all of this was dependent on Petra either sticking in the UK and with her marriage or them letting her go.

In the end she chose her job, which didn't surprise me. There would always be another project for Petra – and Ralph hadn't turned out to be content with being endlessly fixed. From what Wilf said, Ralph offered to have a long-distance relationship with her in the southern hemisphere until Wilf was older, but she wasn't having it. Petra was one of those people that once crossed couldn't see a straight line again.

We all worried that Ralph would revert to the disastrous version of a couple of years back, but in the end he was much more pragmatic. He also didn't seem that broken-hearted, but who was I to judge? He said he was going to get his business properly going again and rented a small flat, but with room for Wilf, in the town centre. It was a bit grotty and not at all executive-home-like, but he seemed happy and Wilf started to crash out there sometimes. Ralph got a bit scruffier too, which made us all like him a lot more again.

The other chill was more obviously in our street itself. It was between number 36 and number 42 and it felt like a frost that would never lift. Short of sitting like a stalker in my front window at all hours of day and night, waiting to see if Patrick would emerge from his door, there was little I could do about this. I'd sent a couple of 'thank you' texts, and, when they'd got no reply, even one more where I said I'd love to see him and explain, but there was no return bubble on my iPhone screen, even though the messages said they were 'delivered'.

In my joy at Wilf remaining and in seeing Lily's face stop looking so apprehensive as the GCSEs finally ended, it was hard not to let a little bit of my mind think about that. Mostly, I wanted to curl up in mortification. Here I was going round kissing him less than twenty-four hours after I'd done much more with someone else... and after I'd given him all that stuff about not having time for a relationship. At the best he would think I was extremely fickle. I didn't want to think about the worst.

Why hadn't I worked out I liked him earlier? It was as if he was invisible to me too, when we met. And now, when I spent quite a lot of time thinking about how lovely it would be to have his eyes on me, it was too late.

Meanwhile the police were making slow progress with working on what made Pete decide to help Wilf disappear. There were psychiatric reports to complete, an investigation and abject apology from the company behind Seymour House and still no conclusion as to what they would charge him with, if anything. This too hung over Wilf. He'd become more teenage-like in the last few weeks, sleeping for longer and longer periods; I would have been worried, but he still gave me his shy smile and spent hours in Jowan's garage making unmelodious music.

Mum and Dad stayed in their own home. They were chastened by their experience of Seymour House, but it didn't make them any more self-sufficient. I went back to fielding random text messages from them throughout my highly satisfactory working days dealing with everyday sexism at Carter's Cars of north London.

I still cleaned up for them at the weekends. They were yet to discover their next passion.

Was it guilt that made me let the girls have a party to celebrate the end of their exams? Probably. After all we'd gone through, I wanted everyone to have another focus. My only proviso was that Wilf was given a decent DJ slot – or at least able to take the credit for a playlist pelted out from an iPod and the speakers he'd set up. It had to feel like his party too.

I imagine if you've ever had a teenage party in your home, you are probably shuddering as you remember alcopops and bottles of cider being thrown all over your floors and curtains, mopping up puke from your bathroom and breaking up amorous couples who'd sneaked past the sign you'd made for the stairs, which clearly said: *No one upstairs please.* Add in the very loud music, the unbelievable crap tipsy teenagers could talk at you all night and there was no reason to think of any teenage house-party experience without wondering why you ever said 'yes' in the first place.

But I did. I wanted Lily to keep the smile on her face; Daisy promised (and actually stuck to it) to stop swearing if she was allowed a party; and the DJ gig gave Wilf a new swagger.

On the night itself, I'd recruited Marvin to help me. I'd banned the AAs on the basis that if they came to the party I would be too drunk to look after the even-more-drunk kids. And the kids had suggested it might be a better idea to have a separate celebration dinner with Lois and Lorca, so they were also effectively banned, much to Dad's chagrin.

So, picture Marvin and me, at about 9 p.m. on a Saturday night in early July, sitting in my scrubby garden, under the pear tree where I'd so stupidly kissed Pat, while the noise of forty kids ricocheting around my sitting room and kitchen to loud beeping came out of the back door.

'It's the calm before the storm,' said Marv.

'They've promised no more drink than I provided,' I said. 'Strictly limited to a couple of beers each.'

'So that kid I saw with the massive pack of Desperados¶¶¶¶¶¶ was breaking the rules?' Marv smiled.

'Didn't you take them off him?' I said in horror.

'Well, as soon as you stopped looking they all went out and got six-packs of the stuff out from under the front garden bushes,' Marv said. 'I couldn't confiscate all of them or Daisy and Lily would hate me forever.'

The noise got worse and we had a good old gossip to try and ignore it. Mostly we discussed how Abby had amazed us all by falling in love. Well, she denied that it was anything as strong as actual love, but the signs were all there: she'd stopped hanging out with us so much, her determined face had taken on a softer hue and she'd even been seen wearing

_____

¶¶¶¶¶¶ A beer that contains tequila that kids are extremely fond of but which they should avoid at all costs.

a dress. The lucky man was the lawyer, Dominic, who'd helped me when I'd first heard about Wilf. It seemed he'd refused to let her non-committal approach to him rest and actually demanded that she make it clear how she felt about him, one way or the other, after a few dates.

'She respected that,' Marv recounted, wide-eyed about Dominic's inability to be terrified of Abby. 'And she realised that he didn't actually aggravate her too much, so she said he could stick around.'

There was some whooping from the side alley then, where a few kids had gone to smoke. I couldn't smell weed and nor could Marvin, so we told them that smoking killed and to be a bit quieter.

'Did you warn all your neighbours?' Marv asked.

'Next door said they'd go out for the evening and not get back till late and the other side said, "Thank heavens, we're away on our holidays",' I recounted. 'I put some notes through some other doors telling them it would finish at 11.00 p.m., even though, according to Daisy, it's social suicide to have such a saddo end time.'

'Did you put one through Pat's door?' Marv asked, pretending to look at the stars.

'Yes, but nothing back.' I shrugged. 'I can't make the man talk to me, Marv, if he doesn't want to.'

I thought it was going pretty well. Jowan and Wilf were standing behind the iPod dock trying to look like superstar DJs and the kids were all pogo-ing around the sitting room or hiding their contraband beer behind their backs in the kitchen when they saw me. Several had come out into the garden and were having 'DMC'******* conversations. Daisy seemed to be arguing with a boy with a quiff just outside the back door; as I passed, I heard her say something about 'western attitudes to conflict resolution' so I figured it wasn't too heated. She was wearing a vest that came just past her bottom and – after an epic row with me, when I'd threatened to cancel the party unless she put more clothes on – a pair of denim shorts. Inside, I could see Lily, wearing a pretty floral playsuit, pressed up against Aiden at the kitchen counter. They stopped snogging for a while when I walked through on a quick patrol before returning to the garden.

'No puking, no underage shagging and no accidents,' I reported back to Marvin.

'Result,' he agreed. 'Are we allowed a glass of wine now ourselves?'

It was then, though, that there was an almighty crash from somewhere inside the house, the music came to an abrupt end and someone started screaming.

I ran towards the noise, Marvin close on my heels. 'Out of the way,' I ordered the kids in the kitchen, and rounded into the sitting room, where the sea of jumping teenagers had parted and there on the floor, clutching his leg in agony, was Wilf.

'Oh, my God. Are you all right?' All the teenagers gathered round in sympathy.

******* See earlier. Or don't – I'll make it easy: Deep and Meaningful Conversation.

'It really hurts, Cal,' he groaned, holding his shin and writhing, his face curled up in pain. His voice was suspiciously slurry.

'What happened?' I knelt beside him.

'I was just jumping around and…' Yes, there was no way Wilf hadn't been drinking – despite having been part of the extensive lecture I'd given to all the kids before the party started, about the dangers of alcohol.

I glanced at Jowan, who looked shell-shocked. 'He jumped off the sofa,' he mumbled. 'He was trying to do a better pogo than me.'

'How many beers, Jowan?' I asked. 'You're not in trouble, I just need to know what Wilf has drunk.'

Jowan held up a half-litre of Desperado from behind the DJ table, which was two-thirds empty. 'But we shared it, Cal,' he said. 'I promise.'

OK, so, even without any alcohol tolerance, Wilf was only likely to be tipsy rather than stomach-pump-requiring drunk. Still, it had made him stupid enough to try and dive off the sofa. The alcohol, however, was going to make him feel much less pain than he would without it, and he was writhing beside me, clutching his leg.

I sighed. It had been going so well. 'We'd better ring for an ambulance.'

So, that was how we ended up back in A & E at Seymour Hill hospital. While we waited for the paramedics, Wilf rolled around on the floor with scared, mildly intoxicated eyes. I tried not to be furious. 'I should've kept an eye on what he was up to,' I told Marvin. Jowan didn't seem that worse for wear, luckily, or I'd also have had another parent to answer to.

Marvin packed all the kids into the kitchen and garden while I made Wilf comfortable on the floor with cushions. The paramedics arrived – by now we'd probably met most of the colleague base of the local ambulance force – and examined Wilf.

'We'll have to take him in, Ms Brown,' one said. 'Probably a strain but he needs an X-ray.'

When I showed them the bottle of Desperado, the paramedic just smiled. 'That's nothing really, Ms Brown, compared to what we've already seen tonight – and what you're about to see in A & E. I'm pretty sure he'll be all right. You've been a bit stupid though, haven't you, Wilf?'

He blushed and started apologising. 'Sorry, Cal, really sorry, I love you though.'

He was even sweet when he was an underage drunk. I smiled on. 'I'll just get a jumper.'

I'd ring Ralph on the way, I thought, as, having given very clear instructions to Marv about alcohol limits and home times, I went down the path following the stretcher containing Wilf.

He was saying, 'Sorry, Cal, again,' while he was lifted into the ambulance. One of the paramedics was already talking to him about his party playlist and he was answering without difficulty, so it was a temporary pissed-ness. The music had started up inside the house again, but this time, more quietly.

'I'll follow in the car,' I said and turned to click the fob to open the car doors. It was as I turned that I saw the unmistakable shape of Patrick, standing under the street light.

'Umm, everything OK?' he asked. He looked browner than a few weeks back; while his face had the familiar look of concern it seemed to have round me, it wasn't as smiling as it used to be.

'Yes, just a sprain probably – Wilf drank a beer and was dancing and showing off and...' I sighed. 'And now we're going to lovely A & E on a Saturday night, which is always a laugh.'

'Is someone with the rest of the party?'

'Yes, no worries, my friend, you remember Marvin? He's got it under control. I'm going to get Wilf's dad to meet me at the hospital and then come straight back. I'm pretty sure Wilf is OK.'

Patrick hung his head for a minute. 'Want me to come with you?' and then there was a flicker of a smile. 'Just in case you're bored of ambulances and A & E departments and...'

'*Drama?*' I asked with my eyes mock-wide.

'You do seem to like a bit of that,' he said. 'Or shall I stay back and help Marvin out?'

'Hmm, A & E on a Saturday night or a houseful of teenagers at a party? It's a difficult choice.'

The front door of the house swung open and two kids could be seen snogging in the hallway, pressed against the coat rack.

'I think, just for now...' Patrick smiled '... Marvin might need me more than you.'

And he went off up the path into my house.

The A & E was familiar, although being there rabbiting on about being invisible seemed an age ago. The waiting room was full of people with minor injuries, some clearly slumped over drunk.

Wilf was wheeled past them into a cubicle and I sat down on the chair by his bed. 'That's one way of getting out of one of the twins' parties,' I joked. 'Your dad is on his way.'

'Sorry, Cal,' Wilf groaned. 'I didn't mean to ruin your evening.'

Just then the curtain swung to one side and there was the glorious sight of Maura, her badge pinned to her ample chest. 'Well, young man…' she started and then saw me. 'Well, if it isn't Mrs Invisible.' We both smiled broadly at each other while Wilf looked bewildered. 'You like it so much here you can't stay away?'

'I'm so glad it's you,' I said. 'This is Wilf, my sort of son, and he decided to go a bit nuts dancing at his sisters' party.'

'Were you *crowdsurfing*?' Maura winked at him. 'Normally we keep that sort of behaviour for well-known stars.' Wilf blushed and started laughing while she carried on. 'I suppose you're going to tell me you are up there with Jay-Z and Kanye, aren't you?' and she fussed around sticking a thermometer in his mouth.

He tried to mumble, 'Do you know Cal?' while it was between his lips, but Maura quickly shushed him.

'You could say so,' she went on. 'Now how are *you* doing?'

While she did all the triage tests on Wilf, we had a good old reminisce about my last trip to the hospital, until Wilf had forgotten all about a pain in his leg and was laughing away with us.

'This woman came in all covered in curry,' Maura told him with quite a lot of exaggeration. 'But mostly, all you kids were driving her wild. I hope you've been making things a bit easier for her lately.'

I could only smile. If she only knew.

Ralph's head appeared round the curtain and Maura caught my eye, raising an eyebrow that only meant: 'This one yours?'

'This is my ex-partner and Wilf's dad,' I told her, shaking my head.

'Well, Mr Ex-Partner of Mrs Invisible, your son might have done something to his leg. The doc will be along at some point and he'll probably need an X-ray. That could take a bit of time, what with him not being an emergency and it being a Saturday night.' These were her words, but she rolled her eyes at me as if to say: 'You seen what I have to deal with out there?' and it was difficult not to be very glad there were people like her in the world.

I was apprehensive about getting back to the party. There was the standard panic about whether Marv and Patrick had managed to control the illegal drinking/puking/shagging and so on; and general exhaustion at the idea of having to clear up so many bottles and crisps trampled in the carpet. But it was more than that.

Patrick had come to help when I needed him most – again. And now, I knew, he would go back into his flat at number 36 and resume the frosty silence with me at number 42.

I felt a compulsive need to explain to him that I wasn't the most awful, lying, treacherous woman that he'd ever met. But, examining my behaviour at that time, it was difficult not to come to the exact same conclusion myself.

It was 11.15 p.m. as I swung into Patchett Road. And after all my worries, my biggest one was that my house was eerily quiet.

There was no music, no sounds of kids flirting, teasing one another or arguing about politics. There was no one fallen over in the gutter near the pavement. No parents angrily waiting for their kids to stop snogging and come outside. I hurried very quickly to the back door.

Bodger met me there, his face surprised behind his grizzled old whiskers. And he was quite right, his doggy facial expressions always a good indicator of what was to come.

Behind him in the kitchen, Marvin was at the sink, wearing my butcher's pinny over his stripy outfit. He was whistling into his goatee beard while round him, astonishingly, the twins and Aiden were busy gathering up bottles from the counter and throwing them into a bucket for recycling. Daisy was wobbling slightly as she did it, but no one seemed really the worse for wear.

There were no stray teenagers in sight. None who hadn't been collected because their parents were at another party and had forgotten about them. None lying in a pool of something regurgitated.

Instead, I was met by a scene of industriousness, which had never been seen in my kid-ridden household. There was a smell of lemon Flash and Aiden had a sponge in his hand, which he seemed to be using to wipe the table.

From the doorway, a smiling Patrick appeared, his arms stuffed with empty Becks bottles. He looked up at me and winked and I raised my eyebrows back at him in wonder.

'All OK with Wilf?' he asked, and the others noticed I was there.

'He's good – they think there's nothing broken but he's with Ralph waiting for an X-ray.'

'We've nearly done all the cleaning up,' Lily said proudly. 'Patrick got everyone out of here on time and...'

My God, the man was a one-man wonder.

'He gave us instructions and when I tried to tell him that hierarchies were a capitalist construct, he just laughed,' Daisy added, sending herself up for once, and only slurring a bit.

'We got squad goals,' Aiden said. I think he meant that he was working as part of a team with a mission, but I couldn't be bothered to interpret.

'Thanks so much,' I whispered.

Marv just looked at me with an evil glint in his eye and then, flicking his Marigolds, carried on washing up.

The pear tree. The scrubby back garden. Midnight, but, as it was July, still with a balm to the night air.

When all the cleaning, teasing and laughing was over and the kids had gone upstairs, supposedly to sleep, but really to have a party post-mortem, Marv very quickly exited left. 'Date,' he said and ran off down the path as I was thanking him. I didn't believe him.

I'm not sure Patrick did either. 'Nice bloke,' he said. 'But not that many women, for sure.'

We both stood awkwardly in the middle of the now-gleaming kitchen and I mumbled on for a while about how grateful I was for him coming 'yet again' to our rescue and we weren't normally this dysfunctional as a family and…

'It's the fun in dysfunctional, though, isn't it?' he asked. It was difficult not to remember how sad he'd been back when he was telling me about how much he'd wanted a family of his own.

'That's a very kind way of putting it.' Then I leapt in. It was a bit desperate, I admit. 'Would you want a beer, maybe? We could sit in the garden.'

Given the generally unloved state of my garden, this wasn't up there with the best of invitations, but he paused, nodded and then said quietly, 'All right.'

Bodger got quickly to his feet and wagged his tail, as if he thought this was a great idea. We got the only two undrunk beers in the house and took them to the old bench. Of course, as soon as we got there and sat stiffly down, memories of the last time we'd stood in that spot came rushing back and I blushed in the darkness.

I tried to think of something to say about the moon, but clouds were over it now. The stars, which had been glistening earlier, seemed to have retreated too. There was only the light coming up from the house and the rest of Patchett Road as the neighbourhood called time on another Saturday night.

'I'm sorry I was an arse,' was what I managed eventually. I said it without looking towards him and then took a swig of my beer.

'In your defence, you were an arse with quite a lot going on,' Patrick said. 'But yes, incontrovertibly, still an arse.' He turned then and gave me a small smile through the darkness. 'And that was probably better than being a nutjob, invisible, a fruit loop or any of the other descriptors you chose.'

He was teasing me, and it felt very good.

'I just want to explain.' The words came tumbling from me; it felt as if they'd spent so long in my head that, being let out of my mouth, they weren't going to stop. 'I was just really confused. I'd spent so long taking no notice of men, just with the kids and my folks and stuff, and I'd forgotten what it was like to like being with someone or for someone to like being with you, and there you were, crashing into my life...'

'Quite literally, crashing.'

'... and I liked you but there was so much happening that I'm not sure I even thought about any of it in that way and then there was...'

'The young activist.' Pat seemed to spit the words rather than say them.

'Yes, and I was a bit blinded, I think, and it took me a while to see that he was just a...'

'Completely self-obsessed wanker?' This last sentence seemed to give him some satisfaction.

'Yes, and by then, I'd already...'

'Not sure we need to go there?'

'It wasn't like that.' For some reason I wanted him to know that I hadn't actually gone completely shagadelic with Sunil and, more importantly, I wanted to tell him that I hadn't liked it half as much as I'd thought I would.

'And then with Wilf running away, I was distraught, and you were there, being lovely and so helpful and…'

'You kissed me because I was *there*?' Patrick's voice was small in the night air. 'I knew that was what it was.'

'No! I don't know what happened. I should never have done it,' I said. 'And I'm so sorry and you thought I was playing you and lying to you and… well, I'm not sure I knew what was going on. I'm sorry, I'm really sorry. I've spent weeks thinking what you must think of me and I just wanted to come round and tell you I'm not that kind of person and how much I missed you and…' My words finally ran out. 'I'm sorry.'

As grovelling apologies went, it was the best I could do. It wasn't going to make him forgive me; it wasn't going to make him ask me out again, but it was my best shot. It was all I had.

There was a silence. A very long silence. I'd like to say something momentous happened, like a shooting star zoomed across the sky or the moon decided to come out again and cast us in a single spotlight. But none of that happened. All there was was quiet and all I could do was wait.

Then Patrick turned to me and said, 'I'm not sorry I kissed you back though.'

It took me a while to realise quite what he'd said. A moment when I recognised the flirty tone he'd used to talk to me in. When, turning really slowly to look at him, I saw the teasing smile he'd always had on his face when it wasn't looking at me or members of my family in concern. And just for a second, I had a little bit of hope.

'Come on, it was my fault too,' he went on then, taking the hand I was holding my beer with, gently extracting the bottle and putting it on the bench. 'I just couldn't believe I'd moved in near someone so... so, well, full of life, as you.'

'Another way to say dysfunctional?' I quizzed.

'And you were so lovely and a bit nutty—'

'I was doing pretty well with lovely,' I interrupted, but my heart was doing a little soundcheck to see whether it was about to sing.

'And I couldn't help wanting to know you. That whole invisible thing, I wanted to make you know that I could see you very well and really liked what I saw.'

My heart did a few more test octaves while he carried on. 'But I should never have been that persistent and obvious. Then, when you quite rightly decided you didn't have time for me, I thought I'd play the friend card...'

'You came round and fixed Wilf's bike and helped my folks move,' I said. 'That was good playing of the friend card.'

'I know, but then you just seemed to need me rather than...'

'I just didn't know what I wanted – just my family to stay together.'

· Patrick paused but carried on holding my hand. 'But when I found out about—'

'No more insults necessary.'

'I thought it was just that you didn't like me, you liked guys like *that*, and even though you kissed me, it was because I was, as you put it, *there*.'

319

'Umm, no, it wasn't that at all,' I said. 'I mean…' I meant a kiss like that didn't happen just because someone was conveniently standing right next to you. 'I really liked the kiss, but it was at such a terrible time, and it was only after it happened that I thought what it must look like.'

'It was a pretty good kiss.' Patrick smiled. I could only nod back. There was a pause and then he picked up my other hand. 'Here we are again though. With absolutely no dramas going on.'

'I noticed the complete lack of dramas.'

'We could have another go? See if that kiss was a one-off or, you know, it had something going for it.'

'Something that other kisses don't necessarily have.'

I can report that the kiss that came next had true distinction from your standard run-of-the-mill-type kisses. It was true, for a while I hadn't done a lot of kissing at all, what with being in my Invisible Phase, as Marv would say, apart from getting it on with Sunil, but you never really forgot what made a great kiss stand out. And I didn't think, *Eww, wet,* once.

In fact, it was pretty much up there with the greats. To put it another way: there were five senses and it hit up every single one of them. His lips were soft, like velvet ice cream to the touch of mine; he tasted of desire; he moaned gently as his lips closed on mine; he smelt of sweet, robust *man;* and before I shut my eyes in bliss, I could see his big blue eyes look at me too, with total abandon.

30

And, I am happy to report, that was not the end of that.

The classic line was 'Reader, I married him,' but the truth really was, 'Reader, I did quite a lot of kissing and, after a while, yep, I shagged him.'

But much more than that, we got to know one another a little better and a little better still. Eventually we became, Patrick and I, much closer neighbours when, the following summer, he gave up number 36 Patchett Road and moved his belongings down the street to number 42.

Everyone came round to celebrate with a barbeque. Patrick had organised the kids to help him clean up the garden one weekend and it was looking – well, a bit less scrappy. There would be pears on the tree this year.

Lois and Lorca sat on a couple of deckchairs. They'd not really got any older or more barmy than before; just existed in an ongoing state of randomness. There'd been a brief spell when we'd had to persuade them that trampolining wasn't really for them, but they'd quickly moved on.

Now, they'd set up a Twitter feed (@boldbutold), which had quickly amassed 3000 followers and was growing. Its aim was to put pressure on the government about social issues by harnessing the anger of pensioners, which was a neat idea, I thought, and particularly one that was safely conducted from their own kitchen table. So far, they had called out the Secretary of State for Transport on the lack of charging points for electric mobility scooters; the Health Secretary for unnecessary plastics use in the NHS; and were in the middle of a showdown involving local 'grey' protestors about the shutting of post offices. They seemed to have found their métier, but still came round often to be fed. My latest innovation was to ensure a daily delivery from Tesco to their house so that they always had food and didn't always need to come to mine, but it hadn't really worked.

Marvin came with a girl called Dilys I'd never met before but that he'd actually been on more than one date with. Ajay came on his own. This was because Abby was driven to the barbeque by Dominic. He turned out to be as tough as her really, at least meeting her on her own terms and, therefore, managing to stay the course.

Daisy and Lily were a year older. This meant that they spent quite a lot of time in Wetherspoons armed with quite convincing false IDs.

Now they were drinking beers in the garden with us, Daisy in a string bikini even though it was evening and Lily with more appropriate shorts and a shirt on. Aiden hadn't lasted through the first year of sixth form. She'd decided, after achieving a string of top grades in her GCSEs (compared to her sister's slightly worse ones) that there were more articulate boys in the world and she should find one of them. He hadn't come along yet.

And there was Wilf too. He wasn't drinking beer, having sworn off it after the leg sprain of the previous year. The police had closed the case on Pete a few months earlier, much to his and all our relief. The kid was disturbed, and we could have brought charges, PC Warren said, but he needed counselling more than he needed a court appearance. Ralph had eventually agreed, and I was very glad to move on.

Wilf had moved in with Ralph by now on a permanent basis but was still found on our sofa or round the dinner table a few times a week. This felt right as his dad continued to rebuild a life with his son. Petra and Ralph eventually got divorced and she was now living with a former junkie near the beach in Cape Town.

And behind a barbeque under the pear tree, was Patrick. Daisy was teasing him about how flipping burgers was the ultimate expression of patriarchy in action, but he resolutely took no notice and then, having got bored at not having the upper hand, she sloped off.

I stood near the house, another couple of beers in my hands. I was wearing a new summer dress in a blue that I really liked; I knew that the smile on my face would have registered with anyone who'd looked my way.

Of course, none of them did.

In the warm, bubbling, messy love that exuded from that garden, I was still being ignored and taken for granted.

Still invisible. But, I knew, I was very much needed. I also knew that I was seen by the people who mattered to me and loved in ways I hadn't realised. One of them, in particular, had been very unexpected but was now very special to me.

I gave Patrick a beer and clinked my bottle with his and we looked round us at all the chattering and eating and drinking as he slid a happy arm round my waist.

'I'm so glad that this is my family now,' he said. 'Even though it's completely dysfunctional.'

'You're part of that now,' I pointed out. 'You can't keep going on about it.'

'Look where we're standing.' He gestured with his beer bottle towards the tree. 'You could kiss me just because I'm there, if you like.'

I very visibly did just that.

Acknowledgements

Thank you for reading this book – it's been a thrill to write and my first thanks have to go to kids – Elyse, Sienna, Laura and Tom. While the book is not based on them at all, it has been really fun to take the loving mickey out of teenagers.

Thanks to super fab agent, Diana Beaumont and editor Lucy Gilmour – and to Laura Palmer, Vicky Joss, Sue Smith, Sue Lamprell and the whole team at Aria, Head of Zeus. Every time I get a little yellow 'best seller' flag I feel you all cheering alongside me.

To my writing group pals, Christina Pishiris, Lisa Williamson, Sara-Mae Tuson and Maria Realf and to the online groups who provide writerly advice and friendship when the going gets a bit tough.

Huge thanks to Natalie and Nigel Stockton who have shown so much love and support as my writing career developed. And to Fanny Johnstone and Rachel Lichtenstein and all my other friends – really appreciate all the love you send out into the world on my behalf.

Biggest thanks of all to my wonderful Mum (who's nothing like Lois in this book, praise be) and the rest of my massive, mad fam.

To Laura, Elyse, Sienna and Tom – you are always an inspiration. And the dog, who smells a bit better than Bodger in this book but is just as judgemental.

Biggest love and thanks to Alan, who has cheered me all the way, even when it meant listening to me moaning when the rugby/cricket/football was on. There can be no greater expression of love than missing Luton play in a league game.

And to everyone who read and reviewed my first book – thank you. Reviews on Amazon and elsewhere make a massive difference to authors, so they are super appreciated. If you want to say a few lines about this one, I'd be so grateful.

Fiona

About the Author

FIONA PERRIN was a journalist and copywriter before building a career as a sales and marketing director in industry. Having always written, she completed the Curtis Brown Creative Writing course before writing *The Story After Us*. Fiona grew up in Cornwall, hung out for a long time in London and then Hertfordshire, and now writes as often as possible from her study overlooking the sea at the end of The Lizard peninsula.

Hello from Aria

We hope you enjoyed this book! Let us know, we'd love to hear from you.

We are Aria, a dynamic digital-first fiction imprint from award-winning independent publishers Head of Zeus. At heart, we're avid readers committed to publishing exactly the kind of books we love to read – from romance and sagas to crime, thrillers and historical adventures. Visit us online and discover a community of like-minded fiction fans!

We're also on the look out for tomorrow's superstar authors. So, if you're a budding writer looking for a publisher, we'd love to hear from you. You can submit your book online at ariafiction.com/we-want-read-your-book

You can find us at:
Email: aria@headofzeus.com
Website: www.ariafiction.com
Submissions: www.ariafiction.com/
we-want-read-your-book
Facebook: @ariafiction
Twitter: @Aria_Fiction
Instagram: @ariafiction

Printed in Poland
by Amazon Fulfillment
Poland Sp. z o.o., Wrocław